Travels With a Whip

Travels With a Whip

G.C. SCOTT

CARROLL & GRAF PUBLISHERS
NEW YORK

TRAVELS WITH A WHIP

Carroll & Graf Publishers
An Imprint of Avalon Publishing Group Inc.
161 William St., 16th Floor
New York, NY 10038

First Carroll & Graf edition 2002

Library of Congress Cataloging-in-Publication Data
is available.

ISBN: 0-7867-0938-3

Printed in the United States of America
Distributed by Publishers Group West

Contents

1
Meeting Strangers

25
A Trip In the Dark

49
An Evening At Home

75
Arrival

99
By George

123
Explanations

147
The Naked and the Nude

169
Horseplay

193
The Line Shack

217
Last Ordeal

Travels With a Whip

Meeting Strangers

1

The great panorama of rock and trees and sky through which the highway ran would have impressed anyone. Janice Singleton, a self-confessed townie with very little experience of anything remotely rural or pastoral, was impressed. She admitted it. The decision to take a holiday at a remote ("secluded" was how the brochure put it) resort with a Western, horsey flavor ("equestrian ambience," said the brochure) seemed like one of her better ideas. And if, after all, it turned out not be to her taste, she could write it off to experience and take her future holidays in more congenial settings. The flight from Boston to Cheyenne, Wyoming, had been boring, as were most flights that did not end in crashes. Flying held no more novelty for her. The airports all looked the same, and the airplanes *were* all the same. But she had begun to feel more sanguine as she drove the rented car out of the city and began to see why they called this "big sky country."

Beneath that sometimes daunting blue dome they used for sky hereabouts, one could begin to grasp one's insignificance in the grand scheme of things. One's perspectives, even those of the most independent-minded persons (among whom Janice numbered herself) changed. One suddenly became a small fish in a big pond, not always an unwelcome situation—provided, of course, there were no bigger fish of the strongly predatory or territorial persuasion in the same pond. But even if there were, Janice believed she had enough skill and self-confidence to cope with them. The time spent in beating her male colleagues to the big news stories (and of being beaten in her turn) had hardened her to competition. Now she was looking forward to the coming break from habit and the everyday routine.

She had never been on a horse, but she imagined it couldn't be all that difficult. She had no intention of becoming an accomplished horsewoman. Horses, she thought, were useful for getting around in country where roads were scarce, as they were where she was going (so the brochure informed her, though not in those words). One somehow got onto a horse, she gathered, and sort of guided it with the reins, assisted by the guides, who, the brochure said, were extra helpful to beginners (check appropriate box indicating level of skill). Janice had duly checked "novice," though she was not altogether happy about it. She didn't like to mention her weaknesses, and besides, admitting to one's weaknesses could be a weakness in itself. But she was realistic enough to know that not everyone could know all about everything. She regretted briefly the overwhelming of the Renaissance man/woman in the flood of information let loose upon the world by said Renaissance and the many subsequent explosions of information.

Watching her mileage, Janice reached the point the directions had mentioned, where a narrower road turned off the main highway and led toward the mountains in the distance. She duly turned off and began to follow the secondary road through semidesert country with outcrops of rock and a steadily rising gradient. Foothills, she thought, the word coming to her from her reading rather than from her actual experience. She was in the foothills. The word was apt, she decided. The scenery grew more rugged and wild as she left the main road farther behind. Finally the road itself, as if succumbing to the ruggedness through which it ran, lost its edges and, finally, its hard surface. She passed isolated farms, most of them deserted and falling down. She recalled scenes from newsreels about the Dust Bowl of the thirties.

The seclusion the brochure had promised was beginning to materialize. Not a good place to be alone, Janice thought, her townie instincts asserting themselves. She was not used to this much silence and emptiness all at once. What if she broke down? As if on cue, the car began to make distressing sounds. She forgot about the scenery abruptly. The engine faltered and she swore at it. Not now, damn it! Not here. Why did I even think of being lost and alone, she asked herself. Clouds of steam began to come from beneath the hood, and rusty drops of water spattered the windshield. She was forced to pull over to the side of the road and stop amid sand and scrub and stones. She switched the engine off and got out of the car immediately, in case of fire.

She swore again at her bad luck. The desert stretched out to the horizon on all sides and did not hear her. There was no house in sight, and the main road lay far behind her. When the car did not immediately burst into flames, she opened the hood to investigate the problem, though she knew there was no hope of her repairing any serious breakdown on her own. Mechanics had not been among the required subjects for newspaper reporters. Clouds of steam rose from the radiator as she peered at the enigmatic bits of machinery that crowded the engine compartment. When the steam cleared somewhat, she saw the broken radiator hose with water still running out.

"Shit!" she said.

The car had been air conditioned, and now the heat struck her like a blow as she stood beside the road, leaning against the fender of her useless vehicle. Being a city dweller, Janice at first did not realize how much trouble she was in. She looked around at the wide open spaces and wondered how long it would be before someone came along to help her. That was what always happened in cities. Stay with the car, was the usual advice. So she climbed back in, leaving the hood open as a sign of distress and opening the windows to allow what breeze there was (not very much, and it, like the land, was hot) to circulate. Janice recalled with dismay that she had not seen another car for almost an hour.

Only when she had waited for several empty hours, taking shelter from the baking sun inside her car, did she begin to realize that no one was coming. The thought was frightening. She had only a half bottle of water, bought at her last fuel stop, and no food. She guessed she would not last long trying to walk in either direction. She knew that she stood a better chance of being found eventually if she stayed by her car, but the idea of doing nothing did not appeal to her. She was decisive by nature, used to making up her mind and getting her own way. So, against all she knew, she decided to walk. She chose to continue on the way she had been going, assuming she would be missed at her destination and someone would set out looking for her when she failed to show up as planned.

She got out accordingly, taking the water with her, locked all her belongings into the trunk, and began to walk in the direction she had been heading. Let there be cowboys and horses, she thought. Or, even better, mechanics and tow trucks. Her vacation idea began to seem much less appealing to her. Next time, she vowed, she would stick to what she knew. But there was the present to get through.

After what she judged to be five miles of walking, the present began to look like taking a long time to get through. For one thing, there were no signs of habitation, let alone civilization. For another, the heat was becoming a real problem. She was sweating, and her clothes clung damply to her body. She was tempted fleetingly to take them off, but the idea of walking in the nude (or even seminude) along what was really a public road (even if the public was conspicuously absent) stopped her. What if the public became suddenly less absent? At least there would be no chance of anyone not stopping, she imagined. But she kept her clothes on. Her shoes, designed for city pavements, were not wearing well in the rocky soil. The rough going of what had become a dirt road in the mountains (foothills, she corrected herself) required different footgear. High country was not high-heel country. The sweat ran down her legs, making dark stains on her tights.

The dusty road seemed to wind on forever beneath the cloudless blue of the sky. The sun beat down without respite. Janice was having serious doubts about the wisdom of having abandoned the car. She was debating with herself whether to go back (thus admitting defeat, something she found very hard to do), when she saw a green oasis of trees and shady overhanging rock in the distance. That would be a place to rest, to recoup her strength, to make fresh plans. More important, it lay ahead of her, not behind, so she did not have to decide just then about turning back, with all its unpleasant overtones of defeat. She walked on, her strength renewed, just by having a goal of some sort in sight.

The road wound in under the shadows of the trees, beckoning her onward. She fancied she could hear the sound of falling water. A waterfall, she told herself, would be heavenly. A swim in cool water would allow her to carry on with renewed strength to her destination—the place that called itself The Last Resort in the brochures she had seen before booking her holiday. She thought the name clever at the time, but now that she had trudged so far in search of the actual place, she found it less so.

The shade under the trees was indeed welcome. Janice felt better almost at once. And, yes, there was a stream running alongside the dusty road in a bed of gravel. She turned to follow it upstream, reasoning that a waterfall, if there was one, would lie in the direction of the higher, rocky ground. Visions of showering in icy, clear spring water led her on. She forgot the sweaty discomfort of the past two hours in the hope of refreshing herself in the clear water that flowed from the rocky uplands. She left the road and wandered among the trees. At last she came upon a small waterfall, where the stream ran over a ledge of stone and fell free for eight or ten feet. It was not the spectacular, free-springing waterfall she had hoped to find, but it was welcome nonetheless. It fell into a shaded pool that invited bathing. There was neither sight nor sound of other humans as she stood on the bank and began to unbutton her damp blouse.

Janice had been told by many men that she had beautiful breasts, but she had not paid much attention. Her breasts were indeed beautiful, springing round and full and firm when she unhooked her bra. There was no hint of droop, and the generous nipples were surrounded by large dark areolae. One of her lovers had enjoyed licking them until they stood up taut and firm, and Janice herself had finally come to admit that they were an important erogenous zone when she had had a shattering orgasm merely from having her nipples tongued and nipped. The warm air caressed her bare breasts, and her nipples erected in response to it—and to the memory of her lover nuzzling her.

Impatiently, Janice dismissed him from her thoughts. That was the past. He was the past. This was now. She unfastened the waistband of her skirt and let it fall to the grass, standing for a moment in her panties and hose before stripping them off as well. Nude, she straightened her back and stretched her arms over her head. As she stretched, she heard a sudden sharp whistle behind her, a loud high-pitched sound. Startled, she lowered her arms and tried to cover herself as she searched for the source of the sound. Another whistle, longer and higher pitched, came from the opposite side, almost as if in answer to the first. Together, they sounded like the sort of wolf whistle she had often attracted as she walked past building sites—and had always resented.

But here there was no one. Janice stood for long minutes, one arm covering her breasts and one hand covering her mons veneris, in the classic pose of Botticelli's Venus rising from the waves. Only in her case, she had been about to step into them. Well, into the pool at least, she reminded herself as she slowly relaxed. No other sounds disturbed the silence of the stream bank. It must have been birds calling to one another, she told herself as she lowered her arms and stepped into the pool.

The water was cool on her heated skin, refreshing her at once. As she soaked, she could feel herself relaxing, her tiredness and annoyance slipping away. Skinny-dipping in sylvan pools, she thought, had its points. The added *frisson* of being naked outdoors was welcome. A pity most of us have to make do with bathtubs most of the time, she thought. Janice lay back, her head pillowed on a smooth stone to keep her hair dry. She closed her eyes and drowsed. She might even have drifted off to sleep if the whistles had not sounded again. This time they were closer. Startled, she sat up and looked around for the birds. There were no signs of them.

Nor, when she got quickly to her feet, of her clothes.

Janice felt a stab of panic as she looked at the empty spot where she had left them on the grass. Wildly, she looked around, doubting her memory. Had she left them *there,* or *there?* Or somewhere else? No matter. They had vanished. Janice wondered if she were in one of those dreams in which one found oneself naked in the street, looking vainly for some-place to hide. This felt like one of those dreams, but the sun shone through the canopy of leaves, dappling her nakedness with shifting patterns of shadow. The wind blew softly. The stream flowed around her calves. This was real. She was naked in what others were wont to call the great outdoors. Janice did not think of them quite that way. Open spaces had always seemed strange, sometimes threatening. Her panic flooded back. She felt extremely vulnerable in her nakedness.

She scrambled onto the bank, breasts bobbing and breath short, to search for her missing apparel. Once clothed, she knew, she would feel more in control of the situation, not so panic-stricken. The matter of being in the wide open spaces on foot did not seem threatening at all when compared to her present situation.

Janice cast about in widening circles for her missing clothes, fighting her panic, telling herself to think logically. Clothes, she told herself, do not simply vanish. Someone or something has to move them. At the thought, she felt a new flood of panic, as if she had been doused with ice water. Some *thing* had taken her clothes. She thought immediately of a large cat, a puma or mountain lion, stalking her, watching her even now from the surrounding bush in her nakedness and fear. Logic once again came to her aid: mountain lions and pumas do not collect their victims' clothing and hide it simply in order to avoid the incon-venience of dismembering a clothed body.

But there was one animal that did. Janice froze in mid-stride, realizing that she was not being stalked by some *thing*, but by some *one*. Being surrounded by men lurking in the brush while she was naked was frightening. Logic was not much help.

Her first impulse was to run, but there seemed no particular direction in which to go to avoid the danger she perceived. Her second thought was that signs of panic—like running—might provoke the attack she feared. But standing still and being *regarded* by strangers was intolerable. However, no course of action suggested itself. *When in danger or in doubt, run in circles, scream, and shout.* The old joke ran through her head as she tried simultaneously to cover herself with her arms while she tried not to look concerned about her nakedness.

The whistle sounded again, behind her, and this time it was definitely a wolf whistle. Janice spun to face the sound but could see nothing in the bushes that surrounded the clearing in which she so nudely stood. From the same direction came the unmistakable sound of a twig snapping as it was trodden on. It was too much for Janice. She turned and fled in the opposite direction.

Running on bare feet is never easy for those who usually go about well shod. Janice constantly stepped on sharp things, twigs or bits of rock, but she could not watch where she was setting her feet if she wanted to make any progress. The whistle sounded again, behind her, but no farther away than at first. Her pursuer was following, guided no doubt by the noise she made as she fled. When the whistle sounded a third time, still no nearer, it occurred to Janice that she was being driven. She imagined that whoever was following could easily overtake her if, as was probable, he had shoes as well as some idea of the territory in which she was a barefoot (and bare-assed) stranger. But if she were being driven, then to what (or to whom) was she being driven? The answer to that question, while important, was less so than keeping out of the clutches of whoever was behind her. She knew he was there, whereas she did not know for sure whether there was anyone else ahead of her. Her pursuer might be merely trying to tire her out.

And he was succeeding. Her breath sawed in her dry throat as she fled. The bushes and the low-hanging branches of the trees lashed her as she ran, leaving red marks on her skin and once, even cutting her. The sweat of her combined fear and exertion mixed with the blood from the slash on her stomach ran down into her pubic hair, trickling between her legs and making her thighs slick. Janice was by now a far cry from the confident young woman who had set out lighthearted-edly for a holiday in the mountains. But she was too frightened to dwell on that unsettling thought.

The whistle sounded again, off to one side, but seemingly nearer. Janice turned her head toward the sound and ran straight into a thick, low branch. The crack on the head was softened by her long hair, but she fell to the ground unconscious.

When she came round, the shadows were longer. It was getting on toward evening, she judged. Then recollection came back to her. Where was the man who had been pursuing her? He must have seen her knock herself out on the branch, and he could easily have taken her while she lay unconscious. At that thought, she became aware of her aching head. When she tried to raise her hand to the injury, she discovered with a new chill of fear that her hands had been tied behind her back while she lay insensible. Her pursuer had not simply aban-doned the game when the quarry had dropped. He had stood right over her, looked at her, touched her, tied her hands. And now where was he?

Janice tugged frantically at the ropes that bound her, fighting panic as she looked wildly about for some sign of the man who had done this to her. There was no sign of anyone nearby, but she knew he would not merely have tied her up and then abandoned her. Or had he? There were people who liked the idea of leaving another helpless, but usually they stayed around to watch the quarry's struggles. Janice tried to stand up, but she lost her balance and fell once again. After yet another failure, she realized that she would never make it with her hands tied. Once again she tugged at the ropes, but they held her. She paused for a moment in thought, then rolled over to the tree whose branch had felled her, the leaves and sand sticking to her sweaty body. Bracing herself against the trunk, she struggled to her feet and once more looked wildly about her. The frou-frou of the wind in the branches was the only sound in all that silence.

Now she would have welcomed the sound of her erstwhile pursuer or the shrill whistle that had driven her in panic through the trees. Anything would have been preferable to being alone. But the silence prevailed. Finally Janice could stand it no longer.

"I know you're out there!" she shouted. "For god's sake show yourself. Help me!" Nothing. "Oh god, I don't want to be alone!" she wailed. Hysteria was not far from the surface. At another time she might have fought it down. But she felt a choking panic in these unfamiliar surroundings, in her bizarre condition. Could one go mad with fear? And how long would it take?

The silence remained unbroken. Janice knew she could count on no outside help. She would have to fight down her own fear. That knowledge helped her regain some of her composure. She was almost sure her pursuer was watching her, but she couldn't help that. She needed to get her hands free. Afterward, she would deal with what came next. Once more Janice tugged at the ropes and twisted her hands behind her back, but to no avail. She could not wriggle free, so the next step was to find something to cut the rope.

In all good adventure stories there is always something lying about that cuts rope. A Swiss Army knife, for instance, dropped by some careless Boy Scout. Or a shard of glass or pottery. Or even a sharp rock. Janice saw none of these things as she looked about. There were only trees and bushes and the sound of the wind—the lengthening shadows that told her night would fall soon. She shivered at the idea of being naked and bound in the woods after dark. She would feel helpless enough in that setting with her hands free. Bound as she was, she would be wholly at the mercy of whatever—or whoever—found her. The primeval fears never really leave us, she thought in some calm corner of her mind. I must fight them, she told herself. The rest of her mind filled with those fears and threatened to swamp what sanity she had left. It would be infinitely more difficult to keep calm in the dark.

Janice fought down her rising panic once again. If there was nothing nearby that would help free her, she would have to look elsewhere. She began to walk in the direction she thought the road lay, not because there was any more hope of finding what she sought there, but rather because it would be more familiar, something made by man, not really a part of the wilderness.

To occupy her mind, Janice tried to concentrate on memories of earlier life—before she had decided to take this holiday that had turned nightmarish—even before she had entered the competitive world of the journalist, where she had carved her own niche by her own hard work. Not unnaturally, she found herself remembering an earlier walk in the woods, not so dissimilar from this one. Only then she had not been alone. William had been with her. She had never forgotten him, as she had forgotten earlier (and later) boyfriends/lovers. She must have been seventeen. He could not have been much older, but they had become an item soon after meeting.

There was something mysterious about William that had drawn her. For her part, she thought he had been attracted by her predilection for wildly improbable schemes and adventures. It had been her idea, for instance, that they go skinny - dipping in the quarry on the night of the football game to which every other student had gone. And it had been her lead that had turned the swim into their first sexual encounter. Every girl remembers losing her virginity, but not every girl remembers it with such pleasure.

Janice had been determined to rid herself of her own innocence and discover what sex was all about. William had been slow and gentle, and she had screamed in ecstasy where she had been expecting at least discomfort, even outright pain . . . and guilt. But there had been none of those things. Even now Janice could remember William's hand between her naked thighs, touching her so surely on the spot that gave her such pleasure. They had lain on a blanket under the stars, and they had made love for what seemed like forever. She had been aroused by the idea of sex under the sky.

They had gone on to have sex in several other venues, always returning though to the quarry or the woods, where they could lie naked in the darkness or the sunshine.

It had been Janice who had broached the idea of having sex

while tied up. She was never sure where the idea had come from, but one day she decided to try it. She had taken the leather laces from her then-fashionable knee boots, putting them into her rucksack, along with a leather dog collar and a chain lead. She had been trembling with anticipation, she remembered, as she made her preparations for the picnic with William.

William had been startled by the idea, but he was eager enough once Janice had explained what she wanted him to do. They had gone to her parents' summer cabin in the Maine woods. It had been a late spring day, with the leaves still fresh and green, before the deeper hue of summer dulled them. A warm day, sunny, full of the promise of spring and the long summer holiday—and the beginning of adulthood. The air itself seemed full of exciting possibilities as they had taken the path into the thick forest. William had brought along the rucksack with the leather thongs, the dog lead, and their lunch. Janice had brought along a tremulous anticipation.

Her chest had been so tight with the idea of new adventure that she could hardly speak. So it was William who turned to her and asked if she was ready. Janice nodded wordlessly.

"Take your clothes off, Janice," he had told her, and she had done so without protest.

When she was nude, he had tied her wrists together behind her back with the leather bootlace, but she had not been satisfied.

"Please tie me tighter, William," she had asked, wanting to feel the bite of the thongs around her wrists and know that she was in his power.

He had untied the knots, pulling the leather cords until they bit into the flesh of her wrists, and then he had secured the ends once more.

"Better?" he had asked.

Wordlessly, she had nodded, feeling the excitement become a hard knot in her belly. Naked in the forest, bound for the first time in her life, she had been wet and parted without even being touched. But there was more to the ritual.

"The collar, please, William," Janice had said, standing still as he buckled it around her throat. He attached the lead, letting it hang down between her breasts. Then, something not in her plans, he had blindfolded her with his handkerchief. Janice had felt a thrill of fear mingle with her excitement.

William had said nothing for so long that she wondered if he had gone off and left her. "William?" she had said in a small voice, "are you there?"

"Yes, Janice. I was looking at you."

"Do you like what you see?"

By way of reply he had brushed against her, letting her feel his erection against her mons. She was surprised to learn that he was naked. He could have left his clothes on while she was nude, but he had chosen to join her.

"Oh god!" she gasped. "I want you inside me now. Please, Will!" She didn't often use the short form of his name, but now it came naturally to her.

"I know, Janice," he had said. "But wait just a little longer." His voice sounded as taut and strained as hers. Briefly, he had let his hand rest on her sex, his finger tracing the line of her labia and drawing a gasp of pleasure from her.

Then William had tugged on the dog lead, signaling her to follow him. Slowly, he led her deeper into the forest, guiding her so that she did not stumble on the uneven ground.

Janice had voluntarily put herself completely in his power, and she had followed without protest. Perversely, she ignored her own independent nature, drawn to surrender responsibility, if only for the moment, as a relief from the necessity of having to always decide things. And in the end, it had all been worthwhile. William had shown an instant aptitude for the game, inventing things Janice had never dreamed of, things that propelled her to screaming orgasm, time and again, that spring day and later.

Deep in the woods—Janice didn't know where because of the blindfold—William had laid her down on the blanket they used on their picnics and commenced to arouse her. He had lain beside her, his erect cock pressing against her flank, his hand between her parted thighs as he rubbed her labia, pausing now and again to slide his finger part way into her sex and tease the engorged bud of her clitoris. Janice, already excited by the game they had begun that day, had begged him to enter her, but he had made her wait, circling her breasts with his fingers, squeezing her nipples between his thumb and forefinger, kissing her all over, his lips and breath hot on her neck, her earlobes, her throat, her breasts. Then he had moved lower, spreading her legs so that he could use his lips and teeth on her parted cunt lips and, oh god! his tongue on her clitoris.

Janice had been wild with the excitement of being aroused while helpless to resist. And when William had entered her at last, making her lie on top of him so that her bound hands were not crushed beneath their combined weight, she had screamed with pleasure as the long length of him slid into her, and she felt herself impaled and ecstatic. Only William's arms, tight around her waist and holding her hands behind her back, kept her from falling off him as they rose and fell to their wild rhythm. Janice was shaken by wave after wave of pleasure until, finally, William could hold back no longer. She had felt him spurt inside her, and she had nearly fainted with the pleasure of it.

Afterwards, they had lain together, joined, for what seemed like hours, the silence broken occasionally by the flight of a bird or the scuttering of small animals in the underbrush. The soughing of the wind in the branches overhead had lulled her to sleep.

And now, as she made her way through the underbrush, her belly and thighs and breasts lashed by the branches she was unable to ward off, she wondered how they had managed to lose contact. If she ever got out of this, she promised herself, she would track him down and make him stay with her. But she had to get out of this. She looked about wildly for anything that could be used to cut through her bonds. Nothing offered itself. Once she staggered on uneven ground, falling to her knees and then struggling to her feet once more by leaning against a tree.

As she struggled to her feet, Janice's breast brushed the rough bark of the tree. Excitement coursed through her, almost like an electric shock, at the contact. Her nipple felt like it had when her erstwhile lover had used his teeth and tongue to arouse her. She leaned against the tree once more, brushing her nipples against the bark, and felt another thrill of pleasure starting in her breasts and working its way down to her belly and between her legs, making her knees weak with its sharpness. She looked down at her nipples. They were erect, taut, and suffused with the warmth of arousal. And Janice welcomed it. Anything would have been better than her terror, and this was far better than just anything. She leaned against the rough bark, pressing her engorged nipples to its hardness, and she let out a low moan of pleasure. She wished William were here now.

The shrill whistle that had been pursuing her sounded again, jerking Janice back to the present and sending her blundering through the bushes again. She fancied it had been nearer this time, and she flushed with embarrassment as she imagined her pursuer watching her in heat as she rubbed her breasts against a tree. Now she fled blindly, forgetting to look for a means to free herself, intent only on getting away.

When the noose dropped from an overhanging branch, settling itself around her chest beneath her breasts and pinning her arms to her sides as it jerked tight, Janice was taken completely by surprise. She felt herself lifted off her feet into the air, and she had a brief impression of someone swinging down to the ground as she was lifted off it. Janice jerked and struggled, kicking her legs as she twisted slowly around in the air, facing first the tree from whose branch she was suspended, then the brush and the surrounding grove, and then a man wearing jeans and a denim shirt who held the end of the rope that imprisoned her. She twisted around further, still kicking frantically. The rope cut into her flesh as she struggled. When next she faced in the direction of her captor, she saw him tying the end of the rope to the tree trunk. He then stepped back to watch her struggles.

Casually he put out a hand and grasped her leg, stopping her slow circling.

Janice gathered her breath and said forcefully, "Let me go! You have no right to do this. Let me go at once!"

Her captor made no move to obey. Instead, he looked at her levelly, in a way that made her go cold with dread. But he made no threatening move toward her.

"Miss Singleton, I presume," he said with a grin in his voice.

Janice retorted angrily, instinctively, "Ms. Singleton, if you please."

"Good, Miss Singleton," he replied. "I wanted to be sure we

had gotten the right one. It would have been embarrassing if we got the wrong person. You've led us a chase, Janice."

The casual use of her first name by this menacing stranger sent a chill of fear through her. With difficulty, she summoned the breath to demand shakily, "Who . . . who are you? And how do you know . . . my name?" Janice was acutely aware of the inanity of these questions as she dangled in the air, but she had to ask them.

"I," began her captor, hastily amending it to "we" as a second man came up, "We are your holiday hosts, Janice. We came to meet you so we could begin as we intend to go on. You know, get you accustomed to being tied up and taking orders . . . and the rest," he finished vaguely. "But," he resumed, "you surprised us by showing up on foot. We had expected you to arrive by car and had set up a different diversion to make you stop. When we saw you walking, we had to change our plans quickly. Still, even if I do say so, we managed to get the job done neatly, wouldn't you agree?"

The question seemed to answer itself. Janice thought she had been taken neatly enough, but she wasn't going to say so. Instead, she insisted again that she be let loose. "And give me my clothes back," she added, as she saw that the second man, undoubtedly the one who had driven her through the woods to this trap, was carrying her clothing and handbag.

She was ignored, as one might ignore a fretful child. And Janice, bound, naked, suspended before the gaze of her two captors, felt herself flush with a mixture of helpless anger, embarrassment, and . . . excitement. To cover her confusion, Janice demanded once more to be set free, kicking out at the man standing nearest to her and managing a glancing blow to his arm.

Casually, he reached out, grasped the foot she had kicked

him with, and spun her in the air. Janice found herself turning so rapidly that she felt dizzy, the limited panorama of trees, brush, and her two captors whirling past. She fought down her giddiness, not wanting to humiliate herself by being sick. She closed her eyes to avoid the confusion of her whirling. Gradually she slowed to a stop, and just as she began to think the worst was over, the twisted rope that held her helplessly off the ground began to untwist, turning her in the opposite direction with gradually increasing speed. The feeling of giddiness returned, and once again she closed her eyes. She was afraid that if she opened her mouth to demand her freedom, or anything else, she would be sick. So she clenched her jaws as she spun.

When she came to a stop, the giddiness subsided. She opened her eyes and found the two men still looking at her. It was getting toward evening by now, the sun low in the west and the air beginning to feel chilly on her naked flesh. Janice felt her nipples harden as the breeze cooled her.

Both men noticed, to her chagrin. "It's only because I'm cold," she insisted.

"And were you cold when you were rubbing yourself on that tree awhile back?" demanded the one who had chased her through the woods.

Janice reddened.

"She was rubbing her tits against a tree," the man told his companion. "But I suppose it was because she really wanted to hug it. You know, like these eco-freaks who go around talking to plants and trees. Only, with her hands tied, she couldn't really do anything except rub against it, friendly-like." Turning to Janice, he asked her, "Was that the way of it?"

Furious and embarrassed, she said nothing.

"Well," he continued, to break the silence, "I guess that's

enough chitchat for now. We'd best be getting her along to someplace more comfortable."

His companion nodded.

"Unless," continued the one who had driven her to this trap, "she'd like to stay here for a bit longer. Would you like that, Janice? We could come back and get you in the morning if you'd like to commune a bit more with nature. If we lifted you a bit higher off the ground, you wouldn't have to worry much about wild animals."

"No!" Janice shouted, her earlier fear about being alone and helpless returning. "Don't leave me here!" Even to herself, she sounded nearly hysterical. She fought to control her voice. "Please don't leave me here," she managed to say, more quietly, hating herself for the submission but unable to face the prospect of a night suspended naked from a tree.

"All right, then. That's settled. Janice agrees to come along with us and have her holiday just as she planned." The man holding her clothes set them down on the ground while his companion moved to untie the rope that held her suspended.

When her feet touched the ground, Janice found herself very shaky on her feet. Noticing her difficulty, the man who had taken her clothes from her put his arms around her waist and let her lean on him until she recovered somewhat.

"I suppose," he said, "we should introduce ourselves if we're going to spend a few weeks together. I'm Harry," and, pointing to his companion, "that's Mark."

"Not our real names," Mark said with a laugh. "After you've been with us for a while we may tell you who we are. But in the meantime, I'm sure you can appreciate the need for discretion. We'll be your hosts while you stay at The Last Resort. And we'll do everything we can to make your stay enjoyable."

"Then how about untying me and giving me back my clothes?" Janice asked.

"Well, now, that might not be such a good idea. We need to know you're responding to the experience more naturally before we can do that. But if things work out as we expect, we'll be able to allow you a few freedoms. Just be patient for a while until you settle into the regime."

"Regime? What regime?" Janice asked. "It sounds more like a concentration camp than a holiday resort."

"I wouldn't put it quite that way," Harry responded. "Most of our guests come to enjoy the sex and the riding and the roping at our place. Many of them come back again and again for more. And the ones that don't mostly don't because they've found someone closer to home to give them what they want, just as we gave them what they wanted while they were here with us."

"And you keep them tied up the whole time?" Janice asked.

"Well, under restraint, you could say, but not always tied up as you are now. Unless that's what they want. Some of them do. But we always begin this way with new guests. Until they settle in, like we said."

"And supposing they don't 'settle in'?" Janice asked. "What if they return with the police, or the sheriff, or whatever passes for the law out this way?"

"Well, our biggest protection is that they don't know where to find us," Mark told her.

"I could find you again. I would only have to follow this road, asking at every place I came to until I got to you," Janice said.

"That would work if we were up this road," Mark said. "But we're not. We're not even in this state. We have a long drive ahead of us before we reach The Last Resort. We sometimes use this place to meet our guests. But sometimes we use other places. We have to be careful, just in case someone does try to return with the cavalry."

"And do you mean that no one has?" Janice asked, incredulously.

"Not so far," Mark said. "Are you planning to be the first?"

Janice started to say yes, but she thought of what might happen if she made the threat at this point. A naked woman with her hands tied behind her back was not in a strong bargaining position. Nevertheless, she could not bring herself to say an outright "no," so she changed the subject. "How do you keep your guests from remembering the roads you drive over to get to the resort?"

"We blindfold them," Harry said.

Janice digested that for a moment, and then she thought of a new objection. "What about my car? Someone will have to come and repair it and return it to the rental company. If I don't go back with it, or at least call, they will surely call the police."

"We'll get your car back on time," Harry told her. "It's all part of the service. And," he added with a smile, "it keeps the police away from us."

"But they know Janice Singleton rented the car. If I don't return it, they will want to know what happened." Janice wondered why she was raising all these objections. It was already clear that she was going to go with the two men, willingly or not. And she was beginning to lean toward the willingly, because her newspaperwoman's (as well as her personal) curiosity was piqued. But her habitual independence forced her to go through the motions of argument.

"One of our alumnae will take it back, and the rental company will be none the wiser. After all, we have to provide transport for our guests when they are ready to leave. So one of the girls going back will take your car, and when you go, you will take someone else's car, and so on. Everyone gets home safely and conveniently in the end," Harry said. "But what made you get out and walk? And where is your car?" he asked.

"The damned thing broke down," Janice said angrily, "about five miles back toward the main road. The radiator hose is broken."

"That's easy enough to fix. We'll take care of it as we pass, and one of us can drive your car along to the resort."

A Trip In the Dark

2

Harry produced a roll of wide surgical tape from his pocket. Janice watched as he cut two short pieces from it. This was the blindfold he had mentioned, she knew. If she were going to run, now was her last chance, before she was deprived of sight. She stood still, knowing that she would not run. She would not get far before she was recaptured. And there was nowhere for her to run where she would be safer than she was here. It was a new sensation for her to be so circumscribed in her choices. She could either submit or try to flee. No other course of action was open to her. She chose submission as the lesser of the two evils, though that went against the grain.

"Close your eyes, Janice," Harry told her.

And she did, standing very still as he sealed her eyes with the wide tape, pressing it firmly against her eyelids and into the contours of her eye sockets and her face. When he took his hands away, Janice tried to open her eyes and found that she could not do so. No ray of light penetrated the darkness in which she stood, not even the residual glow that allows us to "see" the sun even with our eyes closed. She trembled, not wholly in fear.

"No need to be afraid, Janice," Harry told her.

She was angry that he had seen her tremor. "I'm not afraid," she told him in as firm a voice as she could muster.

"No? Then you must be trembling with excitement," Harry retorted.

His reply made her even more furious, as much at herself as at him. She did not enjoy being read so easily. Janice said nothing, thinking that any answer she made would be turned against her.

"Mark," Harry said, "go get the car. Janice is ready to go with us, I think." To Janice, he said, "See how easy it is when you relax? By the time you're ready to leave us, you won't want to go. Many of our alumnae wish they had more time at the resort. So will you, after you've been gentled to the bit, so to speak. I can tell about women. You'll love it."

His easy assumption of control over her and his casual reading of her mood infuriated Janice still more, especially as he had hit so close to the mark. But she kept silent. For once in her life she could think of no effective retort.

Mark's footsteps receded, and she stood in darkness, waiting perforce for her captor to make the next move. The next move surprised her. Harry tied the rope on which she had been suspended around her neck, wrapping it twice around and securing it with a knot at her throat. It was so like the dog collar and chain William had used to lead her into the woods all those years ago. This time she trembled with the force of the memory. She couldn't help herself. She felt herself go wet and knew her labia were parted. It took so little to set her off when one knew the right buttons to push, as William had. As these two did.

Janice jerked in surprise, her breath catching on a gasp as Harry's finger insinuated itself between her legs, tracing the line of her labia and touching, knowingly and too briefly, the hard button of her clitoris. "Will," she said, then went silent.

"Will what?" Harry asked.

When she remained silent, he brought his finger up to her nose so she could smell the evidence of her arousal. Janice felt the quick flare of anger, but mixed with it was the realization that she was now excited too. But she could not—would not— ask Harry to take her, as she had asked William.

As if reading her mind again, Harry said, "You'll come round soon. We thought you might, from the information we got. It's good to know it was right."

"Information?" Janice asked, thoughts of impalement among the tall, green trees vanishing abruptly. "What information? How could you know. . . ?" She trailed off uncertainly, unwilling to complete the thought lest she reveal too much of herself.

"How could we know you'd like this kind of reception? Is that what you were about to ask?" Harry finished the thought for her. "Never mind that now. When we've become better acquainted maybe we'll tell you how we study our guests in advance. If we think it will help you. And us."

Janice found his reply both enigmatic and frightening. She imagined being followed and photographed when she least expected it, her privacy invaded without her knowledge. Maybe they had been behind the burglary of her apartment not so long ago. But she said no more. She, too, might find it useful to reveal knowledge at her own pace.

The sound of a vehicle approaching at slow speed broke the tableau. With a gentle tug on her lead, Harry led Janice in the direction of the car, which had stopped and now waited with its engine idling. Janice caught a faint whiff of exhaust in the cooling air. Suddenly, she realized why she had been blind-folded before being loaded into their car. They didn't want her to be able to identify it (or them) later, in case she decided to seek legal vengeance for her abduction.

Janice found herself taking refuge in inanity in order not to think too much about where they would be taking her . . . and why. She already knew she would be bedded by both of them sooner or later. There was no other point in trapping her as they had done. Abduction, she was thinking, from the Latin *ducto, ductare,* to lead, plus *ab,* away. I am being quite literally led away. She shivered again, again not wholly in dread.

They were very thorough and practiced in their work, if the abduction of young women could be called work. Harry stopped her by letting her halter go slack. Deprived of the sense of direction its pull had given her, Janice stood still. Unable to see, she didn't want to risk injury by blundering into obstacles.

She heard doors opening and revised her guess about her captors' vehicle. The sounds she heard reminded her of the doors on delivery vans, the sliding type in particular. Logical, she told herself. It wouldn't do to transport a naked female, bound and blindfolded, in an ordinary car. Too many people would see her, even in the dark, and questions were bound to be asked. And, Janice thought, if she—I—knew there were people nearby, I might be tempted to call out for help. Unless she—I—were gagged, she added silently.

As is so often the case, the thought was precursor to the deed.

"Janice," she heard Harry (Mark?) say. It was vaguely frightening not to know who was speaking.

"Janice," he continued, "drink some water."

A bottle was held to her lips, and she drank thirstily, realizing how much she needed to. The flight through the woods and her capture had taken a lot out of her. She felt the cool liquid run out of the corners of her mouth, down her chin, over her bare breasts and midriff, trickling finally into her pubic hair and between her thighs. She turned her head away as a sign that she had drunk enough.

"Janice," Harry said again. She decided it was Harry.

"Janice, we are going to gag you now, in case you decide to scream for help at the last minute. Open your mouth," he ordered.

And she did, docile under his hands as he stuffed some type of cloth into her open mouth, filling it. The material felt silky and smelled—tasted—somehow foul. She tried to force the packing out, but a hand clamped across her mouth forestalled her. She fought and bucked, trying to dislodge the hand and the gag. Hands held her. The sound of tape being unwound and torn off lent further strength to her struggles, but she could not break their hold on her.

Suddenly she felt her nose being pinched shut, cutting off her air. She tried to breathe through the packing in her mouth, tasting again the strange, foul flavor of the gag. She couldn't breathe! She became panicky, twisting and writhing, beginning to black out.

"Janice," she heard dimly through the roaring in her ears, "Janice, stand still and we'll let you breathe."

Immediately she stopped struggling, and the hand pinching her nose shut was withdrawn. She sucked in huge greedy breaths, the blackness inside her head receding, the roaring in her ears lessening at once. She waited, trembling, while her captor tore off strips of the tape, covering her face from chin to nose, winding it around her head under her hair, carefully lifting the thick strands out of the way so the tape would stick to the back of her head. Harry made a thorough job of it, cutting off the end of the tape and pressing all of it firmly against her flesh, making sure it stuck tightly.

"Janice," he said, "say something."

"Ummmmnnnnghhhh," was the only sound she could make, muffled and choked back by the packing in her mouth.

"Good. No more noise, eh?"

Meekly, she nodded, tasting the foul gag.

"Mark and I," she heard Harry say, "thought we should use your own panties to gag you, but we added a little flavoring of our own. Can you guess what it was?"

Suddenly the light dawned on Janice. They had urinated on her panties before stuffing them into her mouth. That was the strangely foul taste she could now detect. "Nnnnngggghhh!" she said, throwing her head from side to side, wanting the gag removed.

"Good," Harry said with a short laugh. "I see you understand. So now we'll get on with the next step, which is loading you aboard and whisking you off to your great adventure."

Janice realized then that she would have to endure the foul-tasting gag for some time. The idea dismayed her. Once more she shook her head violently, pointing her face in the direction she imagined Harry was standing. "Nnnmmmmmmggghhhhhhh!" she said, as loudly as she could manage. "Eeeesse aay oouugh!"

"No," Harry told her, from behind her back. "Now shut up, unless you want a taste of the whip."

For emphasis, he stung her bottom lightly with what felt like a cane. Janice yipped in surprise. She had not expected to be beaten, but apparently she would have to reckon on that in the future. She had never been gagged before either. That was something even she and William had never tried. She would have to deal with being unable to speak. That made her feel as if she had lost an important part of her ability to influence the course of events, especially as those events affected her. She felt a touch of cold dread as she realized that these men could do anything to her at any time, while she was powerless to do anything either to them or for herself. At the same time, she felt the excitement of the unknown stirring in her belly and making her knees weak with anticipation.

Janice felt hands under her armpits and at her ankles. She was abruptly lifted off her feet and, slung like a sack of potatoes between Mark and Harry, loaded into the van. They lifted her onto a seat and arranged her so her bound wrists hung down behind it. They strapped her into the seat, wide belts pulled tightly around her waist and chest, just beneath her breasts. She imagined them jutting out, as if offered to her captors.

"Look at those tits," Mark (Harry?) said. "Begging to be felt."

And he did. Hands cupped her breasts from behind her, and she shivered at the touch. Thumbs and fingers pinched her nipples, and she gasped in delight, feeling herself erect, both at her breasts and between her legs. Janice felt an intense excitement, as if her whole body were aflame, begging to be touched, caressed, teased, explored. She moaned softly, deep in her throat, relaxing to the hands, her thighs parting involuntarily to allow access to her melting center.

The invitation did not go unnoticed. Another pair of hands stroked her thighs, from knees to crotch, slowly, up and down, again and again. When the hands settled at the tops of her thighs, she opened them as far as she could. And gasped again as a finger traced the line of her labia, parting them, sliding inside her, meeting no resistance, her cunt already slick and lubricated, ready for penetration. The finger slid deeply into her. She felt the knuckles against her labia, and she moaned again, the sound muffled by her gag, but unmistakable: she wanted more, more inside her, more teasing of her breasts and their swollen nipples, the touch of fingers on her clitoris. She felt the finger inside her being joined by a thumb, and together they rubbed and nipped the hard button at the apex of her cunt, and all at once she was coming, her hips moving backward and forward seemingly of their own volition, her back arched to offer her breasts fully to the grasping hands, the kneading fingers.

The straps holding her to the seat creaked with her movement, digging into her flesh and making her wild as her body sought to move and was restrained, her bound hands twisting behind her back, her fingernails digging into her palms as she clenched her hands into fists. And then the tide of her pleasure surged through her once more so that she held herself rigid, straining against her bonds, moaning as she came again.

Her captors gave her no respite. The fondling of her breasts, the pinching of her nipples, the insistent finger and thumb kneading her clitoris: all this continued when she thought she would have to rest, and Janice realized that she would be made to come again. Weakly, she tried to dissuade the two men who were driving her wild: "Nnnnnggggh! Nnnnnnn!" It was if she had made no sound.

Janice felt the familiar surge begin again in her belly, then travel down her legs and throughout her straining body as she was driven to yet another orgasm. If she had not been gagged, she realized in some corner of her mind that allowed her to play the spectator even as she was driven wild, she would have been screaming, shouting out her pleasure for all to hear. She heard herself moaning, a series of muffled cries that revealed her imminent climax: "Unnnnnnh! Uunnhhhh! Unnnnnnnhhhhhggghhh!" Her body was beyond her control. Even the tiny part of her that was left as onlooker was being swept away as she writhed and bucked against her seat, against her bonds, surrendering herself finally, fully, to those insistent hands that gave her no surcease, that seemed determined to leave no part of her untouched or unstirred.

When the hands withdrew from her body, Janice slumped in her seat, held up only by the straps that bound her to it. She was vaguely conscious of movement, the sudden brush of the wind against her sweaty flesh, the rocking of the car as one or both of her captors got out. She heard the doors close, heard the motor start, was aware of the swaying of the vehicle as it made its way back up the road she had walked that afternoon. That afternoon? Only then? It seemed already like some distant memory, years old. What would William have done if he had been here? Driven her wild as her captors had done? Set her free? She drifted in and out of an uneasy sleep, memories of William and their days in the woods mingling with the events of this extraordinary day.

She roused herself briefly when the car in which she was being transported—yes, that was the word, transported; one could hardly say she was traveling in the normal sense—when the car in which she was being transported turned onto a smoother road. Janice surmised that they had reached the main road, and she distinctly felt the vehicle make a left turn, which meant they were traveling back toward Cheyenne. She imagined she should make some effort to learn where she was being taken. Despite the blindfold, she could feel changes in direction, sense slowing down and speeding up. But she would have no way of knowing the speed they were making, and so she would not know at what points these changes occurred. They had been wise to blindfold her. She would never be able to reconstruct this journey in the dark or identify their destination when they finally reached it.

How long would that take, she wondered. Not much longer, she hoped. Her body was stiff from lack of movement, but the straps that held her to her seat allowed none. Her shoulders felt cramped from being held so long in the same position by her bound hands. Her eyelids itched under the tape. She tasted the sourness of the gag once again. She could smell the dried sweat and the other, slightly fishy odor she knew as her own musk, the evidence of her arousal, now drying between her thighs. Janice twisted her wrists in the ropes, not so much in the hope of escaping but more to get the circulation going faster and to relieve the cramps.

And, a part of her sardonically observed, to prove to yourself that you are in fact helpless. You like that, don't you? Yes, she answered herself. You've known that for a long time, she continued. Not always helpless, but some of the time, a few hours or days (or weeks?) in which someone must make all the decisions—assume total control and care of you—a respite from the need to conduct your own affairs, a surrender of your whole self to another. She had known that since her days with William, when she had allowed him to take control. Was that why she was thinking of him so intensely now?

And where had he gone? They had both gone on to university after the summer days in the woods—she bound, led on a chain, both of them naked under the sky, coupling joyously—on the verge of growing up and moving on. She had gone to New York to get her degree in journalism. William had gone west, to California, to Berkeley, to study history and, perhaps, to see for himself the places that had made student history in the sixties: the steps of Sproul Hall, the quadrangle where the students had defied the National Guard and their guns, the home of the Free Speech Movement that had promised so much more (and had faded entirely as its leaders had reached the age of twenty-five, beyond which, they had said, no one was to be trusted)—those historic places, remembered mainly by the young, if at all.

Letters. Yes, there had been letters, mostly of the remember-when variety, but they had not been enough to sustain such a long-distance relationship. The letters had become less frequent, had stopped entirely as each of them found new friends and new interests. Had he married someone, and did he now take her for wild days in the woods? Or had they started (oh, no!) a family? Or—most congenial thought—was he still single, did he still think of their time together? Once he had advised her, "Stay single, Singleton." She had. Had he? She really must find out. After all this was over.

They drove for a long time on the smooth road, the sound of the tires and the gentle rocking motion of the vehicle lulling Janice once more. She slept despite her discomfort, waking only when she sensed another turn, this time to the right and onto a slightly bumpier road. They continued along this for several minutes, as far as she could tell, though she had no way to judge time. Blindfolded, she lacked all visual clues and could not have guessed what time of day—or night—it was. She felt disoriented, the effect, she knew, of sensory deprivation, and one of the methods used so effectively against prisoners, an insidious form of torture against which there was no defense.

But she wasn't a prisoner. She was a guest, wasn't she? Janice was not so sure. Was there some form of torture to come? she asked with the by-now familiar mixture of dread and anticipation. If the recent experience had been torture, then she was ready for more of the same. But there was the disturbing presence of the cane that had stung her, the threat of the whip Harry had used. Would they really beat her with a whip? Once again the ambivalent shiver. It was all a matter of how hard, she told herself. And where.

They stopped, and Janice heard the silence as the motor was switched off. She strained her ears for other sounds—traffic, pedestrians, the growling of lions, the hoofbeats of zebras. Don't be foolish, she told herself. Hear hoofbeats, expect horses, not zebras. The sounds that reached her were too faint to identify. She could be anywhere. Was this their destination? The doors slid open, and Janice felt a cool breeze and warmth on her foot. Sunlight? Yes. That was it. They had traveled through the night, and now it was morning.

How did her captors propose to move her without arousing suspicion? Janice did not mind if they aroused her, but the sight of a naked woman, bound, gagged, and blindfolded, being led about in broad daylight, was certain to make people curious. By now Janice's feelings about being seen had changed. At first seeking rescue, or at least release, she now just wanted to be invisible—sure sign of a change in her mental attitude toward captivity. Harry had said she would soon begin to like the regime. Apparently he had been right. She no longer felt angry. Tremulous, maybe, like a virgin on the big night, but not angry.

There was the sound of doors closing, and the sunlight was cut off. Janice could feel the change in temperature on her foot. Hands touched her in the dark that surrounded her, and she felt the straps that held her to the seat being loosened, falling away. The hands helped her stand and disengage herself from the seat entirely. She was guided forward, heard the injunction to "mind the step down," and stepped onto a cool floor that felt like concrete. She smelled oil and gasoline fumes and surmised they were in a closed garage.

The hands led her forward, a door opened, and she was inside a house of some sort. Up the stairs, the hand holding her elbow, and down a carpeted hallway. Into a room, the door closing behind them, and Janice stood still as the guiding hand was withdrawn. She imagined this was how the newly blind must feel in a strange house: disoriented, afraid to move for fear of stumbling over some obstacle. A sense of helplessness flooded in upon her again.

"I imagine you'd like to have a bath, Janice," Harry said.

"Ummmmmm!" she said, nodding her head.

"All right. Just a moment while I fix you up."

Janice wanted a bath very badly, now that he had mentioned the possibility. She could smell herself, and she felt gritty all over. Lying in a hot tub was like a promise of heaven. "Ummmmmm!" she said again, more loudly, turning her head from side to side as she tried to place Harry by his voice.

She felt the touch of something hard and cool on her left ankle, heard a metallic click as the steel band closed and locked. Harry made her bring her legs closer together and locked the other band on her other ankle. When Janice tried to move, she found that her ankles were chained closely together. Afraid of falling, she stood still.

She sensed Harry standing close beside her, then she felt his hands lifting her hair from behind. The sound of scissors snipping close to her ear made Janice flinch. Was he cutting off her hair? But no. It was the tape he was removing.

After he had cut through the tape in several places, Harry said, "This will hurt a bit, but it's the only way to do the job. Ready?"

Janice nodded and felt the tape pulled sharply away, a series of jerks that made her wince. But in the end she was able to spit out the sour packing that had gagged her for so long. Her mouth felt dry and foul.

"Water," she croaked. "Please give me some water."

"In a minute," he promised. "Let me get the tape off your eyes. Hold still."

Without further ado, he pulled the sticky tape from her eyelids. Janice almost cried out with the pain and with the dazzling effect of the sunlight coming from above her. She had been so long in the dark that the light hurt her eyes. If her hands had been free, she would have covered her face. Janice closed her eyes convulsively, then opened them very slightly. The dazzle effect subsided as her eyes adjusted to the light. Harry was standing behind her, loosening the rope on her wrists.

As the cords fell away, Janice's arms fell woodenly to her sides. They felt lifeless, cramped, and sore; she groaned at the agony of returning circulation. Gradually she was able to raise a hand to her face, push the hair back from her cheek, feel the grittiness of her skin. She had to have a bath.

Her eyes were feeling more or less normal, and she looked around the room with curiosity. It was a bedroom. (I might have known that, she told herself.) The light that had dazzled her came from a skylight through which only the sky was visible. The windows were barred and shuttered from the outside, so that nothing of the neighborhood was visible. Her captors were being careful to keep her from knowing where she was being held. She would never be able to find this place again.

Janice knew that her captor was looking at her, and she flushed again, not entirely with embarrassment. Even though her hands were now free, she made no effort to cover herself. It was much too late for such gestures. Instead, she turned to face him. Mark or Harry? Harry, she decided, when she heard him speak.

"Actors' make up," he told her. "I don't really look like this," he said. "Some of our guests thought I really looked handsome, even though I shouldn't say so myself. But later we may be able to drop the masquerade—after we get to know one another better. We'll see." He chuckled at the pun.

"Where is Mark?" Janice asked, striving for something to say that might make the bizarre seem less so.

"He's taking your car back to the resort. You'll see him there. In the meantime, I have you all to myself." He moved away. "For your information," he told her, "I'm leering at you behind your back." There was another chuckle in his voice.

"You'll find everything you need in the bathroom over there," he said, pointing to a door across the room. "If you care to shampoo your hair, we have loads of Wash 'n Go. So Go 'n Wash." He turned and left the room, locking the door behind him.

It was a substantial door. Janice didn't think it would give way if she threw her weight against it. Nevertheless, she felt impelled to try, shuffling across the soft carpet in her leg irons. The chain was quite short, perhaps no more than a foot, so that she had to take extremely short steps. She glanced at the shackles and saw that they fit her ankles closely and seemed to be made of stainless steel. Just as well, she thought, if I have to wear them in the bath.

The door, when she reached it, proved to be as substantial as she had guessed it would be. There was no slack in the knob or the lock. She tried to rattle it, but it was the nonrattling kind. No escape that way, she concluded. But the matter was academic anyway. A naked female in leg irons was not going to go very far before she was missed and recaptured.

Since there was nothing else to do, Janice made her way to the bathroom. She drew a hot bath and added bubbles and herbal scent. When she tried to climb into the tub, she found that the chain joining her shackles was too short. She was obliged to sit on the side of the tub and swing her legs together into the water. After that it was easy to slide down into the warm water and let herself begin to relax. It felt heavenly just to soak. She soaked for a long time, shampooing her hair as well. When she finally got out, she felt cleaner and more refreshed than she had in a long time.

Janice dried herself and, as the water drained away, sat down on the side of the tub to inspect her shackles more closely. They appeared to be have been made by a craftsman, not simply mass produced. All the edges were rounded, and all the rivets were carefully seated and hammered smooth. There were no sharp edges to chafe or cut. Either her captor was a skilled metalworker, or he knew a man who was.

Janice shuffled back into the bedroom to find her captor had laid out some of her clothes. Well, not really clothes, she saw: her peignoir and high-heeled slippers with the fur trim. Seduction gear, she had called it as she packed for her holiday. One should always be prepared for the unexpected. Only, where she had expected to use it to charm a man, it was being used against her instead—to let her know that she was virtually naked.

Shrugging, she put on the filmy garment. She reasoned that her captor liked it—otherwise why let her have it? And it was better than what she had worn on her trip to this place. Dressed, or rather covered scantily, Janice sat at the vanity and did her nails, smoothing the rough edges she had caused blundering about in the wild, applying a soft red varnish to both toenails and fingernails. Even in captivity, she reasoned, one should look one's best. It was a matter of pride.

Having finished her toilette, there was nothing else for Janice to do. She shuffled over to the bed, sitting at first on the edge, then lying back with a sigh. She stretched, unkinking the muscles that had been knotted by the long drive strapped to the seat of the van. Relaxed, she drowsed and woke, drowsed and woke, dreaming, sometimes luridly, of her forthcoming holiday. She imagined herself lying on this bed in the darkness, actually bound to it, spread like a starfish, her wrists and ankles tied to the posts, watching the stars through the skylight as she waited for her captor to come for her.

But when he finally did come, it was only to bid her to dinner. Janice was suddenly hungry, not having eaten anything for nearly eighteen hours. But, she told herself, it had been a busy and not altogether boring eighteen hours. She rose with alacrity and began to make her slow way to the open door where Harry stood. She would have preferred to sweep grandly out of the room and down the staircase, Scarlett O'Hara fashion, but Margaret Mitchell's heroine had never had to walk in shackles. Janice was suddenly aware of her undignified position as the prisoner and was annoyed.

"Can't you take these off," indicating her leg irons, "for the time being? I won't be able to run away dressed like this. And if you're worried, you can keep the doors locked," she mocked him.

"I'm not worried about you escaping," Harry said. "I— we—simply want you to get used to your chains. When you're not tied up or being, er, exercised, you will wear shackles. You will never be free until the end of your stay—if you can call it freedom when you won't want to leave, will beg for more time, will impatiently await your next visit to the resort, your next appointment with sexual torture and ecstasy, your next encounter with your secret self." He deprecated the florid language with a smile and a dismissive gesture. "But," he went on, "something like that is what will happen to you. It's already begun; you just haven't noticed it. It happens to everyone who is chosen to visit us."

There it was again, the intimation that she had been

carefully studied before she even knew about The Last Resort. How had they chosen her, out of all the millions of other young women like her in the country? Janice tried to remember any suspicious men following or photographing her, but she could not. Or had they used a woman to follow her? A woman would have been less suspicious. She would have been less on guard if a woman had done the work. They might have been clever enough to realize that themselves. So far as she actually knew, her secrets remained her own, but she had the uneasy feeling that these men had somehow found them out. It was unsettling to think that such intimate spying could be carried out without arousing the victim's suspicion.

Like all modern Americans—men as well as women— Janice knew that sophisticated surveillance techniques existed and were used by various government agencies. But she tended to believe, without any foundation, that these techniques were used only on spies, foreigners, and others, a practice that, while reprehensible, was necessary to entrap the enemies of the state. She had never considered the possibility that private citizens could or would use the same clandestine surveillance on another private citizen, especially not her. It appeared that she was wrong, but she still could not see how it had been done.

"How . . . how do you know so much about what I like and dislike?" she asked.

"In good time," Harry responded, "I might tell you. Let's see how you react to the regime first. It wouldn't do to tell all our secrets to someone who might use them against us. We aren't infallible. There is always the possibility we have misjudged one of our guests. It would be presumptuous—as well as dangerous—to think we were always right. As we all know, pride goeth before a prison sentence. None of us wants to risk a fall. But we were going down to dinner. Come along."

When she moved closer in her slow, shuffling walk, he offered her his arm. After a short hesitation, Janice took it. It was bizarre: the man responsible for her abduction was being gallant. When they reached the stairs, she realized it wasn't all gallantry. The short chain joining her ankles just allowed her to move from step to step. She was glad of his support as they slowly descended the staircase. Even so, she held onto the handrail tightly as well.

As they came downstairs, Janice saw that the curtains were drawn, leaving the house dark save for the dining alcove, where a table was set with two places. Candles glowed softly. She liked the effect, but her own situation made it seem out of place. Floodlights shining into her eyes would have seemed more appropriate.

"How very romantic," she said, with what she hoped was the right degree of sarcasm.

"Yes, isn't it?" Harry said calmly, ignoring her tone. "And you're dressed to suit a candlelit dinner *a deux*."

Was there just the hint of mockery in his tone? Janice decided there was. She would try to match it then. She could be distant, even if she couldn't escape. When they were on level ground, she released his arm and drew the peignoir close about her, holding the front shut with her hand as she made her slow way toward the table. It was set with care, the fine white tablecloth smooth, the china and cutlery gleaming. The candles were in silver candlesticks in the center of the table.

Harry indicated her place at one end of the oval table, pulling her chair back so she could be seated. As she took her place, Janice glanced at the table. There were two knives, two forks, and two spoons at each place, indicating that something more than just a simple snack was in store. But at her place there was something more, something that made her draw breath with a hiss. She looked up at Harry.

He looked levelly back at her.

Janice indicated the flesh-colored dildo lying by her place, to the right of the knives by her plate. "You had no right!" she said sharply. "That's . . . private. I never said anything when you searched my luggage for this," indicating the peignoir, "even though I resented the invasion of privacy. But this is too much!" Embarrassment combined with anger to make her voice shake.

"You are the one who has no rights, Janice," Harry told her. "So long as you're with us, you will do exactly as we say. There is no appeal to rights and privileges. And no privacy. You can go back to that when you leave, if you wish. But here we are the final arbiters, and even when you find us especially, er, arbitrary, you'll still have to do what we tell you." After a pause to let his words sink in, Harry continued. "We have ways to make you obey." There was a smile in his voice as he paraphrased the old joke, but there was no doubt he meant what he said.

Janice felt a thrill of fear, but she held herself erect. She wouldn't betray herself by asking him what he meant. But she heard his words about "the whip" echo in her mind. Distractedly, she was aware of the stirring of excitement in her belly as she imagined herself strung up for a lashing. She put the thought aside, but it crept back, a slow warmth spreading through her. To conceal her agitation, she sat down, her gaze fixed on the dildo she almost always carried with her—the good friend of every independent-minded but highly sexed career woman.

Harry withdrew to take his place. As he sat, he indicated

the dildo. "Go ahead, Janice. Pick it up. You must be familiar enough with it by now." When she still hesitated, he asked lightly, "Is it in the wrong place? I thought etiquette required the implements to be placed in order, the diners using those farthest from the plate first. And you are right-handed, I noticed. So why the hesitation? Just follow the custom."

Janice colored but tried to keep her equanimity. "But suppose one wanted to save that," nodding toward the dildo, "for dessert?"

"You can try that if you like, Janice, but I want you to pick it up now, switch it on and insert it. If you need lubrication, there is the butter. Thereafter, if you wish, and if you can hold out that long, you can have it for dessert." The double entendre was plain, but so was the steel in the command.

Janice picked up the dildo and activated it. It made a gentle buzzing, and she could feel it vibrating in her hand. She had done this hundreds of times, but never in the presence of anyone else. The silence drew out as she looked at the vibrating instrument in her hand. At length, defiantly, she looked down the table at Harry. He was waiting patiently, his expression neutral. Janice moved then, suddenly, knowing that hesitation cost face. Holding his gaze, she opened the front of her flimsy garment, revealing all of herself if he cared to look. She opened her legs and thrust the throbbing instrument into herself with a single push.

Harry said, "Well done. I didn't think you'd need any butter to ease things along."

Janice reddened with embarrassment, realizing that she had revealed her excitement. Now he knew she had been wet and parted, excited, aroused. But there was no going back. Letting the peignoir fall closed again, Janice closed her legs, pressing the shaft tightly inside herself. She could still hear a faint buzz as it vibrated against her sensitive flesh. "What's for dinner?" she asked, striving to regain her poise.

Harry tapped a fork against his water glass. As the clear, ringing tone faded, a beautiful young woman entered from what had to be the kitchen, pushing a trolley with several covered dishes on it. Janice smelled the delicious odor of the food, and her stomach rumbled in anticipation. But at the same time, she had to stare at the woman who was serving them. She wore a French maid's costume. A black satin dress, with the tiniest of miniskirts, revealed her long, full legs almost to her crotch. She wore glossy black hose and black high-heeled shoes. The obligatory frilly apron and cap completed her outfit.

Even though technically she wore more clothing than Janice, her costume was even more revealing than Janice's own transparent wrapper. The maid's outfit was designedly provocative, only just covering its wearer, and proved that clothing can be more revealing than nudity. The tight-fitting bodice clung to her large breasts and emphasized her slender waist, while the short skirt almost demanded that one stare at her shapely legs.

The most striking feature of her outfit was not the dress but the chains she wore, as if born to slavery. She wore stainless steel handcuffs joined with about twelve inches of chain, so that she could handle the serving things. Like Janice, she wore leg irons that fit tightly around her ankles and emphasized their slenderness by their weight. The handcuffs and leg irons were linked to one another and to a steel collar by a loop of chain that allowed the woman to lower her hands to waist level, but no further. As a result, she had to stoop slightly, as if bowing, as she served them smoked salmon.

Janice forgot her embarrassment as she stared at the newcomer. How utterly erotic, she thought with a twinge of envy. She knew this young woman would attract more attention than she herself would. She almost begged to be taken and ravished as she stood.

As the maid moved with a soft clinking of chains to serve Janice, Harry introduced her. "Janice, I would like you to meet Lois, whom we sometimes call Lois Lane, girl reporter. She, too, is a newspaper journalist, though only on a small-town weekly. She wants to move on to the big time, so you may be able to give her some advice. In any case, you have much in common, so you should get along well.

"Lois, this is Janice Singleton, who writes for the *Chicago Tribune*. Be nice to her, and she may help you get to the big city." To Janice he continued, "For her part, Lois will be able to give you a good deal of insider's information about the regime you will follow while you stay with us. This is her third visit."

To Lois he said, "Tell Janice how you feel about the resort. Janice is on her first visit and sometimes seems worried about what she will be made to do."

"Miss Singleton," Lois began breathlessly, "I'm so glad to meet you. I read most of your stuff. Your piece about the famine in Ethiopia was brilliant."

"Call me Janice, please. The setting demands informality." Janice indicated her own dishabille and leg irons. She said nothing about the dildo inside her, but she wondered if Lois could guess from her slightly flushed face. Even as she spoke, Janice was aware of the device inside her, and in company she felt even more excited than usual.

"Janice, then. Thank you." Lois appeared to have a bad case of heroine worship, but she struggled on. "The place is super. I've never had as much sexual experience anywhere else. At home no one even talks about sex, so I feel absolutely free and wonderful while I'm here. There's nothing but sex, sex of all kinds, almost anything you want. And to get it you only have to do what the men say. I'm sure you'll have the time of your life."

Lois's enthusiasm, while naively expressed, nevertheless made Janice feel a bit easier. If this young woman can take everything they dish out and come up smiling, she reassured herself, then I should have no trouble.

"It's not just Harry here, and Mark, good as they are." She smiled nervously at Harry as she said this.

Harry smiled encouragingly, and she went on. "They have visiting members as well, whose, er, members are memorable. You can have a different experience every night if you want, or you can ask to have a steady, er, member every night." Lois said with a smile.

Janice admired her poise and her seemingly effortless use of alliteration and double entendre.

"But you'll soon see for yourself," Lois went on. "Tomorrow we'll be traveling to the resort together, and you'll have your first meeting with the men in charge of us in the evening."

Harry asked Lois to serve the food, and as she moved about the room in the candlelight, Janice admired her grace and the way she accommodated her movements to the chains that held her. Ah, to be on the right side of twenty again, Janice said wistfully to herself.

An Evening At Home

All through dinner Janice was reminded of the dildo inside her. She fought down her rising excitement and tried to eat as though nothing—except the whole dinner party, of course—was out of the ordinary. Once or twice she caught herself ignoring the excellent food and concentrating instead on the inner reality. Once she saw Harry smile at her when an unexpected stab of pleasure lanced through her. She choked on a mouthful of wine and touched her crotch under cover of closing her sheer nightgown.

Lois moved gracefully about the room in her chains, serving them and looking provocative. Harry ate little. Instead, he steadily regarded Janice as she struggled with the demands of eating and the excitement caused by her dildo. Janice guessed that he would eat later, after the children—herself and Lois—were safely trussed for the night. She accepted now that they would be restrained somehow. Harry had told her that much earlier on. Janice wondered if she would be able to sleep while tied or chained—something she had never contemplated before. She hoped she would not be too tightly trussed.

"Would you like coffee, Janice, or a brandy?" Harry's words broke into another of her reveries as she concentrated on the device buzzing away so insistently inside her. She had

49

been on the verge of another mini-orgasm, and the interruption put her off.

Janice looked up sharply. She said, "No," a little too abruptly. "No, thank you," she repeated, hoping he didn't notice her lapse into introspection. Or intromission, she added silently.

"Then let's move over to the sitting room and let Lois clear up here. When she's finished, she can join us." He rose and pulled Janice's chair back so she could rise, then led the way to the sitting room.

Janice followed more slowly, conscious once again of her leg irons. They seemed of the same workmanship as the chains worn by Lois, and she wondered as she followed Harry whether they had their own blacksmith shop at the resort.

Harry sat in an armchair, so Janice took the other one. She could have sat on the sofa, but that might have been taken as an invitation to him to sit close to her. She was not ready yet to send that signal. She didn't know enough about him. True, he was courtly and witty—well-educated, too, she guessed. But there was something hard and unyielding in him, especially when he talked of the "regime" of the resort and of women "being exercised." She decided to approach the subject directly.

"Tell me about the resort," she said. "I mean, what will I be doing there?"

"It's better to let you see for yourself. Showing's always better than telling."

"But suppose I don't like what I see?" she asked.

"You still don't understand that your likes and dislikes aren't important. From the moment we caught you in the woods, you lost the option of refusal. You will do whatever we say, promptly and without question. Lois learned that lesson on her first visit. All of our guests learn it. Some take more time than others. It all depends on how long it takes for you to accept that we are your masters and that there is no escape until the end of your stay.

"You can't cancel your reservation and walk away. You have committed yourself to one week with us. For our part, we promise that no irreparable harm will come to you. Whatever pain we inflict will be short of permanent injury. We believe that you will come to enjoy the pain after a time. Most of the women do. All of them come to enjoy the coercion, for that's what we apply."

"Why?" Janice asked.

"We're not strong on philosophy. We have found that what we do is fun. Fun for us, fun for you, even if it takes awhile for you to realize that. Call it hedonism if you must give it a name. But experience is the only way to really see what we do. Oh, you can talk to Lois later, or to any of the others at the resort. They aren't under a vow of silence. They may be able to help you over the rough spots by telling you how it was for them, but the best evidence in favor of the regime is that many of the guests, like Lois, are returnees. Recidivism is quite high at the resort. We're proud of that."

Janice was not reassured, but the leg irons ensured that she would not run away screaming into the darkness.

Harry saw her agitation. He stood abruptly and moved to her chair. Kneeling in front of her, he told her, "Spread your legs, Janice."

And she did. A moment later she regretted her easy compliance, but there had been something at once so reasonable and so commanding in his tone that she had obeyed without thought. Now she tried to clamp her thighs together, but he was kneeling between them, and she could not move him.

Harry touched her mons veneris, and Janice felt a jolt of electricity in her belly. Her instinct was to push him away, but another part of her welcomed the touch. After a short internal struggle, she relaxed and spread her legs still further. The buzzing dildo inside her cunt had been arousing her all through the meal, and now she found herself teetering on the verge of orgasm. Harry's hand on her sex was the trigger. Janice felt her belly knotting in the old familiar way, the waves of pleasure spreading through her body and down her legs. The chain was taut between her ankles as she tried to open herself still further.

He rubbed her pubic mound with the flat of his hand, pushing the dildo into her and then letting the pressure relax. To Janice, it felt as if a cock were moving slowly in and out. Her body went rigid, and she grasped the arms of the chair so tightly her hands hurt. She closed her eyes and moaned softly as she came, thrusting herself against his hand. This had been building up all evening, and the release was wonderful. Janice lost herself in the pleasure. "Ohhhhhhh!" she moaned, and then "ohhhhhhhhhh" again.

When she came back to the present, Harry was talking to her.

". . . the dildo is a fine way to soften you up, to get you ready, but it isn't the same as the real thing. The dildo is a fine device for loners, and I suspect you have been using it a bit too often. You have been alone, haven't you?"

Janice started to deny the allegation, but Harry put his finger on her lips, and she subsided. With his other hand he pushed the shaft deeper into her cunt.

He went on, "But you aren't alone now. I'm here. So is Lois. We're going to show you some of the things we do, and you're going to relax and enjoy the exercise."

He stood up, keeping his hand on her cunt. "Stand up Janice," he commanded, holding her intimately as she stood. Keeping one hand against her mons, he led her toward the stairs.

Janice followed in a daze, conscious mainly of his touch and his commanding presence. As they passed by the dining room, Harry called for Lois to finish clearing up. With a soft clinking of chains she moved from table to kitchen, the efficient housemaid.

Harry led Janice to the bedroom she had used earlier. He took his hand away from her cunt, and Janice instantly regretted the loss of contact. But she didn't say anything, waiting instead for him to take the next step, which was so clearly his.

"Take off your peignoir, Janice," he said quietly.

She did so, letting it fall to the floor.

"Lie on the bed. On your back, please." He stooped to pick up the sheer wrapper and laid it on the vanity bench.

Janice meanwhile moved to the bed and lay down as directed. As she did, she saw that someone—Lois, no doubt— had come to the room in their absence and made some preparations of her own. Strips of leather had been tied to each of the four bedposts. It didn't require any imagination to guess their purpose. Janice lay on her back, shivering with anticipation. She stretched her arms up, ready for Harry to tie her wrists. She spread her legs as far as the leg irons allowed and waited.

Harry smiled when he saw that she understood what was happening. Swiftly he tied her wrists to the bedposts, stretching her arms and causing her breasts to stand up prominently. He removed her shackles with a key he took from his pocket, then tied her ankles as well. When he was done, Janice was left spread like the starfish she had imagined earlier. When Harry stepped back, she tugged at the straps and found she could not move. The dildo inside her buzzed and vibrated, making itself felt as she lay helplessly on her back.

"Not terribly imaginative," Harry said, "but the best that could be done at short notice. And the simpler ideas are often the ones that work best." He turned away and walked out of the room.

Janice had expected him to climb onto her and fuck her silly. He looked like that kind of man. She was surprised when he left her. And, she admitted, disappointed. She lay for some minutes, straining her ears for some clue as to Harry's whereabouts. As she lay, she heard instead the soft clink of chains, and Lois appeared in the door of the bedroom.

She smiled reassuringly. "It's only me," she said to Janice. "You're not Mary Kingsley," Janice said. Lois looked puzzled for a moment. Her face cleared as she got the allusion. As she approached the bed, Janice saw that she carried a black velvet bag with a drawstring.

"Harry asked me to blindfold you," Lois said diffidently. "He thought the mystery would be more exciting, so this," indicating the bag, "is for you."

"What, no gag to stifle my screams as well?" Janice asked ironically.

"Oh, no. That won't be necessary. There isn't anyone to hear, no matter how much noise you make. But why would you want to scream? I wouldn't. Well, maybe a bit, but that's only because I love to have him fuck me. I wish I was you right now. I suppose he'll lock me in my room while he does you."

"Well, untie me and take my place," Janice told her.

"Oh, no. He wouldn't want that." Lois seemed embarrassed. She lifted Janice's head and slipped the bag over her face, pulling it down past her chin and drawing it shut with the strings, which she knotted efficiently around Janice's neck. Janice was left in stuffy darkness, but she found she could breathe well enough through the cloth of the bag.

"How old are you, Lois?" she asked, her words reverberating in her ears within the black bag. Now that she couldn't see the younger woman, she felt able to question her.

"Nineteen," Lois answered. Her voice sounded more confident. Perhaps she, too, felt easier now that she couldn't see Janice's face. There was a pause, then Lois suddenly asked, "How does that . . . thing inside you feel? Does it feel good?"

Janice smiled to herself. Lois was trying to act the cool sophisticate, but she obviously had never encountered so simple a device as a dildo. Arching her back and raising her hips, Janice said, "Take it out of me and try it if you'd like."

There was a long silence. Janice imagined Lois was taken aback by the suggestion. "Go on," she urged. "It won't bite you. And I can't."

The silence continued.

"Are you still there, Lois?" Janice asked.

A soft clink of chain. A hand reaching tentatively to touch her crotch, tracing the line of her labia. A sharp intake of breath as the fingers encountered the base of the shaft in her cunt, the hand being snatched away.

"Go on," Janice urged again.

This time the exploring fingers were less tentative. They spread Janice's labia and tugged at the dildo. A brush against her swollen clitoris caused her to draw a sharp breath. The hand was snatched away again.

Janice waited in her enforced immobility for Lois's courage to return, and presently the hand came back, touching her more confidently, the fingers brushing her clitoris as Lois reached inside her and tugged on the dildo. Janice found herself holding her breath. She was acutely aware of her nakedness and the proximity of the young woman who was attending her. She had never been touched so intimately by a woman. She was surprised at her excitement as she thought of Lois's mouth on her sex, the quick hot tongue inside her, licking her sensitive clitoris, the small teeth nipping her. Janice's breasts and nipples made themselves felt as well, aching to be touched, fondled, kissed, nipped by her young attendant.

She pulled herself up sharply, frightened by the excitement that Lois's touch had aroused. Lesbian love had never appealed to her. *It's only the bizarre situation,* she told herself. *So many new things have happened to me in the past two days.* She was not reassured by these thoughts, and her excitement showed no sign of abating. Janice twisted restlessly on the bed, held by the leather strips. She wished fleetingly that she were free—free to flee, free to avoid her riotous thoughts.

In the silent room the tinkle of Lois's chains was loud. Janice tensed, unable to see what the young woman was doing. It sounded as if she were moving closer. Bending down? Janice remembered that Lois couldn't reach very far in her chains. The mattress sagged between Janice's outspread legs as Lois climbed onto the bed. A brush of flesh against her thigh, a shifting of weight, and a hand touched her cunt again. This time it did not withdraw, and Janice couldn't bring herself to tell the young woman to go away—not least because her throat felt tight, as if she would have to force the words out. She remembered that she had encouraged Lois earlier. Her pride would not let her drive the other woman away now. Yes, that was it—a matter of pride.

A moment later Janice felt the brush of Lois's handcuffs

against her inner thighs as the dildo was withdrawn. A pause, then a gasp of pleasure. She guessed that Lois had used the dildo herself. But there was no time for further thought as a pair of lips fastened themselves to her cunt. Lois's tongue darted inside her, finding her wet and parted from the dildo. Janice shuddered as the probing tongue found her swollen clitoris, and small sharp teeth nipped the sensitive bud between her thighs. Janice groaned, just biting back the urge to tell Lois to go on, to use her lips and teeth and tongue and hands. But Lois didn't need any direction. For such a young woman, she seemed to know a great deal about arousing another woman.

Janice felt her body grow hot all over. Embarrassment, or a new reaction to a new situation? She knew all the ways of her body, all the signs of arousal. There was the tightness in her belly and chest, as if she couldn't draw breath. There was the aching in her breasts and nipples as they became suffused with blood and grew warm and tight. There were the sharp darts of pleasure in her cunt that spread to her belly and down her legs. And finally, there was the sharp delight of her orgasm and the sense of release. Only now, and added to the other signs, there was this new flush that made her feel as if she were in a hot bath, or as if her whole body were being warmed before a fire.

Lois used her tongue on Janice's clitoris, darting it against the sensitive flesh. Janice felt stabs of pleasure at each contact. Inside the black bag that covered her head she was cut off from the outside world. There was only the warm, close air around her face and the delicious sensations from her cunt. As her excitement rose, Janice tugged against the strips that bound her. The reminder of her helplessness made her more excited. There was no escape, she told herself. True, she could have asked Lois to stop. She wasn't gagged. But she wasn't going to. Anyway, she was not sure Lois would obey, and she had no way to stop the younger woman from doing whatever she wanted. In any case, Harry had told her that she would have no say in what was done to her while she was their "guest." If Lois didn't make her come, she was sure that Harry would, whenever and however he liked. And with that thought Janice surrendered herself to Lois, and to Harry, and to her own pleasure. She groaned aloud as her orgasm took her, writhing on her back, struggling against the leather strips that held her prisoner.

While her storm was subsiding, Janice heard footsteps coming closer. Lois, her head buried between Janice's thighs, apparently heard nothing. There was a swish and a sharp crack, and Lois screamed and reared up. For a moment Janice was conscious only of the loss of that delicious contact. She knew she would have come again if Lois had stayed on the job. There was another swish and crack, and Lois screamed again, falling forward onto Janice's body, the handcuffs hard against her stomach. She realized then that Lois was being beaten. Harry—it couldn't be anyone else, could it?—had discovered them in flagrante delicto and was beating Lois.

Was he angry because he had wanted Janice for himself? The idea pleased her, but even as she felt flattered, Lois screamed again. Apparently Harry was lashing her across her back and bottom. The struggling body atop Janice suddenly slid to one side, exposing Janice's breasts. The whip struck them both. Lois screamed again. Janice was too stunned to make a sound. The stinging of her breasts was unbelievable. Coming so soon after such intense pleasure, the pain took her completely by surprise.

A second blow landed, catching them both again. This

time Janice screamed, too. Lois was sobbing. She was catching most of the lashing. Janice could feel the girl struggling atop her, probably trying to get to her feet to escape from the whip. Janice felt a moment of dread. What if Lois made her escape? Despite her chains, she was mobile. Janice was not. Might Harry not turn the full force of his anger on her? She didn't think she could stand much more, and she had only taken a few strokes.

Suddenly Lois slid off her, landing on the floor with a thud. Janice tensed herself for the next blow. It didn't come. Instead, Harry dropped the whip onto the bed. It landed across Janice's cringing stomach. It felt more like a cane, stiff, not supple like a leather whip. But she knew what it could do to her if he picked it up again. She heard a voice pleading. "No more, please. Please." She realized it was her own. Janice was mortified that she could beg, and she ground her teeth. But what if he did resume lashing her? Could she stop herself from begging then? She didn't think so. Lois, by contrast, had only screamed. She had not pleaded with Harry to stop. Bound and helpless, unable to see, Janice felt a hot wave of shame and fear sweep over her.

Low sobs came to her in her enforced darkness. It was Lois, lying nearby in pain. Janice would have liked to go to her aid, but she could only lie waiting for the next move from their captor. She expected him to pick up the cane and use it on one or both of them, so she was surprised again by what came next. Lois too was taken unaware. Suddenly, her low sobbing was broken by a gasp of surprise. Then a low whimper. Janice wondered what could be going on, and she wished she could at least see. The next sound was definitely a moan, whether of pain or pleasure she couldn't tell. But it soon became apparent that Lois was not feeling anymore pain.

Her low moans turned into sighs of pleasure. Harry was doing something pleasant to Lois.

Provocatively dressed as she was, and in chains, it didn't require much imagination to guess what he was doing. Janice felt her own imagination running wild as she listened to the sounds of the other woman's growing pleasure. She found it hard to believe she could have changed so quickly from screaming in pain to moaning in delight. Pain must be a turn-on for Lois, Janice realized.

And what about herself? The few blows she had taken had surprised her. They had hurt, too. But as she lay listening to Lois's arousal and satisfaction, she felt a tingle in her breasts and belly. What if Harry used the whip on her in earnest? Would she become excited and aroused? She didn't know, but the uncertainty and the noises from Lois *were* making her excited.

Janice imagined what Harry was doing to Lois to cause such sounds as she was making. Had he stripped her and mounted her, as Janice had been half hoping that Harry would mount *her*? But Lois was still wearing her chains; Janice could hear them clinking as she shifted her position. So Harry would not have been able to strip her without tearing her clothes from her body. Janice had heard no sound of tearing cloth. Harry must therefore be using his hands to arouse the young woman. Janice felt better about that, even as she wondered why she might feel resentment at Harry's arousal of Lois. Am I really becoming the kind of sex slave Harry and Mark had described briefly? Do I really need this entire two week of bondage and sex as much as that?

"Oh god," said Lois. "Don't stop. Touch me there again. Oh! Ohhhhh!" The last was a long drawn-out moan of pleasure that made Janice squirm in helpless chagrin. Lois was making all the sounds she would have made in her place. And, yes, she wanted to be in the other woman's place, not merely an audience for another's pleasure. Janice felt her stomach muscles tighten and the familiar tingling in her cunt and belly. Her breasts, sensitized by the lash, ached to be touched, caressed, nipped. She writhed on the bed, gritting her teeth. But she couldn't bring herself to beg Harry to attend to her. The noises from Lois went on for a long time.

Finally Janice heard receding footsteps and then silence: a satisfied silence, she thought. Shortly, the soft clink of Lois's chains broke it. Janice imagined her getting up, rearranging her clothing, perhaps smiling at what had just happened to her. Maybe (mortifyingly) smiling at Janice, the unwilling audience, left out of the main show. The ache in her belly and cunt was a constant reminder of her own arousal and frustration. The whip or cane with which Harry had beaten Lois lay still across Janice's stomach, its presence a reminder of what had happened and would happen again. To her.

"Janice, are you all right?" Lois's voice sounded tentative.

"Yes," Janice answered drily. "Are you?"

"Yes." A pause, then, "Oh, yes," in a stronger voice. "I'm fine now."

"I gather this was not the first time it's happened to you." A statement, not a question.

"No, of course not," Lois replied. "That's one of the reasons I've come back. The first time I was shocked to find how much it hurt, but later I found I missed it. And as this is the only place I know of where I can get what I want in safety and with any regularity, here I am again. The next two weeks are going to be great."

Lois's enthusiasm made Janice calmer about her own coming ordeal. If this young woman can enthuse about her experience, then who am I to be afraid, she asked herself. A novice, came the reply. A novice who might not like the next two weeks as much as Lois did. But there was nothing she could do about it. Still, she resolved to make the try. "I don't suppose you'd consider untying me?" she asked Lois.

"Oh, no. Harry would be angry. And you'd be angry too, for having missed all the fun. I know you would. If you weren't already half expecting to enjoy it, you'd be fighting to escape at every opportunity. Not that there have been many," she added.

Janice silently accepted the accuracy of the assessment. She remembered that it was she who had first suggested bondage to William. To escape any further misgivings, she changed the subject abruptly. "What did Harry do to you?" she asked.

With a laugh Lois replied, "Why, Janice, I do believe you're a voyeur. Or should that be voyeuresse?"

Janice flushed, thankful that the black bag concealed her face from the other woman.

After a pause Lois began to speak, saving Janice the mortification of having to ask again. "Harry put me on the floor on my hands and knees with my bottom sticking up in the air. He likes taking women from behind—you know, doggy-fashion. I like it too," she added with a giggle.

"It sounded that way," Janice said drily. She was nevertheless interested in Lois's experience, not least because she was likely to have the same thing done to her. Forewarned is forearmed, she told herself.

"He pulled my panties and hose down and knelt between my legs, on his back. From there he could lick my cunt. It was wonderful. I was already wet from the beating. I came almost at once."

"Yes, I noticed," Janice commented, excited at the recounting of the action she had only heard.

Lois continued, "Then he knelt behind me and put his cock up my backside."

Janice felt a shock. She had of course heard of anal sex, but her own asshole was virgin. She wondered how long that condition might last. "Didn't that hurt?" she asked.

"Not really. You just have to relax and let it happen. It helps if the man takes it slowly and uses some lubrication, even if it's only your own juices."

"Is that what Harry used?" Janice wanted to know.

"Yes. And he slipped right in. I quite like it now, especially the way he does it. Harry knows what a girl likes, and he takes the time to ensure that she enjoys the experience. He always reaches around to the front to play with my clitoris or my breasts. Usually both. That way I am guaranteed to have a good time."

"So I heard," Janice said drily. She was thinking of how it would feel to have a cock up her own asshole. Anticipation and excitement mingled with fear.

"So now you know what was happening to me," Lois said. "What about you? What were you doing then?"

"I? Lying here, of course. What else could I do?"

"Not envying me, or wishing Harry was doing you instead?"

This exact reading of her thoughts made Janice glad once more that her face was concealed.

Lois interpreted the silence correctly. "You're turning a nice rosy color," Lois told her.

Janice flushed more hotly as she realized the rest of her body had given her away.

"No need to be ashamed of that," Lois said. "I get the same feeling when someone else is being done in my presence. It's natural."

"Indeed? And do you think it's natural to be abducted and put in chains so strangers can have sex with you against your will?"

"I don't worry about natural," Lois replied. "I know what I like. I know this is great fun. No," she corrected herself, "it's more than that. It gives me great pleasure. And no one, certainly not me, is being hurt. And it's not against my will. Did you hear me begging him to stop?"

Janice was silenced by her answer. Who is the more sophisticated of the two, she asked herself, the big city gal who's been around—or this young woman, hardly more than a girl, from the Bible Belt?

"Poor Janice," Lois said. "So mixed up. And so left out." She picked up the cane that had been lying on Janice's stomach and swatted the prisoner lightly across the breasts.

"Ah!" said Janice, jerking in surprise.

Lois swatted her again, this time across the nipples. Not hard, just hard enough to sting. And to remind her that she was helpless to resist anything that was done to her. She grew warm at the thought. Janice tensed herself for the next blow, not knowing where it would land. It didn't come immediately. Was Lois going to play with her? Then the cane touched her nipples. Its hardness, and the thought of what it could do to her made her flush warmly all over again.

Lois said, "See, you like it already. Relax."

Good advice, but Janice was too tense to heed it. Fear and desire mingled in her. She lay still, but taut. The next blow, harder, landed across her stomach. She let out a yip of mingled pain and surprise, pulling against her bonds. Lois struck her again, across the tops of her thighs, and Janice yipped again. Thereafter the blows landed all over her naked front, from her breasts to her thighs. None of them was really hard, but the overall effect of the stinging cuts was to make the target area feel as if it were the home of a hive of bees. Later, when she could see herself, Janice would discover that the lashing had left a crisscross of faint red stripes, none of which had broken the skin. Lois clearly knew what she was doing. From long experience, Janice concluded later.

Janice writhed on the bed as the lashes were applied, oohing and ahhing as she was struck. To her surprise, she didn't ask Lois to stop. Later, again, she explained her odd behavior to herself by observing that Lois probably wouldn't have stopped anyway. At the time, she simply couldn't bring herself to beg for mercy—a matter of pride, she told herself.

There was a pause in the rain of blows. Janice held herself tense, waiting for the next. She almost said, "Oh, come on!" aloud, but she bit back the words before she could utter them. The pause lengthened. Janice began to think it was over. She was left with a warm flush, a stinging body, and a case of mild arousal, but there were no sexual tidal waves. A curious effect to aim for, she told herself.

The next blow, much harder, carefully aimed, landed directly on her nipples. "Aieeeeeee!" She screamed in pain and surprise. There was a pause, and then another lash, this time between her thighs, directly on her exposed sex. Janice screamed again, the noise ringing in her ears. She was now tugging frantically at her bonds, trying to escape the pain, or at least to cover her most vulnerable spots, Venus de Milo fashion. Another blow to her tits, and another on her cunt. More screams.

Then the cane was lying between her thighs, along her cunt. She tensed herself for another blow. It didn't come. Instead, Lois began to move the cane probingly along her crack, opening her labia and running it between them. Janice lay stunned at the abrupt change. Lois continued to move the cane slowly, teasingly, rubbing it against her clitoris. Janice quieted down, relaxing as she succumbed to the touch of the hard wood against her most sensitive spot. The friction against her flesh eased as she became wet, lubricating the hard cane. The slow shift from pain and fear to sexual arousal surprised her, even though Lois had predicted she would learn to like it.

Soon Janice became aware that she was purring deep in her throat, thrusting her hips to achieve maximum contact with the cane as it slid up and down her cunt, touching the clitoris each time Lois moved it upward and slightly between her parted labia. The first orgasm was sudden and short, a stab of pleasure in her belly. Janice said, "Ah!" as she felt herself come. Lois did not pause, saving her the ignominy of having to beg for more. The next one was longer, a series of waves that caused her body to twist on the bed. The cane by now was virtually frictionless, lubricated by her own juices. The pleasure it gave now was due to pressure against her sensitive flesh. Just enough friction left to make her gasp gratefully as it slid against her. More.

The cane went away, and Janice whimpered as she felt herself abandoned in midstream. A pause, then the cane swished down between her thighs, landing on the same spot it had been caressing moments earlier. Janice was too stunned to scream. All the breath had been stolen from her body. The cane rose and Janice drew in a deep shuddery breath. Then she heard the swish of its descent. A moment later a line of fire was drawn up her cunt. This time her scream almost deafened her, confined inside the black velvet bag over her head. Lois continued to strike her, aiming sometimes at her cunt and sometimes at her breasts and nipples. Janice's writhings and jerks made accuracy difficult, but the blows connected often enough.

Janice was not even aware when the lashing stopped. Her body felt as if it were filled with stinging pain, and her breath was coming in gasps. Her throat felt raw from screaming, and sweat ran down her forehead and cheeks, into her eyes and hair. She could even feel it running down her ribs and between her legs.

This time she did beg Lois to stop: "Please! No more! I can't take any more." Forced from her, she later told herself. But at the time it seemed to work. The blows stopped.

There was a pause, and then the cane found its way back to her cunt and clitoris. A hand touched her nipple, rubbing the place where the cane had struck her. Fingers teased her. The arousal after the pain was too much to bear. Janice came at once, shuddering and moaning, twisting on the bed and pulling against the leather strips that held her at wrists and ankles. She felt betrayed by Lois, betrayed by her own body that had screamed for relief and now was making her come as she had not done in a long time. But she could not stop herself. It was as if part of her stood aside, watching and judging while her body pursued its own course to sweaty orgasm.

Lois continued without pause, having found the thing that drove Janice wild. She more than repaid her victim for what she had missed with Harry. Ages later, when she finished, Janice was exhausted, sinking almost at once into sleep when she was allowed to.

Not surprisingly, Janice's dreams were of pursuit and capture. She imagined herself fleeing naked across the sands of some desert place, pursued by a man on horseback. She somehow knew that, if captured, he would break her to his will, making her his slave. This was not some modern version of *The Desert Song*. So she fled, wildly, dreading the sound of hooves behind her. She knew there was no escape, but still she ran. Capture, when it came, was sudden, from nowhere. Inexplicably, a rope caught her ankle. She tripped and lay stunned, as she had in the grove of trees when Mark and Harry had captured her. When she regained consciousness, she was staked out on her back, spread like a starfish under the high blue sky. She did not need anyone to draw her a diagram to explain what was coming next. She slept fitfully, prey to dreams of flight and capture and sexual delight.

In the morning she awoke to the sounds of movement in the bedroom. Suddenly the black bag over her head was removed and her eyes were assaulted by bright sunlight entering the window. The shutters had been opened and the sounds of morning were dimly heard in the room.

Lois said, "Good morning," not asking how she had slept.

Good manners or prior experience, Janice wondered.

Like herself, Lois was now naked, and Janice wondered if she had had another visit from Harry during the night. The younger woman was slighter of build, with small pointed breasts and a waist that would be the envy of any wasp. Janice knew she was heavier (mature, well-rounded, she would have said) where Lois was, well, elfin. But beautiful. And on the right side of twenty. Janice felt a quick stab of jealousy for the other woman's youth and figure, but her own sense of worth came back to her when she remembered that the two men who had captured her had both said she was beautiful.

"Where is our host?" Janice asked.

"Getting the car ready to take us to the resort," Lois replied. "We'll have breakfast and be on our way. It's only two or three hours from here. We should be there by midday. You'll no doubt be wanting a crack at the bathroom by now.

At once Janice became aware of a pressing need for a pee. "You'd better let me up if you want to avoid a messy accident in the bed." she said.

Lois smiled and began to untie her. As the leather strips were loosened, Janice sat up and stretched. Then she got quickly off the bed and made for the bathroom. She really had to go.

After she had taken care of her most urgent needs, she looked at herself in the wall mirror. Her eyes looked puffy from her broken sleep. Her hair desperately needed attention. She could smell herself. But she decided she would be all right after a wash. You'll do, she told her reflection. The leather thongs had left deep red marks around her wrists and ankles, and the cane had left lighter ones all over the front of her body. She shivered pleasantly as she recalled what had been done to her. Then, she stepped into the shower.

Back in the bedroom, she found herself alone again. Lois had made the bed up. The only signs that she had lain there bound all night—and the rest—were the leather thongs still tied to the bedposts. Ready for the next guest, she told herself. The door, when she tried it, was locked. Janice went to the window, toying briefly with the idea of escape. The nearest house seemed to be at least half a mile away, in the only direction she could see. The glass of the window was thick, and in one corner she could read the legend "toughened." It would take something hard and heavy to make any impression on it, she concluded. She wouldn't be able to break it with her bare hands or with any of the other things in the bedroom. And she had no clothes.

Turning, she surveyed the room once more. Save that she knew better, it looked like any of a thousand other bedrooms. It certainly did not look like a place in which women were bound and whipped and subjected to all-night sex. Even the most ordinary of rooms took on a different aspect when one thought of what could be done in them. She believed she would not look again upon any room, even her own, without imagining the other uses to which it could be put.

There was a built-in wardrobe along one wall. As she looked at the closet, a thought struck Janice. She crossed to it and opened the doors, half hoping she would find her missing clothes. The bare shelves and clothes rail mocked her. The drawers, when she opened them, were full—but not of anything she could wear in public.

The drawers contained handcuffs and leg irons, masks and hoods of leather and rubber, collars and leads of the kind she had offered to William all those years ago. She found a coil of light, strong nylon rope and more of the leather thongs that had been used to bind her last night. And canes. And straps. And whips of many types. The sight of these instruments brought another shiver as she remembered what had been done to Lois and what Lois had later done to her. Which one of these canes, she wondered, had featured in last evening's frolic? No way to tell.

Janice hastily closed the drawers and doors when she heard sounds outside her own door. She just had time to move away from the wardrobe before the door opened. She could not say why she had been reluctant to be seen going through the bondage equipment. Perhaps it was her natural wish not to be seen snooping.

And perhaps it was an equally strong wish not to be seen inspecting the instruments of her own bondage—as if she were looking forward to it. Another thought struck her: the best way to enjoy the next week—and maybe the rest of her life—would be to let others make the choices of how and when to put her into bondage. The independent and self-reliant woman she had been was becoming a memory. The desire to resign responsibility for her actions to others was growing. This, she now realized, had been behind her experiments with William, but over the years since she had seen him, she had grown into the habit of making her own decisions. And it had been a less enjoyable sort of life, she admitted, however necessary. Certainly her relations with men had been less than satisfactory for a long time. Now, she was returning to an earlier mode—like reliving part of her youth.

Harry entered the room. He paused to look at Janice, and she felt herself flush hotly. She was not used to being regarded by men—or by anyone for that matter—and appraised. It made her feel only slightly better when he said, "You look radiant. Come down with me for breakfast now. We have to get on the road soon."

Janice followed him down the stairs to the dining area where they had eaten the evening before. The table was set, and Lois, still naked but not wearing her chains, served them. This time she sat down herself to eat. Janice took a certain amusement in watching Harry try to decide which of his two naked breakfast companions he should concentrate on. Her next thought was less amusing. She once more compared herself to Lois, to the advantage of the latter. She rescued her self-esteem only by remembering that she often compared herself to others to her own detriment. But, she reflected, she'd better get over all that. She could not alter what she was.

They ate silently. As Lois cleared up, Harry led Janice to the living room.

"As this is your first time, we'll get you ready to travel first."

Janice saw a collection of bondage paraphernalia on the

sofa. Despite a flutter of apprehension and excitement, she said nothing as Harry chose a length of rope from the pile. Evidently this was for her. Wordlessly she turned her back and brought her hands behind her. In silence he tied her wrists, pulling the ropes tight before knotting them.

Janice tested her bonds reflexively. She found no slack, nor any hope of escape. This, she was beginning to feel, was how it should be. Tied, she should be helpless to free herself, totally in the control of another. While she stood passively waiting, Harry chose a second item from the pile. It was a stiff leather collar that fit tightly around her neck and up under her chin, forcing her to hold her head erect. It buckled behind her neck and had a brass ring sewn onto the front, presumably to attach a lead. Next came a black leather helmet, with a place for her nose to fit. There were no eye or mouth holes.

When Harry brought it closer, she could see there was a penis-shaped fitting on the inside, doubtless intended to go inside her mouth as a gag. It was wider than the real thing, and much shorter. She guessed it would fill her mouth, trapping her tongue and making speech impossible.

But Harry paused to point out another feature. "There's a hole through the penis gag, to let you breath through your mouth. There are also holes in the nose-shaped bit for the same purpose."

It's good to know I'll be able to breathe, Janice told herself with irony. But that would be about all. She would be blind and speechless as long as she wore the helmet.

Harry produced foam rubber earplugs of the type worn by people who work with noisy machinery. He inserted them firmly in her ears, pushing them well in. The sounds she heard now were muffled, almost inaudible, as if coming from a distance.

Janice stood quietly while Harry fitted the helmet to her head, making sure the gag went into her mouth and her nose fit into the appropriate place. He laced the helmet tightly behind her head, and Janice was left in a soundless darkness she had never before experienced. The only sounds she could hear were the muffled beating of her heart and the soft noise of air being drawn in through the nostril holes of her helmet. She might have been alone in a cavern for all she could see and hear.

She stood until Harry guided her to a chair. When she felt the seat against the backs of her calves, she sat carefully to await the next development. Briefly, she wondered if Lois was going to get the same treatment. The younger woman was probably used to it by now. She would feel none of the mingled fear and excitement Janice was feeling. Or would she, too, tremble as Janice was now doing?

Either they were very quiet or her earplugs were very good. Janice heard nothing that would give her any clue as to how Lois would travel. Presently, she felt hands on her body, urging her to stand. She got awkwardly to her feet, almost losing her balance. The hands caught her. She stood waiting for the guidance she must have. It came in the form of a fumbling at her neck. When she felt the sharp pull on her collar, Janice guessed that some kind of lead had been fastened to the ring she had noticed earlier. She followed its tug, moving from carpeted living room, through tiled laundry room, and into the garage. She felt the concrete under her bare feet.

Hands—Harry's? Lois's?—guided her up the step into the van and into the seat. Her lead was dropped into her lap, and she felt the straps go around her. They tightened, and once again she was strapped in for transportation into the unknown. The familiar mix of trepidation and excitement came over her as she heard the door close. She sat in darkness for an indeterminate time, dwelling on where she was going. Finally, the motor started and the vehicle began to move. She was on her way, to all intents and purposes a parcel being delivered to its destination.

Arrival

The old adage says that traveling in hope is better than arriving, but traveling naked and in bondage was most exciting of all. So Janice told herself as she traveled with mixed visions of sexual delight and erotic torture running through her mind. What had happened so far, and what Lois had told her, had awakened a growing excitement in her. Bondage she had known about (though not enjoyed) since her time with William. But looking forward to more of the sexual arousal and torture that had taken place last evening made her tremble.

In the midst of her anticipatory excitement, Janice thought of her life before her fateful meeting with Harry and Mark and Lois. The regime obviously aimed at the subjugation of female guests, something her feminist colleagues would never submit to. She considered herself a woman of independent mind rather than one of the bra-burning brigade who, as Alistair Cooke had put it, had marched into so many feminist battles that one could no longer be certain of their aims. Her work required her to make decisions and to think things through before she wrote her stories. She was on leave from all that now. If her colleagues ever learned of her sojourn at the resort, she would be ostracized forever. She shifted in her seat, trying to find a more comfortable position.

Janice was thirsty and sleepy when the van came at last to a stop. She had no idea where she was. The helmet she wore allowed her no audible or visual clues. Arrival was the reverse of departure. She was unstrapped and helped from the van to the ground. Janice felt grass beneath her bare feet, then a tug on her lead took her mind away from her surroundings. She followed.

Suddenly she heard a woman's scream, a wild note of agony in it. It sounded distant, but she knew that was because of her earplugs. It had to be nearby. Sightless inside her leather mask, Janice felt a stab of panic. Someone was being tortured, and it was probable that she herself would be next. Yet here she was, bound and helpless, being led into heaven knew what terrors. There was another scream, and then another. She panicked, tugging on her lead, making incoherent sounds of denial through her gag, wanting instinctively to flee from this unknown place.

The lead held her, drawing her toward the muffled sounds of torment. And, fighting every foot of the way, Janice was led through an unseen door into an unknown building. The screams had ceased. The lead went slack, and she came to a stop. She wanted to run but couldn't move from the spot. She turned her head restlessly from side to side, straining to hear any sound that might tell her where she was—and with whom. Muffled footsteps came nearer. A voice spoke nearby.

" 'Arry, mon ami! It is good to see you again. It 'as been too long since my last visit."

He sounded like a Frenchman, or a Canadian Francophone. Janice couldn't tell the difference.

The unknown man continued, "And it is good to see ze lovely Lois again. " 'Ow 'ave you been, my dear?"

Lois made no audible reply, but Harry said, "I'm glad to see you as well, Jean-Claude."

Janice suddenly realized she was standing naked and helpless in the presence of a complete stranger—perhaps a whole room full of complete strangers. The tight leather helmet concealed her face, but she knew the flush that spread over the rest of her body could be seen.

It was. "Look. Our new guest is blushing. 'Ow charming! I didn't know anyone still knew 'ow to blush zese days. Such innocence! Not like Lois, eh? Or 'Ilary 'ere." To Janice he said, "You must be ze lovely Janice about 'oom I 'ave been 'earing so much from Mark. We must 'ave ze mask off so zat we can be propairly introduced. It must be terribly uncomfortable."

Janice said, "Ummmmmmmnnngh!"

"What? Gagged as well? Come, let me free you of zis inconvenience."

The concern for her comfort in the stranger's voice warmed Janice. Neither of her captors had shown any. He might even be willing to help me escape, she thought. She felt fingers behind her head, unlacing the helmet she had worn for hours. As the constricting leather loosened and fell away, Janice closed her eyes against the sudden flood of light. With her tongue she forced the rubber penis gag from her mouth, working her cramped jaw muscles. Her eyes remained closed as the mask came away.

"Yes, she is indeed as lovely as I 'ave 'eard. You 'ave chosen well, 'Arry." Jean-Claude took her face in both hands, lightly stroking her cheeks and earlobes.

He discovered the earplugs, and withdrew them. Sound became normal again. The collar and lead came off next. Janice opened her eyes and found herself looking at a man of her own height. He was nude save for a leather hood with openings for his eyes. He looked like those pictures of medieval executioners. Janice drew back in alarm.

He let her go. When she looked at him once more, Janice saw that he was tanned all over, which bespoke long hours outdoors in a private place. Or the same time in a solarium, but he looked more the outdoor type. He was lean and wiry, but well-muscled—well-hung, too, she noticed. And partly erect. In her honor?

When he took off the hood that concealed his features, Janice saw a handsome face with a slightly quizzical look. Dark blue eyes regarded her from deep sockets. His mouth, beneath a dark moustache, seemed made for smiling. When he did, his teeth flashed whitely in his dark face.

He allowed her to look at him. Then he stepped forward once more and again took her face between his hands. "Welcome to our 'umble abode, dear Janice," he said. "I 'ave been most eagair to make your acquaintance evai since I saw your picture and learned zat you were coming to stay wiz us. I am Jean-Claude. Not my real name, of course," he added with a chuckle. He bent forward and kissed her full on the lips.

Janice was taken aback. What picture? How had this stranger seen a picture of her? But she didn't draw away. Nor did she open her mouth to his kiss. Just what was the etiquette when meeting a stranger who kisses you most familiarly on the lips while you yourself are bound and naked? Resist? How? Bite him? Not the civilized thing. She stood still until he drew back once more. Janice at last had a chance to view her new surroundings.

She was in a large barn or stable with a high ceiling. The beams and rafters were exposed and skylights in the roof allowed in plenty of light. Windows in the walls let in more light, but they were set higher up than normal, giving the effect of a clerestory. Their height also prevented those inside from seeing out—and those outside from seeing in. That was just as well, she thought as she examined her surroundings and her companions. This was not the sort of scene that would reassure a timid soul. A clean, well-lighted place, eminently suited for adult games.

Lois stood off to one side, wearing a leather hood like the one Jean-Claude had removed from her own head. She wore her chains again, but now a short broomstick had been thrust behind her back through the crooks of her elbows. The chain between her handcuffs was stretched tightly across her stomach. Like Janice, she wore a collar and lead, and she was standing still now that she had no one to guide her. She looked as naked and vulnerable as Janice felt, the hard bright chains a contrast to the softness of her body. And although she was unable to cover herself, she (unlike Janice) seemingly had no objection to being stared at. She stood easily.

Even as Janice envied Lois her aplomb, Harry led her away. Janice was left alone with Jean-Claude and the woman who had been the center of attraction before Janice arrived. She, too, was naked, a statuesque redhead in her late thirties or early forties. She was full-figured without being fat. Her large breasts jutted proudly, crowned with large areolae that surrounded her erect nipples. Her hips flared widely below a slender waist. Her long, full legs, ripe of calf and thigh, were made to be stroked. She had long red hair that made a pleasant contrast to her green eyes. Her full mouth, even in repose, invited kisses. Overall, her face was strong, handsome, the kind of face that would stand out among the beautiful people at a party or gala. Even here, stripped naked and strung up by her wrists, she seemed to dominate the room.

The triangle of thick red hair at the apex of her thighs was damp with perspiration. Even from where she stood, Janice could smell the odor of her arousal. She stood on a raised dais, perhaps a foot off the floor, her wrists strung up to a beam in the ceiling by a rope and pulley arrangement. Her ankles were spread apart and lashed to a round wooden broom handle. Her magnificent body was stretched tautly, on display, every inch of her exposed and ready to receive whatever Jean-Claude chose to do to her.

But Janice was most struck by the steel pole that penetrated the woman's anus. Its bottom was bolted to the wooden dais, and a telescoping mechanism allowed it to be adjusted to fit anyone. Even me, Janice realized with a shudder. She wondered how it would feel to stand in the other woman's place, spread and penetrated.

And lashed. Janice gasped as she noticed a whip lying beside the dais. Pale red stripes covered the woman's body, belly, breasts, and thighs. Even though she could not see them, she knew the woman's back, bottom, and legs would be similarly marked. There was no way the woman could shield herself from the whip. And Janice knew that the same thing was going to be done to her. The same smiling, affable Jean-Claude would lash her. She would scream, but he would not be deterred. Screams like those she had dimly heard earlier would be wrung from her, too.

The woman, hitherto silent, suddenly spoke up. "Jean-Claude, what about *me?*" There was a certain tension in her voice, as if she were barely suppressing intense emotion.

"Ah, yes, of course," Jean-Claude said, striking his forehead with the heel of his hand in the manner of one who has had a sudden recollection. " 'Ow stupid of me. Janice, zis is 'Ilary Anderson. 'Ilary, meet Janice Singleton."

Am I the only one who finds formal introductions bizarre under these circumstances? Janice asked herself.

Hilary burst out, "I didn't mean the introductions, damn you! I meant ME! Get on with it. I can't stand the waiting." She arched her back and thrust herself as far forward as her bonds and the pole up her backside allowed, offering herself to Jean-Claude in front of them all.

Well, in front of me, anyway, Janice thought. He has already seen—and had—her before.

"But of course," Jean-Claude said. "I should nevair 'ave neglected you so." He retrieved the whip and sent it coiling up between her legs with a lazy flick of the wrist. The blow seemed almost casual.

Its effect on Hilary was electrifying. She raised herself on tiptoes and tried to clench her thighs together. The cords in her throat stood out as she threw her head back and screamed in pain. The scream came again, coiling through the open spaces of the stable, as the whip once more found her most sensitive spot.

These were the screams that had so unnerved Janice on arrival, heard now at full volume. Her knees felt suddenly weak. The familiar mixture of fear and anticipation almost made her wet herself. Only by exerting the strongest control did she save herself from that most public of all humiliations.

Jean-Claude noticed her agitation, the slight stagger, the sudden clenching of her thighs as she fought for control. He casually flicked the whip across Janice's exposed nipples.

"Aieeeeee!" Her own scream of pain and surprise was torn

from her throat. The sudden line of fire across her breasts was agonizing.

Jean-Claude struck her a second time. Janice screamed again, the muscles in her throat feeling raw. She staggered, tried to regain her balance and failed. She fell, sitting down heavily, her legs splayed.

Jean-Claude followed her, the whip catching her this time between the legs as it had caught Hilary. Janice's scream was long and piercing, ending in a choking sob as the pain spread through her belly. She closed her legs convulsively, protecting herself from another blow. But she was aware of warmth and wetness in her stinging cunt, the signs of arousal. She remembered the lashing Lois had given her and her response to that. Am I really a masochist? Janice wondered, but without any real alarm.

Hilary broke the silence once more. "Jean-Claude!" Her voice was ragged, on the edge of losing control.

He turned abruptly to her, striking her breasts and nipples, her taut ribcage, her straining thighs. These were not the casual flicks he had given her before. He was putting his strength into the blows, and new red stripes were appearing on Hilary's body. He moved behind her and lashed her back, her bottom, and the backs of her legs from calves to thighs.

Hilary's eyes were closed, her head thrown back to expose the soft tense curve of her throat as she offered herself to the whip. This time there were no screams. Her repeated "Ahhhhh's!" were clearly moans of pleasure. She was straining with her arms to lift herself on the rod that penetrated her anus, pumping herself up and down on it as the thongs bit into her.

Janice, forgotten for the moment, had recovered from her

own agony. She could plainly see that Hilary was teetering on the verge of an orgasm.

Jean-Claude noticed as well. Abruptly he stopped beating her. He stood watching as she writhed on her perch.

Hilary, thrusting her hips, working on the rod inside her, opened her eyes. She looked directly at Jean-Claude. "Damn you!" she hissed. "For God's sake get on with it. You can't stop now!"

Jean-Claude watched her silently, with amused detachment, as Hilary tried with increasing desperation to bring herself to the orgasm that continued to elude her.

"Please," she begged. "Please use the whip. Can't you see I'm on the edge? Please! Let me finish!"

Jean-Claude seemed puzzled. His forehead wrinkled in a frown of incomprehension. "I do not undairstand. When I beat you, you scream and cry. And now you want more?"

Hilary said, "Yes," tensely. "Please, yes. Don't torment me."

"Zen tell me what you want me to do," Jean-Claude said.

It was clear to Janice that he was deliberately toying with Hilary, forcing her to describe in detail what she wanted him to do to her when both of them knew quite well. Is this for my benefit? Janice asked herself. Does he want me to know that I, too, will soon be begging for what I want? And will I be as desperate as Hilary is, humiliated by being forced to tell him what I want him to do to me?

Even as she marveled at Hilary's desire for more pain, Janice was tense with her own craving. In Hilary it was fully developed, this dark mechanism that transmuted sexual torture into ecstasy. In Janice it was embryonic, but she felt, even now, a moist warmth between her legs and a tingling in her belly and breasts as she confronted this new dimension to her own sexuality.

Hilary's voice, low and tense, broke into her reverie: "You know damned well what I want. Don't force me to humiliate myself."

Jean-Claude was silent still.

Hilary spoke again: "Please!" There were tears of frustration and shame in her eyes and desperation in her voice.

"Please, what?" he prompted her.

"Please beat me. Hurt me! Make me come! Please!"

"Beat you where?" Jean-Claude asked.

Hilary looked at him in disbelief. He regarded her silently. Finally she forced the words out.

"My . . . breasts. And nipples. My cunt. My back and bottom. My . . . stomach and thighs. Anywhere! Please!" She twisted in her bonds, begging for the lash.

Jean-Claude finally spoke. "No. I need to deal wiz Janice now. She looks very lovely and very neglected."

Hilary looked despairingly at him as he dropped the whip to the floor and turned away. "Please," she whimpered.

"Don't mind me. You can go on with Hilary." Janice realized she was babbling, the words forced from her by panic. She would have grown to like the pain, given more time for the idea to grow on her. But not yet, surely.

"We must treat our guests well," Jean-Claude told her, "ozerwise zey will not come back. And we do want zem to retairn. And to tell zair friends about us." He paused in thought, looking at Janice but not seeing her. "I think you will be more comfortable seated on the floor." His manner was musing, meant as much for himself as for his captive audience. He moved to the far end of the room, where he selected some rope and what looked like a dildo.

It was. As he approached her, Janice had the urge to run. She tensed, looking around for an avenue of escape. There was none. Instead of going ahead at once with whatever he had in mind, Jean-Claude laid the rope and dildo on the floor and cupped her breast. Janice shuddered. He took her nipple between thumb and forefinger, teasing it until it became taut. He bent to kiss it, and Janice gasped with pleasure as his lips encircled her. His teeth nipped gently. She felt a pang of pleasure in her cunt, a wetness and a growing warmth that belied her fear. Her knees felt weak.

She was on the verge of asking him to continue—as Hilary had begged him, she remembered suddenly. She bit back the plea, glancing at Hilary. The other woman looked despairingly at them, her need plain on her face. I will look like that soon, Janice thought with sudden foresight. They will work at me until I have to beg for release, as she has done. But will I get it?

Jean-Claude straightened up and moved behind her. Once again, Janice nearly asked him to go on. But she managed to remain silent as he tied a length of rope to her bound wrists. With a gentle tug, he raised her hands to the small of her back and bound them there, taking the rope several times around her waist. This posture was no more uncomfortable than the one she had endured for hours, and she wondered why he wanted to tie her more securely when they both knew she hadn't been able to escape.

When he had finished knotting the rope, Jean-Claude picked up the dildo and screwed the threaded base of the instrument into a socket in the floor near her feet. At once Janice realized what was going to happen to her. The purpose of the spike was unmistakable. She was going to have a rod of her own up the Khyber Pass.

As if reading her thoughts, Jean-Claude told her with a chuckle that it would give her more backbone.

"No. Please, no." She heard herself pleading as if from a distance. She wished she could stop, but she suddenly had verbal diarrhea. Now that her own moment of truth had arrived, she was terribly afraid. "Don't do that to me. I have never had anything . . . up there. I . . . I can't take it. Please!"

Jean-Claude paid no attention. He greased the rod with petroleum jelly. He applied another blob of jelly to her anus, briefly inserting his finger to work it up inside her. When he withdrew, she felt slippery inside, and for an awful moment she thought she was going to shit herself. As she struggled for control, Jean-Claude picked her up in his arms and bore her to the instrument of her impalement.

She squirmed, seeking escape.

"Do not squairm so much. I will drop you," he told her.

"Put me down, please."

"But of course. As soon as we reach ze right spot."

Janice looked fearfully in the direction of the upright steel rod to which she was being borne. It was shining and erect, rounded, shaped like a penis. "Please don't do this," she pleaded. "It will hurt. I know it will." She hated the pleading in her voice, but she had to say the words.

" 'Ave you ever done zis before?"

"No," she answered.

"Zen 'ow do you know it will 'urt? Look at 'Ilary. She is not 'urt. Are you, my dear?"

Hilary shook her head silently, but added, "No, what hurts is being left on the edge."

"You see?" Jean-Claude said triumphantly. "You 'ave nothing to worry about." He stooped and set Janice on the floor.

Janice could now examine her next entrant more closely. It was made of stainless steel, like the leg irons she had worn.

It had a distinct rounded head. It was perhaps an inch in diameter. "That is not going to fit," she said fearfully.

Jean-Claude smiled encouragingly at her as he made a loop in one end of the rope and dropped it over the upright rod. He led the end out on the floor. "Think positive," he told her.

Ignoring her squirming protest, he rolled Janice onto her side and applied some more petroleum jelly to her anus. Once again he worked a finger inside, probing her sphincter. "Relax," he told her laughingly when she clamped down.

"You will 'ave to relax when I lower you onto zat," he told her with a nod at the rod that jutted from the floor. "Think of going to the toilet. Relax as if you wair in your own bathroom."

Janice jerked again in protest.

"Does zat excite you?" he asked her. "Some of ze women who come 'ere claim zat taking a shit is like a mini-orgasm. Do you believe zat?"

She did not reply, busy with her own thoughts. *This is really happening. To me. He is really going to make me sit on that thing.* She whimpered softly as she was lifted beneath her arms and guided over the rod.

She wailed, "Please don't!" as the cold steel prodded at her arsehole.

Expertly Jean-Claude guided her into position, and then slowly lowered her to the floor.

Janice tried to resist as she felt the rod part her ass-cheeks. Then it was penetrating her, and the slow relentless pressure forced her to relax in the end. There was a strange electric thrill as the rod went into her, not unpleasant. She slid down the rod until her bottom touched the floor. And as she sat, fully penetrated, she became aware of a very full sensation

where there had never been one before. It didn't go away.
Janice twisted and squirmed in a vain attempt to raise herself
off the spike.

She was unable to use her hands and arms to push herself
up and off the rod. That was why Jean-Claude had tied her
hands in the small of her back. Like her other captors, he
seemed to think of every detail. Janice realized that she was in
the hands of experts who would never let her escape.

Even now, Jean-Claude was making doubly sure she would
stay where he had put her. He bent Janice's knees and crossed
her ankles. With the end of the rope looped around the dildo
he tied her ankles together, pulling them tightly in toward her
crotch. She was left sitting cross-legged on the floor, unable to
use her legs to move herself.

Janice was too busy trying to lose her anal penetration to
notice that every part of her body—all her erogenous zones,
at any rate—were fully exposed to anyone who happened to
pass by. She became aware of her total vulnerability only when
Jean-Claude knelt behind her and began to fondle her
breasts. His erect cock pressed against her back as he cupped
her in his hands, his thumbs and forefingers teasing and
pinching her nipples until they once more stood up tautly,
achingly.

Despite herself, Janice moaned softly as his hands roamed
over her. The familiar tingling began in her cunt and belly and
thighs. The strange full feeling from her bottom subtly combined with the other sensations as Jean-Claude expertly
aroused her.

He leaned closer to kiss her earlobes and the sensitive pulse
below them. His breath on her skin was soft and warm, the
perfect counterpoint to the unyielding rod up her backside.
Janice yielded to the combination, leaning her head back to

allow his mouth to find her other sensitive places. She moaned once again, the pleasure building in her slowly as he shifted one hand to her belly, feeling between her legs until he could part her labia and grasp the hard button of her clitoris with thumb and forefinger.

"Ohgod," she gasped as he teased her. She squirmed under his touch, trying to offer more of herself to him. The rod in her anus made itself felt as an additional *frisson* whose novelty she now found more welcome. Her breath grew short, rasping harshly in her ears as the fingers on nipple and clitoris drove her closer to orgasm. She grasped the fleeting thought that she was once more being forced to submit totally to a man. This sensation she found overwhelming. Bound and impaled, she could take no part in her arousal, could exert no control over what was being done to her, and by extension could have no responsibility for her actions. Absolute freedom, she thought.

Jean-Claude's insistent attention to her nipples and clitoris made her next thoughts much less coherent. She began to clench herself around the rod inside her as the warm tingling of her arousal spread from her belly to the rest of her body. Where before she had felt apprehensive and uncomfortable, she now began to feel warm and dreamy, as if floating out of her body. Little ripples of pleasure swept through her, making her gasp and shudder, the familiar prelude to orgasm.

But Jean-Claude, sensing the onset of her climax, suddenly changed his target. He released her clitoris and slid his finger inside her cunt—which, though Janice found pleasant, was less urgent than his earlier efforts. Where he had been working on her nipples with his fingers, he instead cupped her breasts, holding the warm heavy globes while his mouth touched her lightly about the face and neck. She began to draw back from the brink. And he sensed this also, returning to tease her clitoris and nipples.

As he played upon the instrument of her helpless body, Jean-Claude also whispered a description of what he was doing to her and of what was to come. With her other lovers, she had urged greater or less speed or had told them to come, come now! But no one had ever described in such intimate detail what his hands and mouth were doing to her while he was actually in the process of doing it. "Talking dirty," she said to herself. So this is what it's like. And as he continued to talk dirty, she became more and more frenzied. Like an orchestra conductor, Jean-Claude directed her in what to do as her arousal continued to unfold like a piece of erotic music. "Now we will slow down a bit, my dear. Piano. Clench your pelvic muscles, feel my finger inside you, ze rod up your ass. Now relax. Breathe deeply. Prepare yourself for an orgasm such as you 'ave nevair 'ad. Something truly stupendous, like ze Royal Fireworks Music." But as he spoke, he slowed down, making the "truly stupendous" orgasm he had promised her recede.

Janice, her body aflame, moaned in frustration.

Jean-Claude was whispering to her again. "You are totally mine. You cannot 'elp yourself. You cannot prevent me from doing zis to you." He gave a sudden stab with his finger to her swollen clitoris. "Or zis." He pinched both her nipples hard and suddenly, drawing another gasp from her. "And now smell yourself, little one." He held a finger near her nostrils so that Janice could smell the musky odor of her arousal. He wiped his finger on her lip, urging her to taste the clean, salty tang of her cunt. And then, once more, he drew back.

It was too much for Janice. She heard her own voice as if from a distance, coming from somewhere beyond her conscious control, high and desperate, the words dragged out of her depths, pleading with him to continue, to drive her shuddering and screaming over the edge of ecstasy. "Oh godddd! Please. Please don't stop! Don't stop, not nowwwwwwww! Ohhhhhhh, please!" She squeezed down on the rod in her anus and the finger in her cunt.

And suddenly the finger was gone. She felt empty, abandoned by her guide on a wild mountainside just feet from the summit. Everything was a blur except the orgasm on whose edge she teetered.

Jean-Claude's voice was once more in her ear. "Zat's right. Relax. Wait. Breathe deeply. You 'ave a long way to go before we reach ze peak."

Janice was in no mood to "relax" or to "breathe deeply." Most certainly not ready to wait. Once more she heard her voice pleading desperately with him to go on! Go on!

Another quick probe, his finger on the hard button of her clitoris, his kisses on her neck and ears. Then he was gone once again, leaving Janice moaning and panting, but still on the brink. "Oh god! Ohhhhgodddddddd! Ohhhh-hhhh noooooo!" Long-drawn moans from the depths. She twisted her shoulders, clenching her muscles again, trying to drive herself over the edge—and failing. In a crisis such as this, she had always been able to masturbate, but now her hands were bound behind her back, twisting and clawing as she fought the ropes that held her. If she could only get free, she would plunge her finger into herself and finish the job. But of course that was why she had been bound before they began.

Later, when her thoughts were clearer, Janice realized that bondage was more than just a negative thing, something to keep her from her pleasure. It heightened the pleasure by stretching her out on the rack of frustration. But that came later. This was now.

Suddenly Jean-Claude drew away, standing up, moving away from her. The finger on her clitoris, the hard pinches on her nipples, the warm kisses—all gone.

"For god's sake, don't leave me like this!" she wailed. "Please, please finish me!" She writhed in desperation even as the cry was torn from her.

"I think not," he told her. "I must 'elp 'Ilary, 'oom I 'ave neglected for too long. She, too, 'as need of me. Be patient, my little one. Someone will come for you soon, and zen all will be well."

Janice heard the adult-to-a-fractious-child tone in his words, and through the haze of her desire, she knew who was the adult and who the child. But she was too deeply aroused to resent the words or the tone. Later, she would reflect ruefully on how Janice Singleton, woman of the world, respected journalist, attractive, mature single female of independent mind and habit, had been reduced to begging a man to give her the orgasm she so desperately needed. She was wild, out of control, in a way she had never been when William stripped her naked and bound her all those years ago. Then, she had retained some control over what would happen. She had only to tell him to stop. But would he have stopped? She realized that she had been given some control only because he had wished it. He could have done anything to her once she was helpless. The symbols of domination and control—the rope, the collar, and the lead—had been enough for both of them.

But now she had been manipulated into a position in which she had no control. These men would allow her no choice. She was in restraint, as Harry had told her. They were in total control of her body—no half measures. And no empty symbols.

All this she realized as she watched Jean-Claude walk away, leaving her in such desperation that she almost begged him again to come back. Janice felt shame and the first flickers of resentment at her surrender—a surrender into which she had been manipulated. She bit back another plea for him to finish her, as she remembered Hilary's words: "What really hurts is being left on the edge."

Jean-Claude picked up the whip and swung it experimentally. The swish and crack of the thongs only inches away from her body made Hilary flinch, but she still gazed steadily at him, as if challenging him to do whatever he wished with her. She even nodded slightly in acceptance and encouragement.

He swung the whip again, but this time he struck Hilary. The knotted thongs left new red stripes on her belly, just above her pubic mound. She hissed in pain, but made no further protest. He struck her again, an upward cut to the underslopes of her breasts that lifted and bounced the full globes. This time Hilary did scream, but it was not the full-throated sound of agonized ecstasy Janice had heard earlier. Doubtless, that would come soon.

Janice watched the lashing proceed, squirming in sympathy with the other victim and in desperation at her own frustrated need. She attempted to assuage the latter with the only tools at her disposal—the memory of the words in her ears, the teasing of her taut nipples, the fingers on her clitoris, and the rod in her anus. Her cunt ached and burned with the desire to be touched, filled. But there was nothing she could do about it.

Jean-Claude was lashing Hilary steadily now, moving behind her to strike her bottom and the backs of her thighs.

Janice saw the whip as it curled around her ribcage. He returned to her front, striking her heavy breasts and making them bounce. He lashed her erect nipples, making her moan with that queer mixture of pain and arousal. She writhed on the stake that impaled her as he lashed her belly and the fronts and insides of her outspread thighs. But she never asked him to stop, however wildly she screamed. Jean-Claude shifted his aim and sent the thongs into her crotch, striking her cunt with upward flicks of the wrist. This time Hilary really did scream— a long, drawn-out, wordless howl that echoed through the open spaces of the stables.

He dropped the whip then, moved to her, and took her head between his hands, holding her face steady as he covered her open mouth with his. Her scream was muffled and turned into a moan of pleasure as he pressed himself against her body. He shifted his grasp, holding the mane of her hair behind her neck and using his free hand to explore the places he had just struck. Hilary shuddered when his fingers slid to her crotch, parting her and sliding inside to find her clitoris.

Janice, watching helplessly, imagined him putting his hand inside her. She remembered the exquisite pleasure of the fingers on her own clitoris. She felt herself go all wet again, smelled the odor of her arousal, but could do nothing. She moaned again in frustration, stifling the plea she felt rising to her lips. I have some pride left, she told herself. But it wasn't much comfort.

Hilary moaned again, the sound coming from deep inside her but muffled by the mouth that covered hers. When Jean-Claude ended the long kiss, her moans told the world—and Janice—of her pleasure. She made sharp ohhh's and longer, deeper ahhhhh's of delight, rising in pitch as she teetered on the brink of her own orgasm. With his other hand Jean-Claude teased her nipples, pinching them as he had Janice's.

Watching Hilary's arousal, Janice almost cried out for him to come back to her, but she bit back the words in time. She moaned softly in frustration as she struggled to bring herself to the edge and over into the delights Jean-Claude had promised and then denied her, twisting on the spike of her desire as Hilary twisted in Jean-Claude's hands.

She was moaning almost continuously, in between urging him to go on and finish her this time.

Jean-Claude needed no urging. He, too, was caught up in the arousal of this handsome woman who begged for his attention. His hands were on her thighs, stroking her upward from her knees to her crotch, as if gathering all of her to a single point, which was her cunt. He now knelt before her to use his lips and tongue and teeth on her. He buried his face between Hilary's thighs, reaching blindly upward to capture both her breasts with his hands, cupping them at first and then settling on her nipples with teasing pinches. Hilary shuddered as his tongue found her clitoris, moaning as he roused her to fever pitch.

Janice saw the onset of Hilary's first climax. The older woman suddenly stiffened, the muscles in her legs standing out as she strained at the ropes that held her. Her mouth opened and little mewing sounds of pleasure reached Janice's ears.

The sounds of Hilary's release made Janice more frantic as she imagined what it would be like to have Jean-Claude doing the same to her as she writhed and squirmed to his touch. Janice envied the other woman what she had been denied, and she recognized yet another level of sexual torture as she watched Hilary's ecstasy from a distance. Ignored, Janice squirmed vainly on the rod inside her. She squirmed mentally too. She had never been a voyeur. Or, more accurately, she had never had the opportunity to be one. Now, guilty pleasure was allied to her frustration as she watched the two of them performing before her.

Hilary shuddered again as another climax racked her. Her cries of pleasure were short and sharp now. Her eyes were closed, and her face screwed up in concentration. Jean-Claude must have nipped the bud of her clitoris, for she suddenly stiffened and cried out sharply. Then she was crying out continuously as his head moved between her straining thighs, bringing her to yet another peak of pleasure. "I can't stop coming!" she cried, wonder and delight in her voice, filling the big open space with the sounds of her release.

Janice wished she could come. She was unable to tear her eyes away from the sight of Hilary in full cry. She saw Hilary's eyes open and grow huge and round; she saw her unfocused stare. Saw the O of her open mouth as waves of pleasure swept through her.

Hilary slumped after the last spasm passed, hanging limply from her wrists. But Jean-Claude continued, his mouth busy on her cunt, his hands insistent on her breasts.

It took a moment for Hilary to realize that he was still with her. Then she looked down in disbelief. Janice imagined her thinking, not again? Surely not? And she saw the moment in which Hilary, disbelieving, knew that, yes, she was going to be made to come again. And again. She began to strain at her bonds as her body obeyed the old signals.

Jean-Claude stopped suddenly, and for a moment Hilary seemed not to notice. But then she stared down at him, and cried, "Oh god! Don't stop NOW!"

Rising, he said, "Of course not, cherie." He guided his stiff cock into her.

Hilary gasped as he slid home, burying himself in her. Her face went slack as she felt him thrusting, probing her depths, and she moaned softly in satisfaction. "Ohgod it feels so good!"

He slid his hands between their joined bodies, grasping her breasts, cupping her, stroking, then finally squeezing her so tightly that her nipples stood out tight and shiny. When he bent his head to nip them, she screamed her pleasure aloud, full-throated, as she had screamed when he had struck her. But this time her screams were of pure pleasure, wild, untrammeled delight, ringing through the stables. "Ohhhh! Jean-Claude, come now! With meeee! Nowwwwww!" This last was an animal growl.

And he did. Janice saw him stiffen and then begin pumping against Hilary while she writhed, twisting herself from side to side, her head flung back and the taut skin of her throat working as she screamed again and again, wild, beyond control, lost. Jean-Claude groaned as he spent himself inside her, and Janice moaned her frustration as she watched their mutual release.

They stayed locked together for long moments after the climax of their coupling. Jean-Claude shifted his hands to Hilary's waist, holding her against him as she made her unsteady way back to earth. Her head rested on his shoulder, eyes closed, face relaxed, all intensity gone now. She sighed.

At last he withdrew, and set about releasing Hilary from her bonds. First he unscrewed the telescoping arrangement on the rod that impaled her, withdrawing the head from her anus and allowing her to relax. Janice, almost in tears of frustration now, stared at his cock, still erect, glistening with the mingled juices of their coupling. She could almost feel it sliding into her. He untied Hilary's ankles and slackened the rope that held her suspended. Janice watched him support Hilary, whose knees seemed inclined to buckle.

When she could stand on her own, he finally turned to Janice. Now me! she thought wildly.

"Be patient, little one," he told her. "Someone will come for you soon." He turned away, leading Hilary by her bound wrists toward a door in the back of the stable.

Janice, helpless, watched them go. She wondered who would come for her, and how soon, and what he would do with her. She hoped it was something as earth shattering as what she had just witnessed.

By George

5

When Hilary and Jean-Claude had gone, Janice sat on alone in the big building. The silence grew until she thought she would scream. But something—the remnants of her pride, she thought—kept her silent. They knew exactly where she was, and they knew she couldn't move from the spot without help. She knew that no one would come, no matter how loudly she screamed. So she remained quiet. More dignified, she told herself.

Because there was no clock to mark the passing of time, she had no way of knowing exactly how long she waited. The changing pattern of the sunlight on the floor told her that about two hours had passed before she heard the sound of approaching footsteps. She looked up and saw a tall, sandy-haired man coming toward her. He was lightly tanned, fit-looking, nude—and erect.

Her first instinct was to flee, and she began to struggle against her bonds.

"Hello," the stranger said. "I'm George. You must be Janice. I'm very glad to make your acquaintance." Noticing her struggles, he went on, "No, don't bother to get up. I'm not one to stand on ceremony." He smiled engagingly at her.

Janice was suddenly overcome by embarrassment at her predicament, but she summoned a retort. "And do you suppose I'm the type to sit around on steel rods?" she asked him caustically. Then, angrily, she went on, "Get me off this thing!" When he still regarded her smilingly, she added plaintively, "Please. It hurts."

George replied, "No, it doesn't. You should relax and stop fighting it—as Jean-Claude told you. Don't be so uptight—as they used to say in the sixties."

His erection showed that he was interested in her, and Janice took that as a hopeful sign. But she wasn't going to let him off the hook lightly. "And does the sight of naked women sitting on steel rods turn you on—as they used to say in the sixties?"

"Yes, as a matter of fact it does," he retorted. "Also their sounds and their smells. And their repartee. Yours indicates a woman of some spirit. I like that."

"But not enough to lift me off this thing?"

"Well, not just yet. One should take the time to savor the aesthetic aspects of the pose. And removing you from your, er, perch would also remove much of the piquancy from our conversation. You would become just another helpless naked woman. Though a very lovely one," he added.

Janice thought, this is insane. I'm not having this conversation. But the solid rod in her anus and the ropes that held her helpless could not be talked away. In order to restore some sanity to their colloquy, she changed the subject. "Are you George, as in 'let George do it?' "

"No, I'm George as in George Washington. But I'll be very glad to do you when the time comes."

Ignoring the last remark, Janice asked, "Is your name really George Washington?"

He looked slightly crestfallen. "Well, no. I cannot tell a lie." He smiled. "That's not my real name, but never mind that. Call me George anyway. We all have to have some name."

"You seem to know my real name. And what about Hilary Anderson and Lois Ames? Are those their real names?"

George nodded.

"I think I see. The women have to go by their real names, and the men can be just anybody."

George nodded again, smiling. "That's right. You don't need to know our names. It's better that way. Safer."

"Better and safer for who?"

"For us, of course. It wouldn't be so much fun if some dissatisfied customer decided to call in the local sheriff just because we're doing to women what they all want anyway."

"*All* women?" Janice asked sharply.

"Well, some women," he admitted.

"Me, for instance? And Hilary and Lois?"

"Well, yes," he said thoughtfully. "And other women who come to us from time to time. And the ones who come back again for more—like. . . ." He seemed to think better of naming further customers.

"How can you be so sure?"

George said, "You're all carefully chosen before the initial, er, abduction."

"Chosen how?" Janice wanted to know.

But George refused to be drawn further. "Later. If you're really interested in how we choose our guests, we'll have another chat. After you've become more accustomed to our ways. But now there's you." As Jean-Claude had done with Hilary, he took her head between both hands and covered her mouth with his.

Janice, taken by surprise at the sudden shift from words to action, nevertheless responded, opening her mouth to him. When he moved his hands and began to stroke her labia and probe her cunt, she felt herself melting. The tingle of arousal was unmistakable.

Further resistance—any resistance, she knew—was foolish. She felt the blood flowing to her breasts. They became warmer, heavy and leaden. Her nipples began to erect without any further encouragement.

George noticed the signs. He moved both hands to tease them, then when they were hard and tight, he bent to kiss them.

Janice, the memories of her earlier arousal flooding back, felt herself growing wet again. She thought she could even feel her labia opening like the bud of a flower. When they broke for air, she was breathless and panting.

"I think it's time for a change of location," George said. "These meditation stations are OK for preliminary games—foreplay, if you like—but unless you're completely anal-erotic, there's no way to proceed much further." He untied her ankles and helped her straighten her cramped legs. Then he took her beneath the arms and lifted her slowly off the spike that had kept her nailed to the spot.

Janice felt the rod sliding out of her with a curious mingling of relief and regret. But this was short-lived, changing quickly to dismay as she realized she was about to shit herself. "Oh god, George, get me to a toilet—quickly. I can't hold it in!"

He helped her to her feet, and then supported her as her legs threatened to buckle. Half-carrying her, he guided her across the wooden flooring and toward the toilet enclosure at the back.

Janice, struggling to contain herself and keep some shred of dignity, thought they would never get there. Each step, each movement, threatened sanitary disaster. They were halfway there. Three-quarters. George was opening the door and guiding her inside. The nearness of relief undid her. Brown liquid mixed with lumps shot from her arsehole and ran down the backs of her legs. She felt the flood of urine at the same time.

"Oh, shit!" she wailed, smelly, slippery, dignity in shreds.

"Well, yes, I guess that's what I'd call it, too," George said. "But never mind. This almost always happens to new-comers the first time they meet Spike Jones. It has some-thing to do with the anal sphincter being held open too long. It doesn't want to close properly afterwards. But it soon gets better."

"Do you have to do this to all women?" Janice asked heatedly.

"Well, not all of them," George told her. "Some of them are just sensitive, like you. But a surprising number of our ladies want us to stick an enema up the backside while they're tied up and make them shit themselves. Some even like to be forced to lie in it. They claim to like it almost as much as the regular stuff. It takes all kinds. But with some like yourself, well, it's like they say, shit happens. But it's not intentional, not part of the breaking-in process, I mean. If we wanted to break you down that way, we could always lace your food with laxatives or diuretics and just stand clear. With some women—and you appear to be one of them—the combination of sexual arousal and the old rod up the back passage just seems to loosen things up a little too much. The only remedy I can see would be to leave the plug in place when we let you loose. But that," he finished with a grin, "would only be a stopgap remedy."

Even covered with her own excrement, Janice could appre-ciate the pun. She groaned in response as George guided her past the now redundant toilet and toward the shower enclosure, which appeared more immediately useful. He urged her inside and turned on the water, adjusting the temperature.

"Could you please untie my hands?" Janice asked. "I need to do more than just rinse off."

George shook his head. "Rules," he said laconically, then added, "Anyway, I like to wash a naked woman. It's a lot more fun than washing a pickup truck." He stepped into the enclosure with her and reached for the soap.

Soon Janice felt cleaner and a lot more contented than she had in a long time. The warm water and the slickness of the soap on her body both relaxed and excited her. The presence of an attentive and erect man whose hands, moreover, seemed to know what a girl liked may also have had something to do with her mood.

George cleaned her thoroughly, even shampooing her long hair. She submitted to it all. Then, when she was clean, he took more soap and began to lather her belly and breasts once again. He stroked her slippery skin, making her tingle. His hands lingered to pinch her nipples and to stroke her belly, sliding between her legs to probe her cunt. Being aroused in a shower while bound and unable to resist was another new experience for Janice. When he slipped a finger into her cunt, she spread her thighs for him. She leaned back against him. With his other hand he stroked her belly and pressed down on her pubic mound. This produced a disturbing interplay between the finger inside and the hand on the outside.

The soap on her breasts made them excitingly slippery. George moved a hand to rub her nipples. His roughened palm produced a friction effect that was even more delightful than the teasing she had enjoyed earlier.

He saved the best for last. Moving slightly away from her, he withdrew his finger and guided his erect cock into her from behind. When she was fully penetrated, he used both hands to stimulate her tits. At the same time, he began to thrust slowly in and out, all slippery from the soap and her own juices.

With a sigh of pleasure, Janice slumped against him, straining to take more of him inside her. Being taken from behind had been one of her favorite fantasies, all too seldom realized over the years. Mostly, she knew, the lack resulted because most men are not long enough to go the extra distance comfortably. This made her feel both deliciously primitive—an animal—and terribly excited. They began to move in the ancient rhythm beneath the cascading water. Her moans gradually became louder, deeper, as the first spasms of pleasure rippled through her, spreading outward from her cunt. George took his time, letting her set the pace.

Janice's arousal was slow and thorough this time. And unlike her last one, it was not interrupted. When he felt her tighten around his cock, George thrust into her and held the position while she came. This time, perhaps because she had been denied for so long, she let out a sharp cry, surprising herself. But George was not done. As soon as he felt her tension lessen, he resumed his thrusts, playing upon her full breasts and nipples with both hands.

Janice matched his rhythm, eager to experience another climax like the last. She had wanted something like it all during her earlier arousal and denial, and now she wanted more. And still more. The denial had merely whetted her appetite.

Slow, deep thrusts from George brought more small, sharp cries of delight from Janice. Suddenly she heard a voice in her ear: "Go on and scream if you want to. I like women who scream when they come." And soon Janice found that she wanted to scream. As she felt the next spasm begin, she tensed her stomach muscles and took deep, rapid breaths. She clenched herself around his cock and let the pleasure flow through her. And this time, she did scream. The sound of her release rang in the small enclosure that seemed too small to contain the wonder of this long-delayed orgasm.

She slumped against him with a sigh of satisfaction, thinking there were few things so satisfying as a shattering climax. When George did not withdraw, she realized with a pang of guilt that she had been concentrating so hard on her own pleasure that she had forgotten him. "George, I'm sorry," she found herself saying over the noise of the water. "You didn't come. Come now." And she settled herself to let him make use of her now for his own pleasure.

After a short respite, George began to arouse her over again. She thought she was exhausted, all screamed out, and she settled herself to let him come. But to her surprise, she found herself beginning to respond again as his hands roamed over her body and his stiff cock slid in and out of her cunt. Surprise soon gave way to excitement. She began to scream early at this last assault on her resistance. "Ohgod! Ohhhhhh! Ohgodddd! Georggge!" Once more, the sound of a woman in full cry filled the tiny shower stall.

And this time George did not hold back. She felt him thrust deeply into her as his own climax began. When she felt the hot spurt inside her, Janice came again, straining her lungs and throat as she gave vent to her pleasure. His grunts of effort matched her cries as he emptied himself into her.

Afterwards, they leaned together against the streaming walls for a long time.

George withdrew slowly from her. Janice felt regret, but at the same time a deep satisfaction. He turned her around to face him and smiled lazily. Then he bent to kiss her mouth. Janice leaned against him and returned the kiss.

He dried them both, Janice first and then himself. With a

clean towel he made a turban for her still-damp hair. Then he led her back through the stable and out the same door Hilary and Jean-Claude had used earlier, out into the golden sunlight of early evening.

Janice was surprised at how much time had passed since her arrival. Was it only that morning? So much had happened. She felt weak, but happy. Much happier than she had felt in recent years.

She followed him docilely across the lawn and into the sprawling ranch house that was apparently the resort's main accommodation. The rooms were big—light and airy—with mission-style furniture. He led her down a long hall and into (naturally, she thought) a bedroom. She felt torpor steal over her as she looked longingly at the big bed—the perfect place to end a busy day.

Only, of course, it wasn't quite over. A selection of food was laid out for them on a table in one corner of the room. Janice heard her stomach rumble as she caught sight of it. She realized that she hadn't eaten since early that morning. The day had been so eventful that she had not thought of food since. But now that she saw it, she was ravenous.

"Oh, George, I'm starving. Untie me quickly so I can eat."

"Sex does kind of take it out of you, doesn't it?" he said with a smile. "But you sit down and I'll do your hair. Then we can eat."

Janice looked at him in disbelief. "I'm ready to eat a horse, and you want to do my hair?" When she saw his grin, she had to grin back. "Okay. Good joke. Now untie my hands so I can eat." She turned her back, presenting her bound wrists to him.

And nothing happened. She turned to face him again. "Let

me guess. You're not going to let me go. So how do you expect me to eat? Do you intend to put the food down on the floor and make me eat it like an animal?" she asked indignantly.

"Now why didn't I think of that?" George said. "I'll pass the idea along to the management. They're always keen to get ideas from the guests. Good feedback they call that in management-speak. But tell me what you want to eat, and I'll put the plate down on the floor for you." He paused thoughtfully. "I don't know how you're going to drink, though, unless you think you can lap from a cup without spilling any." He delivered this suggestion deadpan.

Astounded, Janice looked at him. She had been ready to blaze at him, but she saw his grin once more. "Okay. Another good joke. But just how *do* you expect me to eat?"

"I'll feed you, of course," he replied. "But," he added with a regretful shake of the head, "I sure did like the idea of you eating doggie-fashion off the floor. That would speed up the breaking-in process to no end. Women would learn their place a lot quicker that way." When he saw her anger rising once again, he held up his hands placatingly.

Janice nevertheless burst out, "You're a Neanderthal! What's all this crap about a woman learning her place? This is 2002, not the Stone Age!"

George assumed the manner of a good ole boy confronted by a prickly female. "You're sure purty when you're mad, ma'am. I like a gal with spirit, jest like I told you awhile back. And you've surely got plenty of it. We'll git along like a house afire, just as soon as you stop shoutin' about yore rights." He grinned and continued in his normal voice, "In any case you've got it wrong. As you can see, I belong to the species Homo erectus." He indicated his cock. "See what an angry gal does to me?"

Janice, exasperated and amused at the same time, tried to

conceal her chagrin at being taken in so easily. Finally she asked, "Do you really intend to feed me?"

"Of course," he told her. "One should always take care of his pets."

His grin was meant to be disarming, but it was clear that he was not going to untie her. She would have to submit to being fed like a . . . well, like a pet. Or she could stand on her pride and go hungry. Once again she would have to face the consequences of her choice. A naked woman with her hands tied behind her back was not in a good position to bargain with her captor. That should be almost a motto by now, she thought.

George beckoned Janice over to the table and pulled out a chair for her. When she was seated, he pulled his own chair close beside her and asked her what she wanted to eat. He fed her finger sandwiches of ham, turkey, and smoked salmon, and she ate greedily. Pride was not as important as hunger.

With the turkey sandwich, George gave her a spoonful of cranberry sauce. Inevitably, some of it dripped as she took it off the spoon. A dollop landed on her breast. "Please, will you wipe it off before it runs?" she asked him.

"One of the advantages of the captive feeding program," he told her, "is that the captors get to lick the captives clean. I must arrange for something tasty—at least as tasty as what's already there—to fall between your legs."

He grinned so lewdly as he said it that Janice was forced to laugh. Nevertheless, he arranged for more spills and runs: her breasts caught most of it, but some fell between her thighs. The wine he gave her naturally enough ran down that far. With dessert, some of the fruit trifle landed in her crotch, where it stickily remained.

Janice finally had eaten enough. "A gal's gotta keep her figgah or the fellahs won't follow," she told him in a Southern drawl.

George retorted, "Don't worry about your figgah. One of the more pleasant side effects of a stay with us is that most women leave ten pounds lighter. And a good deal happier than when they arrived."

Janice asked mischievously, "Do you just screw all that weight off them? How do you survive?"

"We just do our duty, painful as it sometimes is," he replied with another grin. "But no. We don't just screw it all off." In a mock-German accent he said, "Ve haf uzzer vays to make you sveat. You must not take the *Geschlect macht leicht* sign over the gate too seriously."

"I arrived blindfolded," Janice told him.

"Oh, well. Remind me tomorrow to take you on a little tour of the outfit. Or spread, as it used to be called. But now it's time for me to eat." He looked lasciviously at the various blobs that had fallen onto her breasts and thighs. He added a drop of custard to the trifle in her crotch. "Prepare to be eaten," he told her with a leer. George moved closer to her and bent his head to her exposed breasts.

The morning light filtered slowly into the room. First, the darkness lessened, then became grey dusk, and, finally, golden shafts of sunlight. Janice woke early. Despite the exertions of the day before, she could sleep no longer. She was stiff from sleeping propped up in a corner of the bedroom. George had not offered to untie her, and she had been too stiff-necked to ask him again. She had tried sleeping in the bed next to him but had not been able to get comfortable in any position while lying down. Sleeping on her back was out of the question, but she had found that sleeping on her side was not much better. Her hands and arms kept going numb. At last she had struggled to her feet and made her way to a corner, where she had sat down with the wall supporting her head. There, she had slept fitfully until the dawn.

Janice got awkwardly to her feet, leaning against the wall until she got her feet firmly under her. She could see that George was still asleep as she made her way across the room to the window. The remnants of their evening meal were still on the table in the corner. She remembered him licking her clean, and then going on to. . . . Janice shuddered as she remembered her cries and contortions and her pleas. Such thoughts weren't the best way for a woman of independent mind to start the day.

She stood by the window, a shaft of sunlight making a vertical line on her body. It felt warm and comforting. She stood in the light, working the stiffness and the pins and needles from her hands and arms, rolling her shoulders and working her upper body. Voices drifted in from the yard outside—a man and a woman talking easily and comfortably. The woman's voice sounded familiar, the man's less so.

Janice drew closer to the window and peered through the space between the curtains. In the background rose forested hills, the near slopes still in shadow. Sunlight through a wide valley, mist in the trees, the cool breath of morning through the open window—all raised gooseflesh on her naked body.

In the foreground, a woman was being harnessed to a cart. Lois, dressed in tight-fitting leather and high-heeled, knee-length boots, stood between the shafts of a light cart, across the yard from Janice. A man had just finished tying her hands behind her back and was moving her into position in front of the . . . what was it? Janice asked herself. Then it came to her. The cart was much like the light ones she had seen at a harness racing some years ago: long poles at the front between which the horse—or woman—was fastened; a light aluminum frame with wire-spoked wheels, like those on a bicycle; a single seat. A sulkey, she recalled. That's what it was called.

Lois, smiling and talking to the man hitching her up, obviously liked what was happening to her. The sight of the younger woman in her outlandish costume made Janice catch her breath. The tight, glossy leather fit Lois like a second skin, hugging her slender figure and outlining every curve. The outfit was designed to display the wearer to best advantage. For a moment, Janice imagined herself in Lois's place, her body tightly confined in the leather costume. She shivered with vicarious excitement.

She wanted to see more. Using her teeth, Janice slid the curtains back. A thought came to her: I've been tied up for so long I've almost forgotten what it's like to have arms. The sunlight fell fully on her naked body, the cool breeze fluttering between her legs and hardening her nipples as she watched the couple in the yard. But she forgot her own sensations as she watched Lois being readied for . . . what? Janice could not guess.

But she knew someone who could. She turned away from the sight outside and called softly, "George." He stirred but didn't wake up. She called more loudly, moving closer to the bed.

He opened an eye and closed it again with a faint groan. "Not again? You're insatiable. And it's too early."

"George, come look at this. Tell me what's happening."

"Come back to bed instead," he said.

"George, get up!" Janice insisted.

Reluctantly he got out of bed and moved closer to her. Janice was by now looking out the window again, so she was taken by surprise when George stood behind her and cupped her breasts as he kissed her in the angle below her jaw.

"Not now," she told him impatiently. "What's he doing to Lois?"

George looked at the scene in the yard. "Getting her ready for her morning jaunt as a pony-girl," he said matter-of-factly. "She comes here mainly for that—and for what happens afterwards up at the line shack in the hills over yonder."

"Pony-girl?" It was the first time Janice had heard the expression.

"Didn't you ever play cowboys and Indians when you were little? We used to sing a little song to the girls—whenever we allowed them to play, that is: 'Come and be my pony-girl.' "

"And is that what you meant?" Janice asked.

"Well, no. We were considerably more innocent in those days. But it's good fun when you're grown up. Lois thinks so, at any rate."

"What is he going to do to her?" Janice wanted to know.

"I expect he'll let her pull him a ways into the hills, to the place we call the line shack. It used to be a place for the real cowboys to sleep when they were away with the cattle. We've fixed it up a bit, and now it serves as another base for those who like to get a bit farther from the madding crowd. Lois goes there often with Harry—that's him hitching her up—and they play the sort of games she likes."

"What does she like?"

"Well, sex, of course. Only hers is all mixed up with dressing up in her leather gear and hauling her master around for the day while he encourages her with a whip. It's not my idea of fun, but she likes it well enough. Well enough, at any rate, to have bought her own outfit for her visits here. They do get down to the basics later, I imagine. It's just that she likes the preliminaries to be just so—to get her into the right frame of mind, I suppose."

Janice looked more closely at Lois. First she had seemed an innocent. Then she had attended to Janice like a lesbian veteran. Then she had been fucked by Harry. And now she was playing at pony-girls with him. A woman of many parts, clearly.

Harry backed Lois between the shafts and fastened her in place. She wore a wide belt around her waist, and he buckled her into place with straps attached to it. Then he climbed into the seat and gave her a flick about the bottom with a long leather whip. Lois jerked at the touch and leaned into her harness. She broke into a trot as the cart began to move, Harry flicking her now and again as they disappeared from view.

George turned Janice around as the cart dwindled into the distance. She saw that he was getting erect. "Is that for me or for Lois?" she asked.

"For you, of course. Lois is Harry's toy."

"And I am yours?" she asked tartly.

"Don't get up on your high horse. It was only a manner of speaking. I was trying to be gallant."

"Well, I don't like your manner of speaking. I'm not a thing. I'm a person." Janice had regained some of her independent manner, having had enough sex the preceding day to satisfy her for some time: she felt as if she was now more or less on even terms with her captor. Except, of course, he *was* the captor. She was the one whose hands were tied. She tried again. "Are you going to untie me at any time in the near future?" she asked sarcastically.

"Funny you should mention that," George replied. "I was thinking of letting you go take a shower, and I thought you might find your hands useful for that. Unless you'd rather I washed you."

Janice suddenly remembered the shower of the previous day, and her independence suffered a tumble. I can't admit it now, she told herself, but I wouldn't like that to be the last shower *a deux*. "Thank you," she said, the sarcasm somewhat subdued. She turned her back to George and waited for him to untie her hands.

He loosened the knots, and suddenly she had arms again. But they were so cramped from long immobility that she could do little with them. They hung at her sides as the circulation gradually returned. Janice flexed her fingers experimentally, and gradually she felt able to raise her arms, first bending her elbows and then extending them before her. She swung them in slow circles, clumsily at first, and then with more control. "I think I'm ready for that shower now," she announced finally.

"Just be careful you don't fall," George told her.

His remark made Janice more determined than ever to show him that she was capable of taking care of herself. She marched into the bathroom and turned on the water, adjusting the temperature to a comfortable level. Over the sound of the running water she heard the door close, and she turned just as the lock clicked. She was locked in the bathroom. No wonder he had so readily untied her. She felt a flash of resentment, immediately looking around for some other means of escape. The window was high up and too small to wriggle through. The door, when she tried it, was unyielding. There was nothing for it but to take the opportunity to get clean.

Janice made a long job of it, both because it was a pleasure and in order to make George wait as long as possible. A small act of rebellion and self-assertion, she told herself. A shampoo and a session with the hair dryer prolonged the process nicely. It also improved her temper and, she thought, glancing in the mirror, her appearance. She now felt ready to make her grand entrance. Knocking on the door, she waited for him to let her out.

Nothing happened. Janice knocked louder. Still nothing.

"George," she called, without result, then louder, "George!" He did not rush to open the door. Janice pounded her fists against it, yelling his name at the top of her voice. This was ridiculous, she told herself. *Locking me up in the bathroom like a small child is going too far.* After a few minutes of yelling and pounding, she was sweaty and angry—and still locked in. She gave the door a kick with her bare foot and immediately regretted it. "Owwww!" she shouted, balancing on the other foot. "God damn it! Let me out!" She sat down abruptly, landing in the bidet and turning the water on full force in an attempt to break her fall with her hands.

Immediately she was wet again, wetter than before, if that was possible. Wet in the way a cat gets wet: spitting and fighting. The time spent drying her hair was wasted as it became wet once more, straggling down over her eyes as she tried to shut off the taps.

As if he had been waiting for that moment, George opened the door and stuck his head into the room, which was by now all steamed up, with water dripping from the walls. "Did you call me?" he asked.

Janice angrily threw a bar of soap at him, hitting the door jamb instead. "Get out!" she screamed at him, looking for something else to throw. Before she could take aim with a jar of bath salts, he pulled his head back and closed the door. Weeping in anger and frustration, Janice tried to jerk it open. It was locked again. Pounding with her fists brought no response.

"George! I know you're out there. Let me out! Now!"

"Are you presentable?" he asked her. "I wouldn't want to embarrass a lady by making an entrance before she was ready to be seen."

"God damn it!" she screamed, out of control but not caring. "Stop screwing around and open the door."

"Only if you're ready to declare a cease-fire and agree to stop the missile attack. Okay?"

"Yes, damn it. Open the door!"

He did, looking quickly to see if she were taking aim again. "Like I told you earlier, an angry gal sure looks pretty—even if she does resemble a wet cat." He ducked as she threw a tube of toothpaste at him. Retreating, he called out, "Come out when you're drier. And less aggressive. I can see why women should be kept tied up or locked up."

Janice dried her hair again, brushing it until it shone. Normally she found it soothing to brush her hair, but not today. She was still seething. She stormed into the bedroom with fire in her eyes.

George was sheltering behind the wardrobe door, only his head showing. He was also laughing.

Janice had intended to throw something else at him in her anger, but the sight of him ready to pull his head in like a turtle in a shell made her laugh, too. She dropped the can of aerosol deodorant to the floor, fighting not to break down completely.

"Truce?" he called from across the room.

"Truce," she agreed finally.

He came out of hiding and they laughed at one another.

"You really are prettier when you're mad," he told her, "but you're lots easier to deal with when you're not."

Janice noticed that he had gotten dressed in a comfortable-looking outfit of denim shirt and jeans. He wore shoes rather than the boots she would have expected. Maybe he was halfway reasonable. She decided that the time was right to extract another concession from George. After all, he had readily agreed to untie her, when he could have refused (citing "rules," vaguely). As she saw it, George both owed her a favor and had been manipulated into a position where he looked upon her as a special guest (if not, why had he spent so much time with her?). She had always been able to charm men in the past. Why not George?

"Might I have something to wear for a bit as well? I have been kept nude ever since the abduction. It gets a bit wearing, don't you think?"

"Not to me, it doesn't," he replied.

Was he being gallant, or merely difficult? She tried again, telling herself that this was not really begging. It was merely a reasonable discussion between two reasonable people. Wasn't it? "I really would like to have something. Please."

"Well," he said, "I was thinking it's about time for you to have something, too. Great minds think alike." He opened the wardrobe door behind which he had been hiding and beckoned her closer.

Inside the large closet were several versions of the same outfit, obviously intended for women of different sizes. What they all had in common was a deep decolletage and a very short (and tight, by the look of it) skirt. They were, in fact, all maid's outfits, of the type Lois had worn when she served dinner to Harry and her. There was a stack of frilly aprons on a shelf above, together with several lace caps. On Lois, she remembered, she had thought the outfit deliberately scanty and provocative. Lois had not seemed to mind. Nor had Janice, so long as *she* was not wearing such a dress. Now she was being offered the same outfit, and she found that her attitude had changed, not for the better.

"I can't wear that," she objected. It's too . . . too . . ." She didn't know how to finish the thought without appearing either too naive, too prudish, or too shocked.

George, no doubt being deliberately obtuse, said, "I don't see why not. I'm sure we can find one to fit you. What size are you?"

"Twelve, but it's not a matter of size," Janice told him. "It's . . . it's . . ." Again she did not complete the thought.

"A woman always looks sexier when she's wearing something short and tight," George said.

Janice could feel her anger rising again. Men! she thought. Chauvinists, pigs, all of them. From being relatively reasonable and accommodating, she thought, George had reverted to type in a single instant. "I can't . . . won't wear that," she said indignantly, pointing at the offending garments.

"All right," George said reasonably, closing the doors. "I can stand the sight of you in your birthday suit well enough. It's just that we're going to meet some of the other guests in a few minutes, and I thought you might want to dress before going out in public. But if you're happy . . ." This time *he* deliberately didn't complete the thought.

Far from manipulating him, Janice herself had been outmaneuvered. However, it was this or nothing. With as much grace as she could manage, she said, "Oh, well, all right. I suppose I can get used to it."

But George made no move to reopen the closet. "I don't want you to be unhappy. You can go as you are, if you like. The others won't mind."

The thought of being the only nude person at a gathering was not very palatable. "No, I really don't mind. I'll take the size twelve."

"No, it's really all right. I don't want to force you like this. If you're ready, we can go now." He started for the door.

"Please," she said, the word catching in her throat. God, how I hate sounding like this, she thought, even as she said please again.

He stopped, turned to her. Looked at her appreciatively, in a way that made her think of a stock appraisal. With a quizzical expression he asked her, "Have you changed your mind again? A minute ago you were dead set against a dress. Just what is it you want to do?"

"Please," she said, "let me have the dress. I'd really rather wear that than . . ." She indicated her nakedness.

With a look that plainly said, "Women!" George motioned her to open the wardrobe and make her choice.

Gritting her teeth, Janice took down one of the scanty maid's outfits and held it up against her body. The skirt was very short. It would have to do, she decided. To George she said, "Is this . . . all?"

"Well, no. There's the apron. And the cap to go with it." As he spoke he handed one of each to her.

"I mean . . ." she said, "I mean, what about . . . underwear. Panties. A bra. Maybe a slip. And shoes."

"Most of the women just put a bit of rouge around their nipples and slip into the dress," George told her. "But if you really must have the other stuff, look in the drawers of the bureau and see if you can find something that suits."

Looking, Janice found a selection of brassieres, all of the push-up type and all with barely more than half-cups, so the tops of her breasts would be exposed. The cups, she judged, would barely cover her nipples. But it could have been worse. She found brief slips, short enough not to show below the hem of the skirt. But she could find no panties. She decided the omission was deliberate, but said nothing when she found a supply of hose. That would have to do. At least she wouldn't be flashing her cunt every time she sat down.

Janice laid the dress on the bed and sat down herself to put on the hose. Sheer, shiny black, she noticed. How typical, she thought. Then she discovered they had no gusset. The crotch was open. She flung them down and chose another pair. They were the same, as were all the hose. Nevertheless she put on a pair, concealing her chagrin as best she could.

As she began the contortions every woman undergoes to fasten a bra behind her back, George said (in a disappointed-little-boy voice), "Aren't you going to put some rouge on your nipples?"

Janice saw that he was grinning as he looked at her discomfiture. Best ignore him, she decided, settling her breasts into the sheer half-cups and tugging the shoulder straps tight. The bra really did present her tits as if on a plate for all to look at, but it, too, would have to do. Next came the slip, barely covering her bottom. The dress was as short as she had feared. And as tight. It clung to her, outlining every curve and line of her body from tits to midthigh. She glanced at herself in a mirror and was surprised to find a stranger looking back at her—a tarty stranger, she thought ruefully. But at least not a nude one, even though she felt the cool air on her cunt where the crotchless hose left her bare.

The shoes were all black, to match the dress and hose, and all of them had stiletto heels. She chose a pair and put them on, teetering for a moment on the high heels before she struck a balance. She was as ready as she would ever be, she guessed. She turned toward the door, expecting George to follow. When he didn't, she turned to glance back at him. He held the apron and cap out to her, obviously wanting her to put them on. Janice felt a flash of anger at him. Not satisfied with dressing her like a whore, he also wanted everyone to know that she was a mere servant as well. Angrily, she put on the cap and apron. "Ready?" she asked tartly.

George gave the same sort of wolf whistle that had harried and pursued her through the woods into the arms of Harry and

Mark. It sounded genuine, a sign of his admiration, and she soft-ened momentarily, even though she managed to look grim-faced.

George made no move to follow her. Am I going to have to find my own way, she wondered.

But no. There were two more items she had not yet donned. From another drawer George extracted a pair of leg irons and a pair of handcuffs with a faint clinking of chain. He held them out to her. Obviously she was meant to take them and put them on as another mark of her servitude.

Janice refused to give him the satisfaction of another show of anger. Wordlessly she took the fetters from his hand and sat on the bed once more. She raised her left leg, feeling the skirt ride up to her crotch as she crossed her leg and locked the steel band around her ankle. She bent down to lock its twin around her right ankle, not bothering to pull the skirt down. Let him look, she thought with as much bravado as she could muster. She turned the key and withdrew it from its socket, leaving it on the bed.

The handcuffs presented a bit more difficulty. Looking at George steadily, she asked, "Hands in front or behind my back?"

"In front, I think," he said. "Easier on you."

Silently she locked the cuffs around her wrists, turning the key and withdrawing it from its hole. This, too, she left on the bed. Standing up awkwardly, she wished her skirt would slide down her thighs. She tugged it down with some difficulty because of the handcuffs and the tightness of the dress. In the mirror, a tarty stranger looked back at her. A tarty stranger in chains.

At last George seemed satisfied. He pocketed the keys to her manacles and indicated that she was to precede him out into the hall.

With a clink of chain, she led the way.

Explanations

6

George stopped her at a door that had a sign on it: Social Director. Exactly what this madhouse needs, she thought: a social director. Madam, meet your new captor. Sir, this is Janice, who has expressed a desire to be beaten and fucked senseless. I hope you will get along well together.

He opened the door and motioned for her to go ahead of him. She moved into the office, taking the small, careful steps of one in leg irons. Across the room was a desk with a window behind it. Like the bedroom window, it, too, faced eastward, letting in the bright light of what was by now almost midmorning. Outside was the same view she had seen from their bedroom. A man rose from the desk and advanced to meet them. With the light behind him, his face was in shadow. As he stepped away from the window, she saw that he was tall and tanned—de rigueur out West, she thought. And he wore the uniform: jeans and denim shirt. He even wore boots with pointy toes.

George made the introductions. "Sam, this is Janice Singleton. Janice, meet Sam Fredericks."

Sam smiled at her. "Glad to meet you, Janice. Call me Sam, please. It's . . ."

"It's not your real name," she finished the sentence for him.

"No, it's not," he said with another smile. "But call me Sam anyway. Please have a seat. And welcome to our little spread."

Janice sat awkwardly in an armchair opposite the desk, her short skirt riding up her thighs. She carefully kept her knees pressed together. The bright sunlight glinted on the sheer nylon of her hose, and she saw Sam looking at her legs. After a good long look, he raised his glance to take in the rest of her.

"I'm glad you're wearing chains, Janice. It shows you have good taste. A lady's hardly fit to appear in public unless she's wearing her handcuffs and leg irons. And so many of them don't. These are decadent times we live in, don't you think?" He moved back to his desk as he spoke.

Janice had been thinking it would be nice to be outside on such a nice day. His words jerked her abruptly back to the room. His face was once more in shadow as he sat behind the desk, so she couldn't tell whether he meant those preposterous words seriously. She was momentarily speechless.

Sam broke the silence before she could think of a retort. "We need to chat about your program while you're with us," he said, sounding like the athletics director of a health spa. "We'd like to know your preferences," he continued in the same tone. "Do you like to be tied with rope, for instance, or to wear chains, as you are now? Do you like leather—like Lois—or rubber? We can cater to most tastes, and we will treat what you say as a guide to dealing with you during your stay with us."

Janice had no idea what reply to make to this insane speech. She looked at Sam. Was he joking? He seemed serious enough. She had the impulse to get up and walk out, but the steel bands locked around her wrists and ankles reminded her that that was not an option. Then she remembered the thorough fucking she had enjoyed since her arrival at this bizarre place, and the idea of having more of that kept her seated as well. Finally she said (exactly as if making a normal reply to a

normal question), "What if I don't have any preferences?"
Listening to herself, she thought, I sound as crazy as he does.
Maybe we're both crazy.

"Don't worry about that," Sam said. "This is all new to
you. Take your time. Experience a little of everything, and
then, when you've made up your mind, just let us know." He
paused. "Maybe I'm going too fast for you just now, so I'll outline the general ideas that govern the resort. Maybe that will
help you decide what you'd like.

"This is a sort of a ranch," he continued. "In fact, it was a
real working ranch not too long ago, until it fell upon bad
times—or on good, depending on your point of view. Now it's
sort of an adventure/discovery center for women like yourself.
In the past, the ranch used to round up wild horses and break
them to the saddle and bridle for domestic use. To continue
the ranch analogy, we now take in women who come to us as
comparative unknowns—rather like the horses—all needing
to be broken to the idea of enjoying sex with bondage and
pain. You need to be taught how to enjoy greater fun and
freedom in bondage to others—paradoxical as that may
sound."

Seeing her about to erupt, Sam held up his hand placatingly. "Please hear me out. We want you to learn to enjoy sex
more fully by exploring your penchant for the outré. By
taking away all choice, and by keeping you tied up all the
time, we are taking away all your responsibility for what
happens to you—and hence any residual guilt you may feel
as a result of your pleasure. So, you will be free to enjoy your
sexuality completely. That's the philosophy part of it. More
practically, we do what we do mainly because it's fun—for us
and for you."

At last Janice had her chance to speak. "I'm glad you didn't try to be too philosophical about what is, quite simply, abduction, rape, and torture. Slavery, in fact."

Sam, rising from the desk, came across to stand over her. Now she could see that he was smiling.

"I admit to abduction," he told her. "Sometimes it's necessary. People don't always know what's good for them. But as to rape—have you been raped? Did you see anyone else being raped?"

Janice was silent for a moment. Then she said, "I saw Hilary Anderson being tortured. And I was struck, too."

Sam retorted, "Yes, and you will be again, perhaps many times, before you leave here. But torture? Wait and see. Or ask Hilary if what Jean-Claude did to her was torture. I think the answer will surprise you. Or maybe it wouldn't. After all, you were carefully chosen to come here. And you came. Under a misapprehension, I'll admit, but many of our guests do the same. They discover afterwards that they really don't mind our little trick. And our scout convinced us you were a good candidate for the sort of regime we operate. The report said you'd really enjoy your stay."

"Your scout?" Janice asked.

"The person who looked you over and decided to submit your name to us. Usually the scout is an alumna of our ranch. While she is here we ask her to be on the lookout in her everyday pursuits for suitable candidates. They are in the world, as the saying used to be, while we are somewhat more cloistered. As often as not they spot a friend or acquaintance or, as in your case, a colleague who would benefit from a sojourn with us. So the name comes in."

"A colleague?" Janice interrupted him. "Someone I work with?"

"Well, yes. That's what 'colleague' means. But it could also be someone in a similar line of work, perhaps even working for another newspaper—someone who knows you, at any rate, in your professional capacity."

"Who gave you my name?" Janice demanded.

"I'm not at liberty to disclose that. If he—or she—decides later to reveal his—or her—identity, then that's another matter. Some do, some don't.'

"It could be a rival," Janice suggested. "Someone wanting to do me a bad turn."

"Possibly," Sam replied. "That's something we have to guard against. It wouldn't do to take in an unwilling guest. Not everyone would appreciate what we do here, as I'm sure you would agree. But before going any further, let me ask you to ask yourself whether you have enjoyed your stay so far."

Sam paused to allow her to consider her answer. Janice felt she should say she wanted to be set free, but the matter was more complicated than that. The silence stretched out.

Sam resumed. "I won't go so far as to say your silence amounts to assent—though some might. Rather, I would suggest that you haven't made up your mind yet. And that's a good sign. It shows you have an open mind and a sense of adventure. That shows we weren't far wrong about you. But as I was saying, we do have to be careful, so we don't rely solely on the scouting report. No one is infallible, so we sent someone we trust to look deeper into the matter and make a final recommendation."

"Who? I didn't notice anyone snooping into my affairs."

"I'll take that as a compliment to our operative. But we don't reveal our operatives either. In your case there were other indications of your suitability. We have seen the Polaroid photos of you and . . ." Sam paused to consult the folder on his desk, "and William."

Janice flushed with embarrassment and anger. She opened her mouth to protest but could not at first find the words.

Sam hurried on. "You were going to say that we had no right to invade your privacy. But we had to know as much about you as possible before we involved you further. A stealthy means to a happy end?" he suggested, Jesuitically. "But," he continued, "let me add that you were a very attractive girl—who has grown into an even more attractive woman."

"And that flattery is supposed to disarm me? How . . . how did you get those photos?"

"We have our ways," Sam replied, smiling mysteriously. "We copied some of the best." He handed Janice several thirty-five-millimeter prints from the folder on the desk.

Janice stared at the images of herself, naked and bound in the Maine woods. She was the center of focus, but all around her youthful body the greens of the trees and the vivid hues of the wild flowers seemed more vivid than she remembered. She was suddenly transported back in time, remembering those days of exuberant experimentation with a sharp pang of nostalgia. Where, she wondered, had the wild joy and youthful innocence of those days gone? Nothing since then had given her such wild pleasure and release. Somehow, she had strayed from the path she might have taken, into the weary byway of work and career and social obligations. Wordsworth's lines came to her from her student days:

> But all is fled. Nothing shall bring back the hour
> Of splendor in the grass, and glory in the flower.

The phrase was exact, summing up for her the splendor and the glory of her early sexual experience in a way the poet might never have imagined. Where had all that gone? Where was William now? Could one ever recapture even a small measure of the joys of those days—when we and the world were both younger?

"Brings it all back, doesn't it?" Sam asked gently. "Do you still see the boy who took the photos?"

Janice shook her head silently. "I wish . . ." she began, and then she fell silent again.

"Wish you were still seeing him?" Sam asked. And then answered his own question. "Yes, I suppose you do. We all have regrets of that sort. The road not taken, and all that. And we wonder why we did what we did. If you want to track him down, I can suggest several people who might help. But it's always risky, trying to go back. Remember Jay Gatsby and the green light at the end of the dock. But think it over. Let me know what you decide before you leave."

Janice had been lost in nostalgia. Sam's last words brought her back, and she nodded. Was he offering her a second chance to recapture her youth—here at the ranch, if not with William?

He resumed the tone of the social director. "Our reports, and these photos, suggest you are very highly sexed. I—we— believe you will enjoy the chance to develop your penchant for B&D. We will do our best to assist you."

Janice caught the last words, and the independent female part of her was provoked—all the more because she had been half assenting to what he said. "Assist me? Toward what? You sound just like the headmaster at my boarding school, with all that about helping me progress. You don't know what I want to do."

"And you do?" Sam asked. "Don't answer that," he went on. "But you have hit on an important point. In a way I *am* a headmaster, and this is a sort of finishing school. Or maybe I should say, a re-finishing school."

Janice asked ironically, "And I'm the new entrant? In just what way do you consider me in need of finishing—or re-finishing?"

"In your approach to sex," Sam replied at once. "You're entirely too prickly about it now. Not accepting it—like a lot of women."

"My sex life is my own business, and I'm quite satisfied with things as they are, thank you very much." Janice's anger showed clearly.

"Are you?" Sam asked. "It was just yesterday, in the shower, that you said something like you had never come so strongly before—or words to that effect."

Janice's anger became dismay. "How do you know that?"

"I can replay the video for you if you'd like to refresh your memory."

Janice flushed hotly, shaken by the idea of all that caught on tape. "You . . . you have a video of *that?*" What would she do if it ever became public knowledge?

"Relax," Sam told her. "We never blackmail our guests. You will receive the tapes when you leave. You can view them at your leisure—a sort of revision, if you like. Or simply destroy them. But I don't think you'll do that. Almost all our returning guests say they keep the tapes and enjoy them. Sort of like you kept these photos."

"Where else do you have cameras?" she asked him.

"Practically everywhere," Sam replied. "We never know when or where our guests will suddenly be inspired to an impromptu performance. But ignore them, and enjoy a good fuck when it comes your way. The best actors always behave as if the camera weren't there."

Janice was on the point of objecting to the cameras and the idea of being filmed in her most abandoned moments, but once more she felt the steel bands on her wrists and ankles, and she knew that her objections wouldn't carry any weight with these men. Instead, she thought back to the time with George. She had to admit that her responses—no, my climaxes, she told herself—had been much stronger than any she could remember in the recent past.

It was no good comparing her present performance to her time with William. Memories fade, and the memory itself edits the past. The important connection between her (remembered) orgasms with William and her latest at the ranch was the element of bondage. Being tied up augmented her pleasure. She had to admit that. Lesson one. She would try not to forget it again. But finding someone to cater to her newly rediscovered fantasies might not be so easy. There were definite dangers in encouraging just anyone to tie her up. The world was full of strange people. Janice could see now at least one reason why the guests came back for more safe fantasy.

"George will take you to lunch now," Sam said. "You'll have a chance to meet one or two of the others there, and you can decide what you're going to cook tomorrow, when it will be your turn to show us what you can do in the kitchen."

"You mean I'm supposed to cook tomorrow?" Janice asked incredulously.

"Of course," Sam replied. "All our guests take turns in the kitchen. No one gets a free ride here. There are certain chores to do, varying with the day. How well you perform yours will determine in part what rewards and punishments you receive, although 'punishment' may not be the exact word. Not everyone has the same ideas about punishment. We'll have to discover what yours are, so as to provide the right stick for the occasion—as well as the juiciest carrot whenever that's called for. We need to find out how you react to the whip, for instance. That's the most common form of punishment. I see from your videos that you don't react well to deprivation or frustration. That's another avenue we can explore. But all in good time."

Sam stood up. The interview was over. Janice felt as if she hadn't been able to say anything of what was on her mind, unusual for one who considered herself more than usually articulate. These last few days, she reflected, had been queerly passive ones for her—everything being done to her, nothing by her.

George opened the door and led Janice down the hall, she taking short, careful paces to avoid tripping on her leg irons, and George matching her hesitant stride.

The dining room turned out to be somewhat like a large family room in an ordinary house. There was one long table in the center of the room. The ceiling was high, with exposed beams. Large windows on two walls overlooked the front lawn and the backyard, with the stables just visible. The service was buffet-style. About what one should expect out West, Janice thought.

Hilary was cooking. She wore a French maid's uniform that matched Janice's own, save that she wore opaque black hose (as Janice noticed when she stooped over to take plates from the dishwasher). She also wore leg irons.

There was no one else in the room at the moment. Hilary smiled when she saw them. She beckoned them to come in as she said, "The early crowd has already come and gone. You'll have to take what's left, but at least you'll have plenty of time to enjoy it."

George selected his food quickly and carried it to the table. Janice took longer, curious to ask Hilary how she had borne up under yesterday's ordeal. "How are you?" she asked, offering the other woman an opening to discuss more than the banalities the question usually elicited. What Janice really wanted to know was how it felt to be beaten and then thoroughly fucked. She could see fading red lines on the upper slopes of Hilary's breasts, but the rest of her body was covered by the tights and the uniform.

Hilary said, "All right," adding at once, "but I felt better yesterday after Jean-Claude came back to finish me. That was great. I usually go off like a bomb after a good whipping. You'll see what I mean in a few days."

Janice was not so sure. Watching while Jean-Claude lashed Hilary was all right as a spectator sport. It might not be such fun if she were the main participant. Nevertheless, she had a strong feeling she would make the first-hand discovery soon, and her feelings would not weigh too heavily in the process. The thought gave her a queer empty feeling in her stomach, accompanied by flutters of excitement elsewhere.

Hilary, meanwhile, had no inhibitions about describing her feelings, from whose enthusiastic insider's account Janice found out more than was really comfortable.

"At first it hurts like hell," she admitted, "especially if Jean-Claude decides to use the riding crop. But later it fades into a background glow. And when he fondles my breasts and cunt, I forget about the pain. Even when he begins lashing me again, I know that sooner or later he'll stop and begin to arouse me. When he touches me after the beating, I can't stop coming. If he touches my clitoris I go wild. Of course it hurts badly when he lashes my cunt. You heard me screaming yesterday. But even then, I know there's more pleasure to come when he stops and enters me.

"I've been doing this for so long I can't distinguish between the pain and the pleasure any longer. Each one acts as a trigger. When I am being whipped, I know the fondling will come later. And when he's arousing me, I always know that the next whipping isn't far away. Either way I'm in a state of exquisite suspense. It's all terribly decadent and terribly delicious."

"Are you always tied up when you do this?" Janice asked.

"Always," Hilary replied. "It wouldn't be a proper fantasy if I could simply run away. I need to know that I can't escape what is being done to me. Of course I struggle to get free, even though I know I can't. It's all part of the game, and it's very exciting. I sometimes imagine that I am a helpless slave girl who is being tortured before being forced to undergo the most unimaginable orgasm. I know that the alternation of pain and pleasure will wring from me the ultimate surrender. And it does. I love it. Trust me; you will too."

"Weren't you embarrassed by the audience?" Janice asked.

"No. Knowing someone's watching at first is a turn-on for me. And when I begin to come, I forget about everything else. You'll see."

"I suppose I will," Janice said, selecting her food to hide her agitation.

"Yesterday," Hilary said, changing the subject, "Jean-Claude was being mischievous when he left me hanging on the edge to attend to you. And I saw that he left you hanging, too, in the end. But it all finally worked out well for me. Did things go well for you too?"

Janice nodded, reddening.

"Hey, George," Hilary called across the room, "she says you're a great fuck." Seeing that Janice had finished loading her tray, she led the way across to the table.

There George nodded his thanks to Janice. "A compliment I'll always treasure." To Hilary he continued, "Did you know that she's a screamer—just like you?"

"I am not!" Janice said hotly.

"Would you like to hear the soundtrack?" he asked.

She subsided. She was digesting the thought that she had not screamed like that since her days with William—if her memory served her correctly. When Hilary launched into a description of her first meeting with Jean-Claude, she was grateful to the other woman for drawing attention to herself.

"Jean-Claude and I go back a few years," she was saying. "He was the one who brought me into the resort back when there was no place like this. I had seen an ad for an adventure holiday and signed up because it sounded different from anything else I had tried. The brochures I got said nothing about what sort of adventure I would have. Maybe that was why I chose the holiday—the mystery involved. I was promised something extraordinary, and that's certainly what I got.

"I was in my office at the end of the day, finishing up so I could leave the next day from home. The cleaners were doing the other offices, waiting for me to finish so they could do mine. There was a knock on the door. It was Jean-Claude. I had never met him before, but I thought he looked devilishly handsome. I felt my heart rate go up as he stood in the doorway.

" 'Mlle. 'Ilary Anderson?' he asked. When I nodded, he continued, 'Bon. I 'ave come to escort you on your 'oliday.'

"He never gave his name. I never thought to ask, even though the idea of someone escorting me on a holiday was completely unexpected.

" 'May I come in?' he asked.

"I stood aside for him to enter. As he closed the door, I

noticed that the cleaners were nowhere around. Strange, I thought. But when he locked the door, I felt the first stab of alarm. The world is full of dangerous people, and I thought he might be one of them. But he smiled at me and I felt a melting somewhere in the middle of me."

"She means between her legs," George interjected.

"Well, yes, about there," Hilary conceded. "Anyway, he announced that he was going to tie my hands and that I was to keep absolutely quiet. He produced a short length of rope from his pocket and told me to place my hands behind my back. And I did. The element of surprise was complete. He tied my hands then, quite tightly. I protested that the ropes were cutting me. He said I would soon forget about that. And he was right."

Janice shivered in sympathy as she recollected waking in the woods to find herself similarly bound.

Hilary continued, "The next thing he did was even more surprising and alarming, but the spell he had cast was already working on me. Jean-Claude raised my skirt and removed my hose and panties, and I let him do it without making even a token protest. Things were developing a certain momentum of their own. If this was going to be a rape fantasy, I told myself, then it was just as well the rapist was so handsome.

"He bent me over my desk without a word. My skirt was somewhere around my waist, and my bare bottom was sticking up in the air. 'Hold still,' he told me. And I did. I watched in a kind of dull amazement as he picked up a thick measuring stick from my desk and moved around behind me, out of my sight. But I didn't have to see him to know what was coming next.

"The first stroke was an upward cut to the bottom slopes of my bottom. The force of it lifted my ass-cheeks. I screamed in pain and surprise—nothing like those screams you heard yesterday, but nevertheless loud enough.

" 'Be silent,' he told me.

"I bit back the scream when the next stroke came. The stick made a flat smacking sound as it met my bare flesh. I could feel the blood rushing to the injured areas, but I kept quiet as he struck me again and again, all up the backs of my thighs, all over my bottom, across the small of my back. And all the while, I could feel the most amazing excitement building up inside. I could smell myself, and I knew I was wet between the legs.

"I imagine he could smell me, too. Suddenly he laid the stick on the desk where I could see it—a reminder that he could use it again at any time he chose. But instead, he touched my clitoris. I squealed and came immediately. And he kept it up. I suppose I was moaning and making other loud and unmistakable noises, because he told me once more to be quiet. He said he would gag me if necessary.

"By then, I was beside myself. Jean-Claude never let me stop coming. I didn't have to beg him to go on. It was only later in our relationship that he began to consciously make me wait, as he did yesterday. But then his hands were all over me and I was out of control. Just when I thought there couldn't be anything more, he entered me from behind and fucked me doggie-fashion right there across my own desk. You've heard the old joke about the secretary not being permanent until she's been screwed on the desk. Jean-Claude made me permanent that day. Even when they promoted me to be manager of the women's wear department I kept the same desk, and every so often I have the loveliest image of myself bent over it while he drives me wild. That, too, causes a meltdown of the central core."

George started to interrupt, but Janice beat him to it. "She means between her legs." They all laughed.

Hilary continued, "Every time I have that feeling, I know it's time to get back to my home on the range. So I call the emergency number they gave me, and I tell them this is an emergency. They say all right, be ready to go within the next week. Then I pack hurriedly because I know Jean-Claude could arrive at any time and sweep me away. I want to be always ready for the sweepers."

"Don't let her fool you," George said. "She's so hot she keeps a bag permanently packed."

"What a wonderful idea," Hilary said. "I'll start doing that from now on. But I was describing one of my better climaxes when you interrupted. Jean-Claude was inside me, and his hands were spreading my cunt lips and massaging my clitoris. I remember at the end, when I could feel him about to come, I broke my temporary vow of silence and shouted for him to come with me. He clamped a hand over my mouth to stifle my screams as the lightning bolt struck both of us. I was whimpering and bucking against him as he drove me over the top and then followed me.

"Ages later, it seemed, he withdrew from me. And ages after *that* I stood up, leaning against the desk while the room steadied down and regained its familiar dimensions. The odor of our rut was in the air, and I remember thinking that the cleaners were sure to smell it. Even as I had the thought, someone knocked at the door. It was the cleaners, wondering whether I was ready for them to do my office, just after I had been so thoroughly done in my office.

"I called out to them to wait a minute while I made frantic untie-me-now signals to Jean Claude. It took only that knock on the door to transform me from abandoned woman back into the embarrassed nine-to-five person everyone there knew. I had a vivid picture of one of our regular cleaners walking in to discover the assistant manager of the department with her hands tied behind her back and her underwear in an untidy heap on the floor. Even without all that, the unmistakable smell would give the game away by itself.

"Jean-Claude took his time, enjoying my discomfiture. Jerking his head toward the door, he asked if the cleaners thought me a nun. Would they not understand that the boss needed to have a bit of fun like everyone else? He can be maddening at times—as you saw yesterday. 'Untie me,' I hissed frantically, turning to present my bound wrists to him. To my horror, he picked up the measuring stick and swung it experimentally. The cleaners were sure to hear the sound of it smacking into my flesh, even if I managed to stifle all other sounds. I shook my head wildly at him, mouthing No! while indicating with my body language the cleaners just outside. Jean-Claude looked straight at me and raised the stick.

" 'Please!' " I whispered frantically. "Don't beat me here—now. Do it later if you must. I beg you.'" The fear of discovery was upon me.

"He smiled lazily, still hefting the stick. 'You are begging me to beat you later?'

" 'Yes! Any time, but not now!'"

"He nodded and laid the stick aside. 'Tomorrow, then. Or the day after. And not with that. I think you will enjoy the taste of a real whip. It will drive you mad. Remember to beg me again tomorrow. Or ze day after.'

"Then he untied my hands. I rubbed my wrists where the ropes had left angry red marks. Jean-Claude remarked that I would have to wear long sleeves and bracelets in public. 'And pick up your underwear. I hate an untidy woman,' he said.

"I got dressed again, still smelling of fucking. He wouldn't let me wash. He said the smell would remind me of how much I had enjoyed it.

" 'What will it remind others of?' I asked him.

" 'It will remind zem zat you are an 'ot numbair.'

"We left the office. I collected my car in the parking lot and drove with him back to my house. I felt like a schoolgirl, giddy and excited by the thought of traveling with this handsome man who had just done me so thoroughly—and gave every indication that he would do it again soon. With a real whipping thrown in."

George said to Janice, "You have probably guessed that she loves to be beaten—can't come any other way."

"Not quite true," Hilary said, "but that's the essence of it. But don't try to frighten Janice beforehand."

Hilary continued her story. "As I drove, I was conscious of his eyes upon me. In the confined space of the car, the reek of our fuck was overpowering. I was glad I didn't have to use public transport smelling like that. Every male in smelling range would have been on alert. Jean-Claude said I smelled just wonderful. He made me raise my skirt to my bottom so that all my legs—and my crotch—were exposed. He rested his hand on my thigh, right at the top, and began to toy with my clitoris through my hose, pressing the sheer material against it and rubbing me. I drove in a wild state of arousal and embarrassment. What, I thought, if a truck drew up alongside us at a traffic light? And, of course, one did. From his high cab, the driver could see everything: my legs, Jean-Claude's hand, and my frantic attempts to control myself. He grinned widely and blew his air horn, making pumping gestures with his arm. I went red as a beet, but Jean-Claude just smiled back and acknowledged his salute with a casual wave.

"When we finally got home, I wanted to rush straight to the bedroom, grab the suitcase, and go straight to the ranch. You might say he had whetted my appetite for more whipping and fucking. As they say out West, I was rarin' to go. He slowed me down at once—the first sign, did I but know it, of his now infamous technique of making me wait just when I want to charge ahead.

"He told me that there was no hurry. He had made travel reservations for the following day, and we would travel on then to an unknown destination (unknown to me, that is). How was he going to keep our destination secret from me, I wanted to know. I pointed out that I would only have to look around on arrival to know where we were—or simply listen to the loudspeaker announcements. He only smiled and told me to leave things to him.

"Jean-Claude made me take a shower while he prepared dinner for us. I washed off the smell of rut with a certain regret, but I suspected it would be renewed shortly. The red rope marks on my wrists had faded somewhat but were still visible—and unmistakable. As he had said, I would have to wear long sleeves in public.

"We ate dinner by candlelight, with heavenly champagne he had brought for the occasion. All very romantic. We made small talk, became acquainted, in an atmosphere of eroticism so thick I thought I would suffocate in the ambience. We watched TV, all very cozy on the sofa. He kissed me softly, and his hands were everywhere on my soon-naked body. But he stopped short of making me come—just as he did yesterday. I was panting and heaving and begging him to go on. He told me to be patient. All I could think of was how we would spend that night. He settled that soon before bedtime. He would sleep on the couch, he said, as a gentleman should. I would sleep chastely in my own bed, to which he would tie me before retiring. 'And sometime during ze night,' he told me, 'when you least expect it, I will visit you—solely to assure myself zat you are all right.'

"At bedtime he led me to the bedroom and made me lie on my back on the bed while he tied my wrists and ankles to the bedposts. He kissed me good night and left me burning with desire, as they say in the romantic novels. Needless to say, I didn't sleep well that night. I dozed and woke and pulled at the ropes and dozed again.

"And sometime in that endless night, as he had promised me, he 'visited' me. He didn't spend the entire time assuring himself I was all right. With his hands and his mouth he made me frantic, and this time, when I begged him to finish me, he did. He climbed on top of me, and the feel of him sliding into me was indescribable—like dying and going to heaven. We fucked for what seemed like ages, and I came for most of that time, moaning and heaving and pulling at the ropes. At one point, he told me I would have permanent rope marks if I didn't learn to relax—while he made it impossible for me to do anything of the sort. He made it impossible for me to do anything except come, and come again, and then again. I thought I would die of pleasure—not a bad way to go, I must say—when I felt him stiffen against me. I felt a scalding flood inside me as he came, and I think I set new highs for screaming incoherence.

"When we were finished, he proved to be a real gentleman. I begged him to stay with me, and he did. It was nice having him in bed with me. Not so cold and lonely, but rather frustrating since I couldn't touch him. But he made up for that too. He put his hand on my pubic mound, and I drifted off to sleep as he massaged me gently.

"In the morning, he untied me and announced he had 'to make some preparations zat I think will excite you' before we traveled to the ranch. He shooed me into the shower again, and when I came back this time, he had laid out what looked like a small electrician's shop on my bureau. He asked me if I had a pantie corselet. I showed him the three I had in my wardrobe. He chose the red one. 'Think of ze red as a fire against your skin, warming your body as we travel toward ecstasy,' he said. He accompanied this purple prose with a self-deprecating grin. Next, he told me to find a pair of opaque black hose—to conceal the rope marks on my ankles. And they would also conceal certain other things that would have been difficult to explain if they had been visible. Finally, he asked me to choose a pair of high-heeled shoes. He was insistent that they have metal heeltaps. He said he liked the distinctive tap-tap of high heels. I believed him.

"At first I wondered why he wanted me to wear the corselet and hose. It was a bit like locking the barn door after the horses have vanished. Or putting on a chastity belt after the fact. But I let him have his way."

Janice nodded knowingly. She, too had let them all have their way since her arrival. There's definitely a streak of submission in us both. And in Lois as well, she thought silently.

"Instead of having me get into the stuff right away, Jean-Claude had me lie face down on my bed. Then he proceeded to wire me up. He used thin bare wire that came on a small reel. He attached wires to the middle toe on each of my feet, wrapping it around and taping it. Those wires were then led under my feet, taped under the arch and at the heel and ankle to hold things steady. He led the wire up the backs of my legs like the seams of stockings, taping it below my knees and around my thighs. I had no idea what he was doing at the time, but I didn't ask any questions.

"Things got a bit more interesting when he used some rather large dildoes to plug me fore and aft. I squirmed a bit, liking the full feeling they gave me. Jean-Claude paid no attention. He connected the dildoes to the wires and had me turn over on my back. He led the wires up my belly and taped one to each nipple. The ends he led up to my neck and let lay. Then he put the tights on me, and I saw at once why he had chosen as he had. The opaque hose concealed the wires running up the backs of my legs. And the tight crotch of the pantie corselet held my plugs in place.

"It was extremely sensuous having a handsome man dress me. I liked it at once. When he eased my breasts into the cups of the corselet, I hoped he would pay more attention to them. But he was all business. Pleasure later, he promised me. Lots of it. 'Be patient,' he said again.

"Jean-Claude had me sit on the side of the bed while he put my shoes on. The movement reminded me quite forcefully of the two plugs. They felt quite pleasant as they shifted inside me. As he buckled the ankle straps of my shoes, I tightened my muscles around the dildoes. I felt myself growing warm all over again. Glowing, my great-grandmother would have called my state. He finished with the shoes and had me stand up, which brought more pleasant shiftings and slidings from the dildoes.

"Then he produced a thick leather dog collar with an enigmatic electronic device attached to it. He buckled it around my neck and locked it in place. I had no idea of his intentions, but I went along with whatever he wanted. He connected the ends of the wires to the collar and stepped back to admire his handiwork. Nothing was visible except the collar. Jean-Claude told me to select my shortest and tightest skirt—'because I am at 'art a leg man, and yours are truly *magnifique*'—and a top with a roll-neck collar, to conceal the other collar I wore.

"When I had done so, feeling quite the tart in my tight skirt, he told me that I was now completely within his power. I looked blank. What did he mean?

"I found out when he put his hand in his pocket. The dildoes began to vibrate inside me with an almost inaudible buzzing. 'Oh,' I said, or something equally inane. I reached instinctively for my crotch, and felt the invading plug vibrating under my hand. I pushed gently against it, and it touched my clitoris. I said, 'oh!' again, this time more sharply. I kept my hand in place while I experienced the strangest arousal I had ever undergone. The electronic age had arrived for me.

"Jean-Claude watched as I became more excited. When I came, he smiled and said, 'You are an 'ot numbair indeed. Ze reports wair right.' I was too busy with internal matters to register the 'reports.' Standing there in my bedroom, fully clothed and with my hand pressed to my crotch, I had a series of orgasms that left me weak and sweaty.

"At last he switched me off and I sat weakly on the bed. I could smell myself again, and I guessed there would not be another chance to wash the odor away before we traveled. Jean-Claude did indeed have me within his power, if he could make me do all that simply by pressing a button.

"But as I sat there thinking of the implications of my situation—not all of them unpleasant—Jean-Claude did something else with the thing in his pocket, and I felt a flash of white fire run through my body, from my toes to my tits and neck, a sudden agony that caused all my muscles to knot up. My nipples were being stabbed by jolts of electricity, and the two dildoes were stabbing me as well. I would have jumped in surprise but I couldn't move. I would have screamed, too, if I had not gasped out all my breath. He switched me off after only a moment—which nevertheless seemed like an age.

" 'Now you 'ave seen ze carrot and ze stick, and you will do anything I tell you,' he said in a menacing tone. His smile took the menace out of his words."

The Naked and the Nude

Jean-Claude entered the room from the outside door. Hilary did not see him, so when he leaned over to kiss the top of her head, she was startled. But she recovered quickly. "Speak of the devil," she said.

" 'As she been telling you lies about me in my absence?" he asked.

Janice answered, "Not really. She has been telling us how you dragged her, kicking and screaming, to this vile place, and how much she wants to escape from your clutches."

"Well, no 'arm has been done zen. 'Ilary is always complaining. You should not pay too much attention to 'er." To Hilary he went on, " 'Op over zair and get me something to eat. I am starving."

"Say please," she told him.

By way of reply Jean-Claude reached into his pocket and laid a small box with several buttons on the table. Hilary looked at it quickly with a mixture of anxiety and interest.

"Well, since you put it that way . . ." she said, getting up from the table.

Janice was suddenly aware that Hilary was dressed in the same sort of costume she had described to them earlier: short, tight skirt; high lace collar; opaque black hose. A leather collar was visible through the lace around her neck. Hilary was wired up again. No wonder she moved with such alacrity to do Jean-Claude's bidding. The box lying so innocently on the table was obviously the control box for the collar she wore.

Jean-Claude put the control box back into his pocket as Hilary returned with a laden tray for him. She sat down again but didn't say anything more about her first trip to the resort. Janice was disappointed. Hilary's story had been interesting, and her excitement was infectious. Janice wondered what it felt like to be wired up as the other woman was, at the mercy of someone else who didn't even have to touch her to make her obey him. She shivered with the same mixture of excitement and apprehension Hilary had exhibited.

George and Jean-Claude discussed football while the latter ate his lunch. Janice was bored rigid, and so, apparently, was Hilary, for she winked across the table and indicated they should take a stroll outside and let the men get on with it. They went out together, each walking carefully to avoid tripping on their leg irons. Janice, hampered additionally by the handcuffs, was especially careful. The two women paced slowly across the lawn. Through the windows they could see the two men eating and talking.

Janice asked Hilary if she was afraid of what the collar could do to her.

"Not really," she replied. "Of course there is a certain amount of suspense, and the shock is not very pleasant by itself, but when I think of the whole plan, the mixture of apprehension and anticipation, pain and pleasure, the suspense, the feeling of being subject to Jean-Claude's whims— well, I like it a lot. And that's not counting the nice feeling I get from the plugs as they shift about inside."

"But what about the shock?" Janice wanted to know. "Isn't that dangerous?"

"Not really," Hilary said. "It's all low-voltage stuff, battery powered. Jean-Claude told me there is an additional fuse in the collar that will go before any dangerous current can flow. They are used on dogs for obedience training, and it doesn't hurt them—otherwise the S.P.C.A. would be down on them like a ton of bricks. So it's even safer for humans. And it sure teaches you obedience. It makes you sit up and take notice in a way words never can."

"Yes, I saw," Janice said drily. "But tell me, how did Jean-Claude manage to get you here without you knowing where you were being taken? Traveling blindfolded would get you noticed on any airplane. Not to mention your, er, electrical gear."

"Yes, of course it would. But Jean-Claude had thought about that. It turned out that he is a pilot as well as a great fuck. We drove to the local airport, but not to the commercial entrance. He had me park the car in the long-term parking lot, and we took a bus to the light aviation section, where the small private planes are kept. He had flown in to get me, and he flew me out as his captive passenger. It was dark when we got to the airport, and we got out of the bus to walk to his plane. As soon as the bus had driven away, he blindfolded me and led me to his plane. So I never even saw the type of plane he used, let alone its registration number. He strapped me in and warned me not to touch my blindfold, reminding me of the consequences with another short, sharp shock. And that's how we traveled."

"And you were brought here?" Janice asked.

"Yes, but 'here' was nothing like what it is now. There was only a cabin in the lower foothills. It's still there, but now only as an alternate place to stay. They call it the line shack, though that's somewhat of a misnomer. It's not a shack."

Janice remembered George saying that Lois was going there when she set off in her pony-girl role.

Hilary was saying, "We landed near here and drove up to the shack—where we shacked up as a cozy threesome. There was Jean-Claude and me and the whip. We fucked our way through a lovely timeless fortnight. It was a real wrench when I had to leave. But I come back whenever I have the time and the inclination—not as often as I'd like, but maybe that keeps it from becoming a dull routine.

"We . . . Oh!" Hilary said suddenly. Her body stiffened and her muscles knotted briefly. When the spasm passed, she was left gasping and shaking. Her face was pale.

Janice looked questioningly at her. "Are you all right?"

"Yes," Hilary finally managed to say, "but I hear my master's voice. I have to get back. Excuse me, please. See you later." She made her way back to the dining room as quickly as her leg irons allowed her to travel.

Janice watched her go, trying to summon up pity for her abject servitude. But the emotion was stifled by a rising sense of being left out. She was as attractive as Hilary, wasn't she? She tried vainly to pass her dismissal off as a tribute to her prickly independence. The steel bands on her wrists and ankles reminded her that she was just as subject to the whims of others. She turned back toward the dining room herself.

When she got there, it was empty. That made her feel even more left out. Hilary had been summoned to an afternoon session of pain and delight, probably with both men, and she was left to devise her own entertainment. She poked about the room in a desultory fashion, noting the equipment and the supplies of food in anticipation of her stint as tomorrow's cook-designate. But she had no real interest in the place and none at all in cooking. Her habit when working was to eat in the nearest restaurant or have a sandwich at her desk when she was really busy. Janice did not consider herself the domestic sort. She was, she believed, too independent to change. She supposed she would be coerced into it, but she would prefer to face that when it happened, while hoping it wouldn't.

What, she wondered, does a single gal in handcuffs and leg irons do with nothing to do and the whole afternoon to do it in? Nothing suggested itself to her. Idly, she wandered out to the lawn again and around the side of the main house toward the stable block, her high heels sinking into the turf and making walking difficult. She supposed walking shoes would be more sensible, but much less sexy—at least in the eyes of the men who ran the place. Their opinions were the only ones that counted.

Janice walked to the smaller rear door they had used yesterday afternoon. The door was not locked, and she passed through into the big building. Her footsteps on the wooden floor echoed under the high roof, the only sound in the whole place. She glanced at the raised dais on which Hilary had been strung up. The rope hung down from the pulley in the roof, and the rod on which she had been impaled lay on the floor where Jean-Claude had left it. Men, she thought. Untidy. Leaving it to women to clear up after them. Well, I won't do it.

She turned to the meditation station, as George had jokingly called it. The dildo that had gone into her own anus was still there, jutting from the floor. The rope that had bound her ankles was still looped over it. She touched the unyielding steel rod with her foot, recalling with a shiver how it had felt when she had been impaled there. Janice shuddered as she recalled her struggles to escape—and her arousal by Jean-Claude and George, who were now doubtless doing the same to Hilary. Damn them! she thought, turning away.

Along the walls were shelves and cupboards that, Janice discovered when she inspected them, held a collection of whips and straps. Coils of light braided rope, handcuffs, leg irons, steel and leather collars, gags and blindfolds, and dildoes. Enough for a small army of women. She knew they would not be used on anyone else. On a shelf, thrown aside carelessly, Janice saw a pair of leather helmets with gags—those she and Lois had worn while being brought here. She remembered the darkness, the silence, the feel of the penis gag filling her mouth. Not a fearful memory. It's as well I never led a really sheltered life, she thought.

Janice turned away and saw a row of hooks set into the adjacent wall. She went over to investigate. From their height, it was obvious that they were intended for stringing up people—women. For whipping, she guessed, that being the favorite method of instilling obedience in these parts. They were set at various heights. She stood under one and stretched her manacled hands up toward it. It was just out of reach.

Later, Janice worked out the reason for her next act. At that moment, she wasn't thinking too clearly. Then, she only had a vision of herself hanging there, helpless, while she waited for someone to come for her with a whip. She imagined the hiss and crack of leather on her body, the white-hot stripes, the pain, her heaving struggles and cries of mingled pain and ecstasy. And the whip finding her secret places—the slash of leather between her legs, on her exposed cunt. Would she scream as wildly and come as unstoppably as Hilary had done?

Facing the wall, she bent her knees slightly and jumped, just managing to hook the chain between her handcuffs over the hook. She came down with a jerk that wrenched her arms, hanging by the chain with the steel bands biting into her wrists. With a gasp of pain, Janice stood on tiptoe to relieve the strain on her wrists. That was better. She twisted and jerked, trying unsuccessfully to free herself. Her calf and thigh muscles were taut as she supported herself in that awkward position.

It was no use. She would have to jump again to get the chain off the hook. Gritting her teeth against the bite of the handcuffs, Janice bent her knees and jumped. No luck. She tried again and was left hanging as before. After several fruitless attempts, she realized she could not get enough height as she hung suspended. She had trapped herself neatly.

Her first reaction was chagrin, but further thought revealed her true predicament. She was trapped, and no one knew where she was. It was then that she gave way to something close to panic. "Help!" she screamed, as loudly as she could, her voice echoing in the big building. It didn't matter what anyone thought about her precipitate action. She had to get free. She screamed again, and again no one came. She had visions of herself hanging there all night, and this time she did panic, screaming and jerking against the chain.

Janice had no idea, later, of how long the panic had lasted. It seemed to go on forever, a nightmare from which she couldn't wake, drowning her reason and making her a helpless, screaming wreck. After an age, she heard footsteps approaching. Twisting her head over her shoulder, Janice saw Jean-Claude through the fringe of damp hair hanging in her eyes. Relief surged through her. "Thank god!" she said. "I thought no one would ever come. Please get me down."

Jean-Claude looked at her with amusement. "What 'ave you done to yourself?" he asked, shaking his head.

Janice was not in the mood for discussion. "Just get me down!" she pleaded.

Again he shook his head. "Women 'oo 'ave lurid sex fantasies should be prepared to pay ze price. Besides, you look very appealing 'anging zair. Does your body cry out for ze whip? Wair you thinking of zat when you got yourself into zis?"

It was as if he had read her mind, but she wouldn't admit her riotous thoughts to him. She shook her head, denying his words. Her heart pounded from her exertions, and her breasts heaved as she tried to catch her breath, straining against the tight material of the maid's uniform.

Jean-Claude noticed. He stood behind her and cupped her breasts. Janice was helpless in his hands, and she was embarrassed to have been caught in her present predicament. At first, that was all she could think about, but gradually she relaxed. And as she relaxed, she felt the first stirrings of excitement. This was something like she had imagined when she first saw the hooks. She began to forget the bite of the handcuffs on her wrists and the discomfort of her straining legs as Jean-Claude's hands stroked her breasts.

"Mmmmmmm." She moaned softly as she felt her nipples becoming erect. When he teased them, she moaned again. With her arms over her head, she was stretched tautly and her breasts were thrust out, freely accessible to him as he stood behind her. Janice began to wish she were naked so that her whole body were available to him. Her cunt burned at the thought.

"Your pretty nipples are getting 'ard, ma cherie. Does it feel good when I pinch zem—like zis?"

"Oh!" Janice said. His voice in her ear and his hands on her breasts were terribly exciting.

"You like zat, I see. Zat's good."

Jean-Claude raised the tight skirt until it was bunched around her waist. Her bottom was stretched tight by her position, and she shuddered when she felt his hands caressing it through the sheer nylon of her hose. As she arched her back to press herself against his hands, Janice remembered that her hose were crotchless, her cunt exposed and vulnerable. He had only to reach between her thighs and . . ."Oh! Oh yesss!" She spread her legs as far as her leg irons and her strained position allowed so that he could reach all of her.

Jean-Claude took time to appreciate her body, stooping to stroke her legs from ankles to straining ass-cheeks, his hands moving over the sheer nylon of her hose, over her taut calves, up the insides and around the fronts of her thighs, stroking, caressing, his hands sliding over the smooth material. And finding "Oh!" her cunt again. His fingers on her there, parting her labia and sliding into her cunt and ohgod her asshole too. Janice moaned when he touched her clitoris briefly, wanting him to go on, to drive her crazy, not merely to touch and move on. "Ohgod, Jean-Claude. Ohgod, don't stop!"

"Slowly, ma cherie. We 'ave all ze time we need. No one will distairb us, and I will be ze only one to distairb you. Like zis." His fingers slid into her again, pinching her clitoris while another finger slid all the way into her asshole, slowly, slowly, while she clenched her pelvic muscles and anal sphincter in her excitement. "Would you like me to whip you now?" he asked

Janice couldn't decide, couldn't answer. She wanted both his hands on her and the whip on her body. She wanted him inside her. She wanted everything, all at the same time.

Jean-Claude interpreted her silence correctly, "Nevair mind. We will introduce you to ze whip later, when you are naked. It is more effective when you are completely exposed. So relax and think of zat as you come."

As if his words were a charm, Janice felt her belly tighten against his hand, and she came in short, sharp spasms, moaning with the pleasure of her release . . . and wanting more. Later, she thought about her behavior, wondering at her responses. It was as if she were seeing a stranger for the first time when she recalled how the episode had begun. But just then was not the time for coherent thought. It was a time for untrammeled feeling. The unexamined life could very well be worth living.

Janice turned her head to look over her shoulder during a pause in her arousal. Jean-Claude had taken his clothes off and was standing to one side looking at her. Admiring her, she hoped, wanting her. He was erect, if that was any indication. He broke the tableau, coming behind her. Janice lost sight of him, but that didn't matter. Now touch became again the most important sense. He spread her ass-cheeks and she felt his erect penis prodding her anus. She had never had a man inside her there. But she guessed that she soon would. Another loss of virginity, she thought as she waited helplessly for him to penetrate her.

But there was one more thing he had to do. Quickly, he pushed a finger into her cunt, giving her clitoris a short pinch that drew a gasp from her. He rubbed her juices onto his cock and guided himself slowly into her anus. Janice instinctively closed down, but he was patient, sliding in a bit further each time she relaxed a trifle. When he was all the way in, she felt very full, as if she needed to go to the toilet.

That sensation faded when he reached around to tease her clitoris with his fingers. She wondered briefly why she had waited so long to try this kind of sex as his fingers on her sensitive flesh made her shudder with pleasure. When he pushed his finger into her cunt, pinching her clitoris between his thumb and forefinger as he did so, she cried out as the waves of her orgasm swept over her. She was shaking and coming and crying out, and at the same time, she was acutely aware of his stiff cock inside her asshole.

The dildo she had been made to sit upon on her arrival had felt strange and exciting, but it had been dead, merely cold steel. Now, she had a real living cock up her ass, and the sense of fullness she had enjoyed so much with the dildo was augmented by the warmth and the small shiftings of Jean-Claude's body as he aroused her with his hands. The delicious sliding as he thrust in and out in the tight sheath of her anus was maddening. She shuddered in another orgasm as she hung in her chains. And he kept on.

It was too much for her to take in all at once. Janice thought she was going to faint as a roaring darkness gathered behind her eyes and the room became dim. Her cries sounded distant in her ears, as if it were all happening to someone else. The sensations from her cunt and anus were overwhelming. "Oh god! Ohhhhhhhh! Ohhhh!" Then he came, and so did she. And then she did black out for a moment with the intensity of it all.

When she became aware of her surroundings again, he was still inside her, his arms around her waist as he held her up. When he felt her stir, he slowly withdrew and stood back. Janice looked over her shoulder again at him. He was a handsome devil, she thought. I'm glad it was him who took me like this. George looked too much like the boy next door, she thought. He didn't really fit her newly formed image of an asshole bandit. But he had certainly done very well as a shower bandit, she thought, trying to be fair to them both.

But now . . . what next? She was still hanging from her wrists, stretched tightly, the juices of their mingled come running down the shiny nylon of her hose and making a dark stain on the sheer material. Oh god, she thought, I must look like a slut—but a very satisfied one. And she felt an obscure pride through it all, as if she had passed a test. And in a way she had. Where before she had been thinking that this was a mere episode she could (and should) put behind her, she now admitted to herself that she had needed this adventure to release something trapped inside her. And it wasn't over yet, she realized with a shiver of excitement.

But, first things first. Her arms were straining and her calf and thigh muscles felt cramped from being held in that unnatural position. "Don't think I'm ungrateful, but could you please get me down from here."

Jean-Claude smiled slowly. "But why? You look very sexy as you are."

"Please!" she said. "I'm beginning to feel uncomfortable."

Jean-Claude smiled again and stepped forward to lift her from her hook.

Janice sighed with relief as her arms relaxed. While being fucked, she had forgotten all about the discomfort and strain of her position. Sex was a wonderful thing, she concluded— not an entirely original thought, but a satisfying one.

"Come with me." Jean-Claude broke into her thoughts. He turned and led her back to the door she had entered earlier.

Janice followed slowly, the chain that joined her leg-irons clinking as she moved. She stopped abruptly as she realized her skirt was still up around her waist. She tried awkwardly to rearrange it, tugging the tight dress down until it was more or less in place. It still revealed a lot of leg, Janice noted again. A lot of very nice leg, she thought, if she credited George's and Jean-Claude's remarks. It was not something she would wear in her workplace, but it didn't seem terribly out of place here. Her handcuffs and leg irons would not be suitable for work either, but like the maid's short, tight uniform, they fit in with the ambience of the ranch. Janice had never been terribly fashion conscious, and she dressed to suit her own image of herself as an independent and casual person. Being forced to wear this sort of revealing dress gave her an obscure thrill at which, she knew, her more radical feminist friends would be aghast. That felt obscurely good too.

As her legs brushed together with the characteristic sibilant hiss of nylon on nylon, she felt the damp stain running down the insides of her thighs. I was strung up to a hook and had by a handsome devil of a man who took no notice of what I might want, she thought. He stuffed his cock up my ass and made me come and come. And now his juices and mine are running down my legs, and I am following him in chains. And I love it, she thought with a little shiver of remembered pleasure.

Jean-Claude led her to the main house, retracing the same journey she had made with George the day before. I should be angry about being traded around among these men, Janice's independent part insisted. Her newly acquired submissive part told her to shut up and enjoy. He led her down the same hallway, but to a different room. It was furnished much like George's: a bed, of course. A sofa and coffee table, two armchairs. Ensuite bath, for cleaning up afterwards.

"Sit down," he invited her.

Janice chose the sofa. But before she sat, she indicated the damp patches on her hose. "Will that be a problem?" she asked Jean-Claude. "I mean, the couch could end up smelling of you and me."

"What a nice idea," he replied gallantly.

Unable to use her hands, Janice positioned herself carefully and half-fell, half-sat. Getting up again would be harder. Seeing Jean-Claude moving toward the bar, she asked for a

Bloody Mary. She searched the room for signs of Hilary—the new woman looking for evidence of her predecessor. She saw none and wondered if he had tactfully removed the bits and pieces. "Where is Hilary?" she asked, curious to know how she was being handled.

"With George, of course," he replied as he handed her the drink. "Do you mind?"

Janice saw that Jean-Claude was watching her closely, so she was careful to keep her voice and expression neutral. She did not want to sound shrill or jealous. Undignified, she thought. And she wasn't jealous, she realized, as she replied "no" to his question. George had been great fun. But so had this man. And now she was with him. He had chosen her. In the very recent past, she knew she would have been offended at the ease with she had been passed from one man to the next. You're learning, she told herself silently.

Jean-Claude sat on the couch next to her, not obtrusively but definitely there. He appeared quite relaxed. And well he might, Janice thought. He holds all the advantages. She was acutely aware of her chains and her short, tight dress. And the sticky patches on her hose.

"Where are my clothes?" she asked abruptly. "I would like to have something else to wear." One had to make some sort of statement, she told herself.

Jean-Claude replied, "All your clothes are 'ere. We are not thieves. Zey will be retairned to you when you leave. Until zen, you will wear whatever we give you whenever you are not required to be naked."

"And all I will get is something like this?" she asked, indicating her brief costume.

"While you are being . . . reeducated, shall we say, you will wear something provocative—something zat reveals your body and does not impede access to it whenever ze urge strikes one of us. It's a well-known method of teaching people like yourself submission and ze freedom zat comes wiz it."

"Well known to whom?" Janice asked.

"Why, to policemen and abductors, of course. And to psychologists, of 'oom I 'appen to be one. Most kidnap victims are kept naked and in chains. Being naked and 'elpless makes it easier to break ze will to resist and escape."

"So I should be grateful I'm not kept nude all the time?" Janice asked acidly.

Jean-Claude appeared not to notice her mood. "You are still not aware of your position. You will not be nude. If I choose to take off my clothes, I will be nude. You will be naked—even when you are clothed. I can choose to disrobe. You 'ave no choice. It's a subtle distinction. But a very real one."

That made her uncomfortable. Janice changed the subject. "How did you happen to contact Hilary?" she asked.

"Like you, she contacted us—after she 'ad been supplied with ze proper literature about what was zen my idea of an adventure 'oliday. I knew what I wanted in a woman, and so I set out to find a woman 'oo wanted ze same thing. 'Ilary was ze first, one 'oo responded to ze offer. It was important zat ze woman respond to ze offer wizout demanding all ze details. Women 'oo demand to know everything are generally not amenable to our regime. For instance, you did not ask too many questions, did you? And 'ere you are."

"And all this," Janice's gesture included the room, the house, the ranch, "came from just the two of you?"

"We wair ze founder members, but ozairs joined us before too long. Our third member was ze girl from ze print shop 'oo did the brochures I sent to 'Ilary and ozairs. She filled one in for 'erself. And she, too, found ze regime amenable. Like Lois, she returns for a refresher course whenever she can. We 'ope you will too."

"Why?" Janice wanted to know.

"For one thing, we like to find anozair kindred spirit. For anozair, we all seek variety. Finally, you are an attractive woman."

The compliment pleased Janice. We can never hear the word "attractive" applied to ourselves too often, she thought. But she couldn't resist applying another needle. "So only 'attractive' women are selected? Who decides which ones are attractive?"

"You are full of questions today," Jean-Claude said. "Are you sure you're not talking just to avoid ze whip?'

Janice felt a thrill of fear at the word. Yes, she admitted to herself, she was trying to avoid the whip, and at the same time she was looking forward to the experience. Ambivalence was getting to be a habit. But she couldn't admit this to him. She remained silent.

"We all do ze selecting," he replied, finally answering Janice's question about "attractive" women. "All ze men, zat is. Our social director is really a sort of secretary 'oo keeps us in order. 'E calls a meeting before a new female guest is contacted. 'E shows us ze scouting reports, and we discuss whezair ze proposed woman would fit in 'ere, or whether she would be a danger. And, yes, one of ze things we discuss is 'er attractiveness—to all of us. Zair's nothing strange in zat. It is merely another form of ze decision making we all engage in when we meet a stranger of ze opposite sex: we are first attracted, or not, by the physical appearance of ze person. Zat is ze only thing we can know about them until we form a closer relationship. After zat we begin to think of person-alities and shared interests, but zat all comes later. But never mind all zat. You are 'ere."

Janice, still postponing her introduction to the whip, changed the subject once again. "Why did the print shop girl come here?" she asked.

"Now zair is a real cautionary tale," Jean-Claude replied. "She came 'ere in order to 'ave safe sex of ze type she craved. Out in ze big, bad, real world zair are all sorts of strange people who would do serious 'arm to someone like Bridget. In fact, she actually ran into one of zem and was lucky to escape with 'er life. She 'ad been seeking someone to tie 'er up during sex, but no one she met seemed to 'ave ze abiding interest she 'ad. One or two of 'er lovers tried it out at 'er insistence, but zey soon lost interest after the novelty wore off."

"Zen she met a man 'oo 'ad too much interest in ze subject. When she found 'im, she thought all 'er dreams 'ad come true. She dropped several 'ints after she 'ad seen 'im several times. So when 'e brought up ze matter of bondage on 'is own, she agreed, as she later said, wiz a pounding 'eart and bated breath. And it was tremendously satisfying at first.

"Things went well at ze beginning, but zen 'e became violent and abusive. On ze last occasion, he raped her—insofar as ze word applies to 'er situation. Then he tied and gagged 'er and beat 'er wiz a strap. 'E left 'er bound and gagged in 'er kitchen. Zen 'e left. Bridget was in pain and couldn't get free. Luckily, a friend found 'er in time. After zat, she was much more careful.

"Bridget realized she was in danger from randomly selected lovers, but she still needed 'er own special type of stimulation. So, what to do? Zen, by great good fortune, I arrived on 'er doorstep wiz my prospectus. She took one look and decided to give us a chance. We looked, she said later, more responsible zan ze average man in ze street. And we are. She 'as been a regular evair since."

Janice said, "You are telling me that I, too, am lucky to have fallen into your hands?"

"Yes, I suppose so," Jean Claude replied. "You could 'ave found someone like Bridget's lovair. But, yes, you are right. You wair lucky. We will take good care of you. Beginning now." He smiled as he reached for her.

Janice sat quite still, acutely aware of her chains and the way the maid's uniform revealed her figure. The skirt, never very modest, had ridden up her thighs so that her legs were bare almost to her crotch. She felt both very vulnerable and quite excited as he took her in his arms. She didn't resist when he kissed her full on the mouth, opening her lips to his probing tongue with a thrill of anticipation. And it's only been an hour or so, she thought, since the last time he had me. Her recovery time was getting shorter. She had discovered a new reservoir of pleasure in herself.

She raised her linked arms and put her hands behind his neck, pulling him against her. She kissed him back and felt his hands on her breasts, cupping them through the tight material of her dress. He wanted her again. Now. She was flattered to be able to provoke such a response in such a man. And she was terribly excited on her own account.

Without knowing quite how it happened, Janice found herself standing, being led over to the bed that had waited so invitingly during their talk. It all comes to bed, she thought as she lay down on it. Jean-Claude was looking down at her with an expression that made her go all warm and wet between the legs. It only takes a look, she thought . . . and the sight of his erection bulging his trousers.

Quickly he got undressed—got nude, as he had described it—while she lay fully clothed in the revealing dress, feeling quite naked. She wondered how he was going to get at her—

and she wanted desperately to be got at—without undressing her. He would at least have to remove her handcuffs and leg irons to make her literally naked—a state she suddenly, almost desperately, wanted to achieve. So she was surprised at his next move. He raised her hands above her head, and there was a metallic snap as he fastened them to the headboard of the bed by a chain to her handcuffs. Janice strained to see what he had done to her, but her hands were out of sight above her head.

Only when she was secured did Jean-Claude remove her leg-irons. It didn't require much imagination to guess why. But he surprised her again when he merely unbuttoned the top of her dress and removed her brassiere to expose her breasts in the lacy opening. They felt terribly naked. And she felt terribly aroused as she imagined how she must look to him: her hands chained above her head, her dress open, the skirt rucked up to her thighs. The sort of lurid picture that adorns the covers of so many "true crime" magazines, promising sex and violence—and so often not delivering it. No false promises here, she thought.

Indeed, he seemed to relish the spectacle, for he stood back momentarily to admire her. Janice lay still while he gazed at her, her heart pounding and her breath coming in short gasps. When Jean-Claude pulled her skirt up to her waist, she was fully exposed, the air cool on her moist cunt through the open crotch of her hose. Janice made no effort to hide herself or to close her legs. Jean-Claude looked hungrily at her. I think he really likes me, she told herself, flushing with pleasure beneath his steady gaze.

He sat on the bed beside her. Janice's naked breasts rose and fell rapidly with her agitated breathing. She felt them grow warm and heavy as they became suffused with her racing blood, the veins standing proud of the flesh and her nipples becoming taut and crinkly merely from the anticipation of being touched. When Jean-Claude actually touched them, she gasped aloud, a startled "Oh!"

He cupped her breasts in his hands, as if weighing them. His fingers toyed with her nipples, and Janice knew she was lost, out of control as she grew wet between her legs and her stomach muscles tightened in the prelude to orgasm. "Oh god, oh god, ohgodohgodohgod, ohhhhhohhhh ohhhohhhh."

Jean-Claude shifted on the bed, kneeling between her legs. He grasped her breasts again from his new position. That was better, Janice thought. Much better. He bent to kiss her taut stomach, his lips warm against her flesh through the sheer nylon of her hose. His lips trailed up to her waist, down to her pubic mound. She raised her hips and thrust herself against his face. Jean-Claude's tongue probed her labia, opening her up as his hands continued to massage her breasts and tease her nipples.

He thrust his tongue inside her, the tip hard against her clitoris, and Janice went wild. She spread her legs widely, inviting him to explore her depths. He responded by nipping her labia with his teeth as he used his tongue on her clitoris. If her hands had been free, she would have held his face against her as she came. As it was, she moaned and writhed, attempting to thrust her sex into his face. And she came, a shattering spasm that rippled through her belly and spread to her stomach and legs.

Once again Jean-Claude shifted, raising her legs over his shoulders, spreading her wide and bending down until he could again reach her cunt. He resumed work on her with his lips and tongue and teeth, but he also inserted a finger into her and began to probe her depths while his knuckle bumped her swollen clitoris. Janice opened her eyes briefly and saw her legs spread down his back, the sheer nylon dark against his skin, and she shuddered when she saw her vulnerability. Her helplessness and her need overwhelmed her once again, and she surrendered herself to him as he aroused her.

Jean-Claude withdrew his finger from her cunt. It was wet with her own lubrication. He held it under her nose: "Smell yourself," he told her, and Janice inhaled the scent of her own arousal. Then he slowly pushed the wet finger into her anus. She gasped and bucked at the unfamiliar invasion, but she could do nothing to prevent him. She said, "No. Don't," softly, but he paid no attention. And when the finger was fully inside her she relaxed and began to respond to the unusual penetration. Why did I bother to protest, she asked herself. It was an empty form.

He moved his finger in and out while his tongue and lips explored her clitoris, and his teeth bit her labia.

Janice slid into a series of long, exquisite orgasms, moaning as Jean-Claude explored her. She lost count of how often she came, and just when she was on the verge of asking him to stop before she passed out from pleasure and exhaustion, he shifted for a final time and bent her legs up until the fronts of her thighs were pressed against her breasts and her cunt and asshole were fully open to him. Then he penetrated her with his cock. Janice gasped as she was filled with him, the shock of the renewed assault on her taking her breath away.

She forgot her exhaustion as she felt him moving inside her, thrusting in and out of her sopping cunt, and pressing her thighs against her breast with his weight.

"Oh!" she gasped. "Ohgod! Unh! Unh! Unh!" A series of explosive grunts as she felt herself slipping over the edge once more, incredibly. Janice almost blacked out from the pleasure of it, and when she felt him spurt inside her, she couldn't stop herself from coming yet again—not that she tried very hard.

Afterwards they lay joined for a long time. The afternoon silence was complete in the shadowed bedroom. Janice thought of how she would look to an observer: breasts exposed, her skirt up around her waist and her legs spread over the shoulders of the man who lay between them. It was the kind of pose one saw in sex manuals or in magazines from the top shelf at the book store. A fantasy. And I achieved it, she thought proudly.

Jean-Claude finally raised himself, withdrawing from her and moving her legs off his shoulders. He laid them on the bed, caressing her thighs through the sheer nylon of her hose. "Rest now if you wish, my dear," he told her. Jean-Claude didn't seem at all tired by his efforts, but she was worn out.

Gratefully Janice closed her eyes and dozed, oblivious to her handcuffs and to the cool air on her heated, ravaged body.

Horseplay

8

Janice's day in the kitchen had not been enjoyable. Never one to love cooking and cleaning, she had nevertheless done her best. She had been forced to wear again the short, tight maid's uniform with black hose and high-heeled shoes, and she had attracted admiring glances from the men who had passed through the dining room. She had been put into leg irons again for the day to emphasize her status as slave. But no one had so much as pinched her bottom. Were they under orders to leave her alone so she could meditate on the effects of sexual deprivation after so much indulgence? Meditate she certainly did, in any case, concluding that the day was largely wasted without some sexual arousal and fulfillment. Prior to her arrival at the ranch, she had never given this much thought to her sexual needs. There had been a decided change in her outlook in the short time she had been here.

In the evening, she had been taken to a cell in the stable block, handcuffed, and locked in for the night, still wearing her uniform and leg irons. She had books to read if she wished. There was a video and television for her to watch. It was not the cold, comfortless place it could have been. But still, she was restless. Unfulfilled, she would have said. Randy, another part of her replied. She couldn't help but draw comparisons to the previous nights she had spent in the bed of George or Jean-Claude.

169

Sometime during the early evening she heard the noise of someone else being placed in a cell nearby. Janice was curious, but her cell door had only a peep-hole, closed from the outside. She tried calling out to her new neighbor, but there was no response. Either the cells were soundproofed, or the neighbor was gagged. The latter was more likely, she concluded, remembering how she had arrived. At some point, the light was switched off and she was left in darkness. No light entered her windowless cell. She might as well have been in a cave. She slept uneasily in her clothes, waking often in the dark room and wondering how long she would be left there. What would happen to her when they came for her?

And come they eventually did. The sound of a key in the lock woke her. Janice felt her heart beating harder with the familiar mixture of excitement and apprehension. Bright daylight flooded her cell, blinding her after the long hours of total darkness. The jailer's footsteps moved along the corridor, and there was the sound of another door being unlocked. Janice allowed her eyes to adjust before she ventured out of her cell. In the corridor, she saw Mark. He had just emerged from the cell adjacent to hers, leading a petite woman in a tight leather hood similar to the one she had worn. That explained the silence of the evening before. The woman's features were completely concealed beneath the hood, and her wrists were handcuffed behind her back. Like Janice, she wore leg irons.

The woman in the hood made an urgent though unintelligible noise, and a moment later Janice saw a dark stain spreading over her hose. Water ran down her legs as she pissed herself. Janice imagined that she had been trying to say something like "take me to the toilet," but had been taken short. As I was not too long ago, Janice thought, remembering George leading her to the toilet on her first day. By a species of sym-

pathetic magic well known to almost everyone, the sight of the
other woman soiling herself reminded Janice that she was not
very far from doing the same thing. She made a beeline for the
toilet before the dam burst.

When she emerged, Mark gestured for her to follow him.
He led the newly arrived guest through into the main stable
area and left her. Without a guide, she was forced to stand
where she was left. Her shoes and hose were awash, and Janice
smelled the stale odor of urine in the room.

Mark came to her and unlocked the handcuffs she had worn
for more than a day. Janice rubbed the red marks on her wrists
as he unlocked her leg irons. "Where have you been?" she asked
him. I haven't seen you since the day in the woods."

"I'm glad to know you've been missing me. We'll make up
for lost time today. You're with me for a day or so. If you'll take
off all your clothes, we can get started."

"That's the most subtle pass I've ever had," Janice told him
acidulously. "Are you always this indirect with your women?"

Mark grinned but did not rise to the taunt.

Janice tried another tack. "Who is she?" she asked, nodding toward the other woman.

"Her name's Bridget. She came last night. You'll meet her
later, when we get back from our own frolic."

"Oh," said Janice, recognizing the name. "And she will be
standing around in her own piss until then?"

"No. Someone will be along shortly to collect her. Don't
worry. She'll be taken care of."

Janice reached behind her back and, in that double-jointed
way women have developed, managed to unzip her dress. She
wriggled out of it, removed the slip and bra and hose. When
she stood nude—no, naked, she corrected herself—before him,
it occurred to her that she might need a shower before she

launched into any more sexual calisthenics. "Mind if I use the bathroom before we begin?" she asked Mark.

He nodded. "Go ahead, I'll need a few minutes to get things ready anyway."

Janice made her way to the toilet and shower, emerging several times more than a few minutes later. In her absence, Mark had saddled a pair of horses. Obviously the day would include a horseback ride. Janice was no horsewoman, and she anticipated saddle sores and aches before the day was over. My chance to imitate Lady Godiva, she told herself with a tingle of anticipation.

When she mentioned this to Mark, he shook his head. "This is not just a short jaunt through Coventry. If Lady Godiva had ridden any distance, she would have discovered that you aren't meant to ride horses naked for very long." He tethered the horses and went to fetch more equipment, coming back with some clothing that he handed to Janice.

She was surprised and pleased at having something to wear, even if it consisted of jodhpurs and riding boots and a roll-necked top with long sleeves. There was also a pantie girdle and a bra by way of underwear. Among the clothing she felt something hard, and as she sorted through the pile she found two dildoes. Ah, she thought, the clue I've been hoping for. This day, then, would not be as sexless as the last had been. She was pleased.

Janice slid the dildoes into her cunt and anus, clenching her muscles to hold them in place while she stepped into the pantie girdle and pulled it into place. Then she could relax without fear of losing the two plugs. When she turned her attention to the bra, she had a shock. The nipple area of the cups had rows of tiny prickers sewn into them, so that her nipples would come into contact with them whenever they grew erect—which they promptly did as she imagined what it would feel like.

Mark looked on with an amused grin as she put the bra on, once again performing the double-jointed maneuver necessary to hook it behind her back. As she eased her tits into the cups, she winced at the tiny pricks assailing her engorged nipples. These made her more excited, so the pricks became sharper. The effect was heightened whenever she tried to take a deep breath. The dildoes inside her added to her excitement, and Janice knew that her nipples would have to get used to the unusual sensation. They showed no sign of going flat, and she felt the warm glow of her arousal spreading from her breasts, cunt, and anus. And the day hasn't even begun yet, she thought.

Janice tried to ignore the signals coming from her sensitive places as she put on the long-sleeved top and squeezed into the jodhpurs. She was not entirely successful. At the end of the exercise she was breathing deeply and feeling flushed. Socks and the high riding boots came next. She looked like a horse person, even though she was not. She also imagined that she looked like an aroused horse person, though she tried to conceal that detail from Mark.

He led the horses out into the stable yard. Janice followed carefully, highly conscious of her sensitive places. It occurred to her that there were hitherto unrealized things she could wear that would keep her in an almost perpetual state of sexual tension. Something along these lines could be adopted on the job, for instance, and no one but her would be aware of her arousal—unless she allowed herself to get carried away. Even as she had the thought, she felt the tightness in her belly and throat that signaled her arousal. God, she thought, I'm thinking of orgasms and no one has laid a hand on me. Just the short time she had spent on the ranch was working major changes in her sexual outlook. Here everything was related to sex. Only a very cold person could fail to respond to the atmosphere. And Janice was learning that she was not cold.

With an effort, Janice controlled her thoughts and followed Mark. He helped her mount, the movement causing more internal turmoil. When she was in the saddle, she felt the dildoes being pushed deeper into her by her own weight. She gasped as she shifted in the saddle. I had no idea that riding a horse could be a sexual act. I wonder how it feels to come at a gallop, she thought.

Mark's words broke into her reverie. "It looks as if you're learning why so many young women love riding horses," he said with a knowing grin.

"Surely they don't all use dildoes," Janice retorted. She strove to keep her voice calm and level.

"No," Mark agreed, "but they all feel the movement of the great animal between their legs, and that's what drives them crazy—those who aren't sexually dead, that is."

Janice silently disbelieved him. Not all women who rode horses, she thought, felt this excitement. But she guessed it could be arousing to some, even without her own added advantages.

But Mark was not yet finished. He brought two sets of well-filled saddlebags from the stable. "Lunch and other things," he said succinctly, as he fastened them behind the saddles of both horses. "The real old-time cowboys carried everything they needed on the trail in their saddlebags. Of course, we have some needs they never had," he finished with another grin.

Janice sat quietly during these preparations, busy with

internal matters. She made no demur when Mark reached up to tie her hands behind her back. At least she wouldn't have to direct the horse, she thought with relief. She could do nothing but follow wherever Mark led. "What if I fall off?" she asked him, suddenly struck by the thought that it was rather a long way to the ground from where she sat.

"All taken care of," Mark assured her. He tied her feet into the stirrups and passed more rope around her legs on either side of the saddle, just above her knees. These ropes he secured to rings in the saddle skirts, fastening Janice securely in place. "The horsey version of seat belts," he said with a smile as he pulled the last knot tight.

Janice pulled against her bonds and found that she was indeed immobilized. She would not fall off, whatever else might happen. Once again, she felt the exhilarating sense of freedom she now associated with being bound helplessly.

Another thought struck her as she sat atop her horse, waiting to be led away. "What about the other woman in the barn? Are you going to leave her there?" She was thinking of what it must feel like to be abandoned, blindfolded in a strange place. And the other woman must be wanting to get out of her soiled clothes and wash herself.

"George will be along for her in a little while. Don't worry. We always take care of our guests."

"All right," Janice said dubiously. "Where are we going, then?"

"Isn't it a bit late to ask that question?" Mark said. "We're going wherever I want to take you, of course, but our immediate destination is a picnic place I know of. Later, we'll move on. Just relax. Enjoy the ride and leave everything to me." As he finished speaking, he mounted his horse and gathered up the reins of Janice's mount. He turned toward the gates and urged the procession into a sedate walk.

Riding a horse requires a certain skill, which Janice lacked. Consequently, she felt every bump as the animal set its feet down. The bumps naturally brought the two dildoes to her attention as they were pushed into her on the downstroke, as it were. Not at all unpleasant, she discovered. If things went on as they had begun, she might well take up equestrian sports on a more regular basis. It seemed as if riding could be fun if one were suitably equipped. Then she gave up thinking and concentrated on enjoying the ride.

Mark led them in single file out of the stable yard and turned toward the distant hills. The air was clear and cool, and the early sun was warm on her face as she looked at the surrounding countryside. Just the sort of day when it was wonderful to be alive and in the outdoors, Janice thought—even in these bizarre circumstances. Especially in these bizarre circumstances, she thought with a tingle of excitement.

The single-file progress made conversation difficult. Janice didn't fancy talking to Mark's back, but she refused to ask him to bring her abreast of him. Anyway, what does a bound woman say to her captor? Nice day? They jogged along for perhaps half an hour, and when Janice turned partly in the saddle, she saw that the ranch was now a considerable distance behind them. She reminded herself that she was being led into the wilderness by a man she barely knew. And she wasn't afraid.

The silence around them was broken only by the sounds of the horses' hooves and the faint soughing of the wind. In the silence, Janice became more aware of the flutters of excitement in her stomach and the tightness of her breathing. The jogging of the horse caused the dildoes to shift inside her—not an unpleasant thing at all. At the same time, her nipples tingled as they became erect—and in contact with the prickers sewn into her bra. She caught her breath on a gasp as her breasts bobbed inside the bra with the motion of her mount. Soon Janice was paying more attention to inner sensations than to outer scenery.

She squirmed experimentally in the saddle, rubbing her crotch against the hard leather and causing more pleasant sensations as the dildoes were pressed deeper into her cunt and anus. Her face, she knew, was becoming flushed with excitement.

Mark turned at that moment and noticed her demeanor. "Getting to you, is it?" he asked with a smile.

Janice reddened still more, but didn't stop. Didn't want to stop. Nevertheless, the arousal proceeded slowly. There was very little she could do to hasten things. If her hands had been free, she would have been able to press them against her crotch and help the dildoes do their work, or press the bra against her sensitive breasts. They jogged on, Janice becoming more excited as they went. She was panting and red-faced, teetering on the brink of an orgasm the next time Mark looked around. She paid him no mind. All her attention was fixed on making herself come, but try as she might, she could get no further.

At that point, Mark decided to take matters into his own hands. He urged the horses into a canter. The change in motion communicated itself to Janice through her dildoes, bringing her closer to the reward she sought. Just a bit more, she thought frantically, and I'll come. But she couldn't. She would have to have help.

"Mark," she called, gasping. There was no response. "Please, Mark! Help me." Still no response. Her nipples were hard and tight and in firm contact with the tiny prickers in her bra cups. "Oh!" she said, the cry forced from her. "Please help me! I'm about to . . . to come. I want . . . need help." But even as she spoke—perhaps because she had spoken—she felt herself come. "Oh!" she cried in surprise and delight. And "Oh!" again as she felt a huge soundless explosion of pleasure between her legs and in her belly. She squirmed in the saddle, jerking at the ropes that held her.

Mark kicked his horse in the sides, urging the procession into a gallop. And the change of gait proved to be just what Janice needed, keeping her in full cry as the miles flowed by. She thought she would burst with pleasure as they pounded along. The wind of their passage was loud in her ears, and the pounding of her blood matched the gait of the rushing horses. Her excitement rose as the dildoes pounded into her, and her nipples strained stiffly against the prickers in her bra. Suddenly, she reached another peak. She reeled in the saddle and would have fallen off if she hadn't been tied in place. Her hands twisted wildly behind her back as she struggled against her bonds. Mark urged the horses, and incidentally Janice, on and on.

Beneath the high blue of the sky, under the unbelievably white clouds, through the yellow sunlight, Janice's cries of ecstasy broke the great silence of the land. She came again and again as the dildoes were driven into her like nails, and her bobbing breasts inside the ingenious bra felt as if they would burst with pleasure. She screamed again and again to the open sky, driven wild by the plunging horse between her straining thighs and the dildoes inside her.

Her blood was roaring in her ears, almost drowning out the pounding hooves and her own cries. Blackness gathered behind her eyes, the landscape became dim and indistinct. She thought she would faint with pleasure but fought to hold on to consciousness in order to enjoy this ecstatic ride.

Eventually she became aware that they were no longer galloping. The horses were sweating and blowing. So was Janice, pleased at that moment that she, unlike the Victorian ladies, was sweating and not merely glowing. She drooped in the saddle, shaking in the aftermath of her multiple orgasms. She understood much better than before why horse riding was so popular among girls and women. Having that great beast pounding away between one's legs could drive one (this one, at any rate) quite wild.

Mark looked around at her. "All right?" he asked.

Janice was too weak and breathless to reply. She could only nod silently.

Mark stopped and drew Janice's horse alongside his own, looking at her closely. "Most ladies who take this sort of ride end up like you," he said. "I know a girl in Tucson who loves to ride the mechanical bulls in the beer joints. She told me she stuffed herself just as you are now before she climbed aboard. Said it was better than any man she knew. Me, I think she was a lesbian. Or one of those women's libbers. Some kind of subversive, at any rate. Or maybe she just doesn't know the right men."

He spoke with a chuckle, so Janice couldn't tell if he was serious or not. She couldn't see him clearly either. Her hair was damp with her sweat and hanging in her eyes. "Mark, could we stop for a moment? I'm thirsty. And my hair. . . . I can't see." Her voice shook.

He brushed her hair back and dried the sweat from her face and neck with a bandanna. Then, one-handed, he reached under her top and pinched her breast. Janice jerked erect when she felt the prickers against her nipple. She moaned and leaned against his hand.

"You want more?" Mark asked.

"Yes . . . no. Please. Later. I can't come anymore."

"You just think you can't. I'll bet you'd surprise yourself if

I took you over to that stand of trees and untied you. I'll bet you'd even help me get your pants down."

Once again Janice couldn't tell if he was joking. Luckily, she didn't have to reply, for Mark went on.

"But we've got a ways to go yet, and when we get where we're going, we'll have plenty of time for fun." He reached into his saddlebag and came out with a canteen. He made her drink before he took some for himself. "You know, I'll bet that girl in Tucson doesn't know how liberating it is to be tied to a galloping horse. But you could tell her, couldn't you? You'd make a believer out of her.

"You know," he continued as if recalling a favorite memory, "we had one girl here who just about went crazy on a ride like this. She was tied up like you, only we put her in one of those leather hoods like you wore a few days back. So she was gagged and couldn't see. She claimed that made it a whole lot better."

Janice drew breath with a gasp as she imagined herself hooded and gagged on a galloping horse with the dildoes being pounded into her.

Mark said, "You seem taken with the idea. We could arrange that for you if you'd like."

Janice didn't trust herself to speak.

Mark said, "Later. No need to make up your mind now. But if you're feeling better, we'd best be getting on. We might even have another gallop the last few miles. Don't want to be out in wolf country after dark when you're tied up, do you?'

Janice looked at him wild-eyed at the thought of another ride like the recent one. His casual mention of wolves alarmed her. "You wouldn't, would you? Leave me here at night?" she asked in a small voice.

"Well, no, not really. That would be a waste of a good

woman. But I think it's always best if a girl knows what she's getting into—even if she's already into it and can't get out. And if you give a girl a good fright, she'll fall into your bed when you rescue her." He chuckled again.

Shortly after noon, they reached a stand of trees where Mark said they would stop for lunch. "There's a spring here, so you can have a wash. You worked up quite a lather this morning."

"I'm not a horse," Janice retorted.

"All right. A sweat then. But you don't have to bathe unless you want to."

"Well, I *would* like to clean up a bit."

"All right. You can do your impression of Botticelli's Venus in a few minutes."

They passed in under the shade of the trees, and Janice was grateful for the cool shadows after the unrelenting sun of the morning. She was beginning to worry about sunburn, and she wished she had thought to bring along a hat. But maybe a hat would have blown away in the wild gallop.

Mark reined in beside a pool and dismounted. A stream flowed in at the top end and then out again over a short water-fall. It looked inviting. It also reminded Janice of the scene of her abduction. Mark untied her feet and helped her dismount. With her hands tied behind her back, dismounting was a con-trolled fall. Mark caught her as she slid from the saddle.

"Do you want a bath now or after lunch?"

He was holding her in his arms, and up close she was very conscious of his smell—a combination of dust and sweat and the unmistakable odor of man. Janice found herself wishing he would take advantage of her there and then, and then brought herself up short. Either he would or he wouldn't. It was entirely his choice. She shivered with excitement but remained silent. This was supposed to be every woman's worst nightmare—a helpless captive to a stranger in the middle of nowhere—but she was unworried.

"I guess I'd like to take that bath now," she finally said.

Wordlessly, he released her and untied her hands. He pointed to the pool and said, "It might be a good idea to wash out your clothes first. Then they can be drying on the rocks while you get cleaned up yourself."

Janice saw immediately that this would present a further barrier to escape—if she had been still entertaining any such notions. But somewhere along the line she had discarded the idea. Aside from not knowing where to run, she was enjoying her captivity much more than she had ever dreamed she would. She now saw nakedness merely as the prelude to more sexual arousal and—she hoped—fulfillment. And it was fun to be naked in the outdoors. She was able to recapture something of the youthful delight she had felt in the Maine woods with William.

She removed the tight riding boots and peeled the jodhpurs down her legs. Next, came the roll-neck pullover. Standing before Mark in her pantie girdle and bra, she looked questioningly at him. "All of it?" was the unstated question.

He nodded. Janice unhooked the bra and laid it aside. Her breasts bore a circle of red dots around and over the nipples. She inspected herself briefly. No permanent damage, she concluded. But the pins-against-bare-tits idea was a clever invention, she thought—that and the dildoes and the tight pantie girdle that held them inside her. That came off next. "The . . . things too?"

"Up to you," Mark replied. "But if you had any idea of replacing them with anything else—me, for instance—it might be a good idea to take them out. Not that I want to push myself on you," he added.

"But you might want to push yourself *into* me," Janice said, as much a statement as it was a question. "I'm at your mercy in any case, aren't I?" Her gesture took in the deserted wood and the empty lands that surrounded them.

"Well, yes," Mark replied, "but I thought it more polite to ask. You don't have to make up your mind now. Have a bath first."

"How generous," Janice said, pleased nevertheless that he wanted her. She spread her legs and pulled the dildo from her cunt. The one up her backside was more difficult. She needed both hands to spread her ass-cheeks, leaving her with nothing to grasp the plug. She squatted and pushed but still it wouldn't come. She felt constipated. Looking over her shoulder at Mark, she asked, "Would you mind playing the gentleman— even if you're going to force yourself on me later?" She nodded in the general direction of her backside.

"Of course," he said, stooping to extract the dildo with a long steady pull.

It took a definite pull to free it from her anal sphincter, and Janice suddenly knew that she was going to shit herself when it came free—as she had the first time. Lucky I'm squatting, she thought as she felt her bowels move with a great heave. "Sorry," she said to Mark.

"Never mind. With a bit more practice you'll be able to keep control."

"That's what George said a day or so ago," Janice said. "I don't seem any closer to achieving it." She picked up her discarded clothing and walked to the edge of the pool. She knelt to wash the sweaty garments. The touch of the cool flowing water reminded her of how sweaty—and smelly—she herself was, and she hurried to finish the washing so she could get into the pool. The prospect of going skinny-dipping was pleasantly wicked. She was sure Mark was staring at her, and his interest lent a further excitement to the occasion. She laid her wet clothes out on a flat rock. From its warmth, she could tell they would dry quickly. She lowered herself into the water.

The touch of the cool water on her heated skin was like a blessing. She submerged herself to her neck and paddled to a rock where she could sit with the water up to her chin. All quite modest, she thought fleetingly as she allowed herself to relax, closing her eyes to the bright sunlight and luxuriating in the freedom her nakedness conferred on her. The water on her bare breasts and between her legs was like a caress.

She let her mind wander. Thoughts of her other life, the stress and the hurry, seemed completely alien to the new person she had become. What would her colleagues think if they knew she had spent her vacation as the sex slave to a variety of attractive males? Those who would not be horrified would be envious, she guessed. She thought again of William, too. Where was he now? She thought he would like to share this experience with her. Her recent male acquaintances were dim memories to her.

Mark shattered her reverie as he entered the water. Janice opened her eyes. There was a new tension in her now. Moment-of-truth time, she thought, and she braced herself for his advance. But he didn't approach her then. He, too, sat down and relaxed, smiling across the pool at her.

She returned his smile a trifle tentatively, aware that she was his captive to all intents and purposes. The tension she felt now would not be there in other, less bizarre circumstances. Briefly she wondered once again how she had allowed herself to be lured into this situation. Because I needed it, she told herself—even if I didn't know exactly what I needed. She felt wonderfully alive. Her body tingled with her new freedom.

But there was no denying that Mark's presence had changed the character of the pool. Janice knew she was the focus of his attention, and his presence made her alert, ready to detect any change in his attitude or position. Nevertheless, when he finally moved, she was almost taken unaware. Suddenly he was before her, his hands on her thighs under the cool water. She stiffened but made no effort to repulse him. He moved his face to hers and kissed her on the mouth. She returned the kiss, feeling his hands slide to her shoulders and then the sudden fierceness of his embrace as she was crushed against his body.

Breathless, Janice felt the first thrill of arousal flash through her, clouding her judgment and making her gasp with surprised delight. She felt herself drifting from her familiar moorings as she floated naked in the pool with this naked stranger. She parted her legs and Mark settled between them as if he belonged there. But he didn't enter her immediately, as she had expected. Instead he prolonged the kiss, gradually forcing her mouth to open to him. His tongue probed her mouth, and his hand stroked her back from neck to bottom, pausing tantalizingly at the crack that divided her ass-cheeks but going no further.

Then Mark slid his hands under her bottom, and the first phase of her arousal was over. He lifted her so she was sitting in his lap, her legs straddling his waist. He held her there while he explored her bottom, stroking the smooth globes. Janice could feel his cock getting hard, brushing against her belly. This was the first time since her arrival that she had been both naked and unbound. She used both her hands to grasp him.

Mark broke the kiss and looked into her eyes. "That feels good," he said with a smile.

Janice wondered if it was possible for a man to do anything else but smile when a woman held his cock in both hands and stroked it. But she didn't let go.

"Ah," said Mark as she squeezed him.

Janice felt a heady sense of power as she held him. Even in her position she could arouse him. But she knew she wasn't the one in control. The ropes were only a few feet away.

Mark put his hands on the insides of her thighs, squeezing the tender flesh and probing her labia with his thumbs. He spread her and probed her cunt, grazing her clitoris and making her gasp with pleasure.

Janice shuddered and opened herself further. Just touch my clitoris and I spread my legs, she thought. A lot of women she knew would not like the thought, but their opinions had ceased to matter. She was in danger of becoming a slave to the male cock, she knew—just as the women's libbers feared. But Mark was now paying serious attention to her clitoris, and there was no more time for coherent thought. This was the time for pure sensation. She settled herself more comfortably and continued to stroke his cock, feeling him stiffen in her hands and wanting that hardness inside her with a fierceness that took her breath away. She needed no more foreplay.

No maidenly reserve was left to her. It had been stripped away like her clothes and her liberty during the last few days. She hunched herself and guided Mark into her, wrapping her arms around his shoulders to crush her breasts against his chest. She gave a small moan of surrender and delight as she felt him slide into her and fill her up.

Mark didn't move at first. He continued to cradle her bottom, supporting her and holding her against him. Janice had expected him to be more active.

And then she felt a strange sensation as he did something

with his cock. It felt as if he were clenching it as one might tighten a muscle. She felt his cock stir inside her even though he remained motionless. "Oh!" she said in surprise. Then, "Ohhh!" again, this time in pleasure. He repeated the movement, and Janice thought she would faint. Being fucked by a movable cock was completely outside her experience. When he shifted slightly to bring the base of his cock against her clitoris, she gasped in delight and clenched herself around him as her first orgasm took her. Making love in water for the first time in her life, she was amazed at the sensations she could feel when even partially freed from the tyranny of gravity. Fleetingly, she wondered if mixed crews of astronauts had tried this in zero gravity. And if that was why most governments seemed reluctant to send mixed crews into space.

Mark's hands and arms, supporting her and holding her against him, made her feel almost weightless. She found she could rub herself against him and rock her hips to bring her nipples and clitoris into contact with him almost effortlessly. Floating in the cool water with the sun warm on her back and arms, Janice imagined she could go on like this forever. She laid her head on his shoulder and closed her eyes, concentrating on the small movements that were somehow more pleasurable than the wildest gyrations performed in a bed.

Her next orgasm burst upon her like an ocean wave, lifting her high on a crest and holding her there as if she were riding a surfboard on one of the legendary waves of Hawaii. She wondered who was making those moaning sounds, and then the wave broke, sliding away from her, dropping her into the trough, and she realized it was her. It was she, Janice Singleton, who was making wild abandoned love to a stranger in a mountain pool, beneath those limitless blue skies, and coming so hard she felt as if she had left her body behind.

Then, abruptly, she was back together, herself again, and still impaled on Mark's rigid cock. They were clasped together, and now he was rocking his hips, sliding in and out of her. She became desperate at the thought that he would slide too far out and she would lose him—that she would be left empty and quivering on the brink. She pulled herself closer, wrapping her legs around his waist and crossing her ankles behind his back. With her arms around his neck, she pulled her breasts against his chest so that the sensitive nipples rubbed his wiry hair. She began to match his rhythm, her hips pounding and her breath becoming harsh in her ears. The blood pounded in her temples, and she saw the world through a reddish haze as she pumped frantically against him, trying to take all of him inside her.

Mark drove himself into her again and again, almost splitting her with his thrusts, rubbing her clitoris with his rigid cock and grinding his pubic bone against hers as their bodies met. The contrasting sensations, warm sun and cooling water, violent movement and soft support, drove her wild yet again. She threw back her head, the cords taut in her throat as she screamed her ecstasy to the skies. Her body jerked madly, and she thought she would never stop coming. Then, Mark came. She felt the sudden clenching spasm in his cock, and she was flooded with the warmth of his climax. And she came with him, driven by the urgency of his response.

They lay in the water afterwards, both reluctant to break the coupling. I was thinking of escaping? From this? Janice marveled at her first responses to Mark and Harry. She hadn't known sex could be so liberating until she became a prisoner. She had never let herself go so completely. There had always been some measure of restraint, shyness, the was-it-good-for-you ritual, the fear of not pleasing her partner, the disappointment when he had failed to please her. She remembered the times she had faked an orgasm. Not here. Here there was no holding back. These men had forced her to respond. And she had.

At length Mark pulled out of her. "You'll get sunburned if you stay here any longer—and then sex will be really painful."

Janice hated to break their contact as well, but she knew he was right.

He helped her from the pool and they dried themselves off. While he went to set out their lunch, Janice felt her clothing. It was almost dry. Soon it would be time to move on. Time to put the dildoes back inside her, mount the horse, and continue the journey. She wondered if she would have any strength at all left when they arrived at their destination.

Mark called her to come and eat. Janice moved into the shade of the trees and found he had laid out a picnic lunch for them on blankets. She realized she was starving after the sexual marathon and sat down at once to eat a naked lunch. Mark had thoughtfully included a bottle of wine. It lent a festive air to their interlude, loosening tongues and reserves—if there were any left after the morning's activities.

Janice felt bold enough to ask Mark where he had been since helping Harry abduct her.

"On a scouting mission," he told her. "After we got your car back to the rental agency, I looked over another prospective guest."

"And did you approve of her?"

"I'm not sure," he replied. "She has some rather unusual tastes. They may not fit in with our regime."

Janice wondered what she might be into, if her tastes would not fit the unusual—to say no more—regime of the resort. "Is she into snakes or horses?" she asked.

"No. We could manage that if pushed. She likes extreme humiliation."

"And that's not what you've been giving us?"

"Not that extreme. She likes her lovers to tie her up and piss on her. Or shit, when she's feeling really randy. A good time for her is to be covered in excrement and left bound for long periods of time. Alternatively, she likes to be tied up and given an enema. She is then left to provide her own shit, and to marinate in it."

"What, she doesn't like to swallow excrement as well?" Janice asked. She was not exactly shocked, not after her own recent experiences. She fancied her outlook had been broadened considerably these last few days. But this was something she didn't fancy. Or at least not yet, she thought, trying to keep an open mind and reminding herself that she had no say in what was done to her. It was a relief that Mark, too, had his reservations. She might yet escape the ordeal he was describing.

"She may," Mark said. "It's likely she does. Coprophilia is a strange practice. I wasn't able to observe the full gamut of her sexual practices this time."

"So you'll be going back for another look?" Janice asked, fascinated despite herself.

"Maybe. Or maybe someone else will be sent. This kind of thing needs as much input as possible."

"So you object to her preferences?"

"Well, maybe 'object' is too strong a word. We aren't in a good position to condemn other people's idea of fun. I would say rather that I don't see any fun in it—leaving aside the olfactory nuances. Remember, we are doing this for fun. And that isn't my idea of fun. We like to help people achieve a better sex life in our own humble, perverted way," he said with a smile. "Maybe someone else will disagree and invite her along. Horses manufacture a lot of shit, so there shouldn't be any problem keeping her happy. But I doubt if anyone will vote to extend the invitation. We'd be contravening any number of health and sanitation laws, for one thing. And there are the other guests to consider."

"You mean you consider our likes and dislikes?" Janice asked. "You could have fooled me."

"We're not complete chauvinists, you know. We want you to visit us again, so we put our best foot forward while you're here, and we ask you for suggestions to improve the service when you leave—just like the best resorts. Sometimes we even listen to you."

"Name one idea you've adopted from one of us," Janice challenged him.

Mark thought for a moment, then looked sheepishly at her. "His and hers towels?" he offered.

"I see," she said. "I thought it might be that way."

Mark smiled and said, "Well, we think you'll share our aversion to the woman I've been talking about. Will that do?"

"I suppose it will have to," Janice said drily. "Even you guys have to have *some* standards of taste and decency."

"I'm glad to see you appreciate our efforts to set a good example. More wine?" he offered, effectively closing the subject.

Janice held out her plastic cup, and he poured. They finished the bottle in a leisurely fashion. Janice gathered the debris of their lunch while Mark dug a hole in which to bury it. He left the food scraps by the pool. "Even coyotes deserve one easy meal," he said.

Mark shook the blankets and spread them again on the ground. "*La hora de siesta,*" he said, lying down and indicating that she should do the same.

The food and wine had made Janice sleepy too. She was glad Mark also felt inclined to doze. She lay beside him willingly. He drew her close and pulled another blanket over them. She gave a contented sigh, snuggled against him, and they both slept.

When they woke, the shadows were growing long. "Time to saddle up and move out," Mark said.

He gathered his clothes and began to dress. Janice retrieved her own clothing from the flat rock. Everything was now quite dry. She inserted the dildoes, pulled on the pantie girdle, and settled her breasts into the tight leather bra with the prickers. By the time she was dressed, Mark was also ready. He helped her mount, then tied her hands behind her back and her feet and legs to the saddle. Then he mounted his own horse and led her toward their destination. She hoped he did not find it necessary to gallop again.

The Line Shack

To Janice it seemed they were retracing their route to the ranch, but she didn't say anything. She was content to let Mark take her wherever he wanted. In any case, she didn't know the land, and she was tired from the long day. The sun had gone down, and the first stars were coming out when she noticed lights in the distance. They drew steadily closer, finally resolving themselves into a small cabin and a smaller outhouse or stable. The lights came from the cabin windows.

As they came into the yard, the cabin door opened and a voice called, "Mark?" He answered, "Yes," and drew the horses up before the porch. A man came out to meet them. When he came close, Janice saw that it was Harry, whom she had last seen heading for the "line shack," as George had called it, with Lois pulling manfully (womanfully?) at the light cart to which he had harnessed her. This, she reasoned, not unreasonably, was the line shack. Lois was not in sight, but the cart was, leaning against the side wall of the stable with its poles pointing heavenward. Lois could not be far away, Janice thought. It might be nice to have some female company to take the edge off the evening with two men.

Mark dismounted while Harry set about untying Janice and getting her off her horse. As she slid to the ground she stumbled and fell against his chest. The spikes in her bra made themselves felt at once. She acknowledged their presence with a gasp.

Harry steadied her. "Whoa, girl. Wait until you see what we've planned for you before you get all excited."

The two men left her standing uncertainly in the yard while they led the horses toward the stable. They were gone long enough for Janice to examine her surroundings. She had no idea where she was in relation to the main ranch. Dark hills loomed against the sky to the southwest. The land nearby was flat and sandy, semidesert. Somewhere in the distance a coyote howled. Janice shivered at the sound. This was not a place in which to spend the night in the open. The cabin was the only house in sight, and it looked more homelike by the minute.

Janice examined it more closely. She could see one large room across the front that appeared to be a combination lounge/dining room. Light spilled from its windows into the yard. She could see several doors opening off the main room. Bedrooms, kitchen, bathroom, she surmised. She hoped Lois was in the kitchen preparing supper. Sex makes you hungry, she said to herself with a slight smile.

When the two men came back, she followed them into the house. Lois was indeed in the kitchen, and the smells of cooking welcomed them. She was naked save for leg irons and an apron. The apron had several spatters of grease on the front, and Janice guessed that Lois had already learned about the hazards of cooking in naked mode. She herself had made the same discovery years ago in the cabin in the Maine woods when she had set out to cook breakfast for William. She had felt quite romantic and naughty and spontaneous, cooking breakfast for her lover and anticipating yet another day of sex among the trees—until the first spatter of grease, obeying

Murphy's Law, had landed squarely on one of her breasts. She had immediately adopted the less sexy, but safer, apron.

Lois came into the front room to greet Janice and Mark with a wave and a smile. To Janice she said archly, "How was the ride?" She seemed to have a pretty clear idea about its effects, probably from having done the same thing.

Suddenly embarrassed in front of the two men, she said only, "All right," not wanting to say any more.

"Only 'all right?' " Lois asked Mark.

"Well, it was better than that at this end, but I wouldn't want to put words in Janice's mouth."

"Meaning you might want to put something more substantial in her mouth?" she asked.

"Sooner or later I thought we might get around to that, but I always like to save something for a finale."

With another smile at Janice, Lois retreated again to the kitchen. Mark beckoned Janice to follow him. He carried the saddlebags into one of the bedrooms and turned on the light.

"Our home from home," he said as he laid the saddlebags in a corner and began to take off his clothes.

Janice didn't need anyone to explain what she should do. She pulled off her boots, peeled off the jodhpurs and top. Next, she unhooked the tight bra and let it fall away from her breasts. She saw that her nipples were once more surrounded by rings of tiny red dots and felt extra sensitive from the prickers. Finally, she stripped off the pantie girdle. This time she managed to get both dildoes out unaided. And this time she managed to control the urge to shit as the dildo slid out of her anus. You're learning, she told herself.

By the time she was naked, Mark had produced a pair of leg irons from the bureau. She stood quietly while he locked them around her ankles. Her glance took in the room, which was a good deal smaller and more rustic than the bedrooms at the main ranch. The double bed was made of serviceable pine, with the obligatory short posts at each corner. Janice noticed a chain fastened to one of the legs. There was a single steel cuff on the end. That would be for sleeping, she knew. The beams in the ceiling were exposed, and there were several hooks set into them whose purpose was at once obvious to her. A bureau and a closet completed the furnishings.

Mark stood up and moved back toward the front room. Janice followed. You're becoming a proper servant, she told herself. No one needs to tell you what to do around here. With that thought, she went into the kitchen to see if Lois needed any help.

Lois was in the latter stages of cooking, trying to make everything come out right at the same time, but she had time to ask Janice again about her day.

This time, more private, Janice was more forthcoming. "I thought I'd die from pleasure and exhaustion long before we got here. Did you know about the dildoes and the spiked bra?'

Lois nodded. "I was introduced to them on my first visit. They *are* exhausting. But great fun. Harry did the job for me. We came straight here, and I was coming the whole time we were coming. The gallop almost did me in, but that was only the beginning. The rest of the day still lay ahead of us. When I went back home after that, I invested in a spiked bra and a set of dildoes straightaway. It's great to wear them at home or even at work. Sometimes I go shopping that way. I love going out with my secret helpers. It's a real turn-on. I use them whenever I'm feeling horny but unable to get back here. They work wonders when a girl is feeling low. Or even when she's feeling high."

"How was *your* trip here?" Janice asked.

"Long and dusty," Lois replied, "but not without its rewards. My outfit is likewise equipped with dildoes and the same kind of prickers you enjoyed so much in your bra. In fact, I specified these options when I bought the outfit, having learned of their effect here. And they provide the same sort of rewards you found so enjoyable. In addition, I get turned on by wearing the leather next to my skin."

"But what about the whip? Can you feel that through the leather?"

"Well, not really, but it is useful in conveying the message and as a reminder of what's in store for me when I take the outfit off," Lois said with a smile.

"And were you whipped when you got here?"

"Not yet," Lois replied. "But there's plenty of time for that. I have two weeks this time, so I can spread things out and enjoy the anticipation. Mostly I have only a few days, or a week, but this time I decided to treat myself. But what about you? Have you been whipped?"

"Not like you were," Janice said, flushing hotly at the thought.

Lois examined her closely, then said, "No. I can see you've not had that pleasure yet. No marks on you. I thought Jean-Claude would do you the day we arrived. He's the whip man around here. He knows how to string it out and make us beg for more."

"Yes. I noticed how he handled Hilary. But I only got a flick or two that day. It hurt like hell. So I'm a bit afraid of the real thing, to tell the truth."

"Well, it's not my own daily favorite either," Lois admitted, "but every so often I enjoy it. I'm expecting Jean-Claude to show up here tomorrow, and I'll be ready by then. How about you? Maybe we can get him to string us up at the same time. It could be great fun."

"We'll see," Janice said. She still had reservations, but she expected them to be ignored. She recalled Hilary's ecstatic response to Jean-Claude's artistry, hoping that she could summon up a similar response when the time came. She wondered again why Jean-Claude had not lashed her when she had trapped herself in the barn. Lois might know why. She told Lois what had happened, and when she finished, Lois thought for a moment.

"I think it was because you were wearing the maid's outfit. Jean-Claude likes to have his victims naked. A whip against one's naked bottom is not the same as a whip over one's clothes. And there's the symbolism too. You never forget, how it feels to be naked to the whip. Paddling through one's clothes is nothing like it."

"He could have taken my clothes off," Janice said. "I couldn't have stopped him."

"Well, maybe he wanted to have sex with you as you were more than he wanted to go to the length of getting you naked for the whip. Those maid's outfits are provocative. The men like them. I think Jean-Claude was overcome with lust for your bod and took the nearest way to satisfy himself. You must have looked fetching to him, hanging there."

Janice was pleased at the explanation. Like everyone else, she liked to know that men found her attractive. And there was no more authentic demonstration than the one Jean-Claude had given her. I must give more thought to how I dress in the future, she thought. A maid's outfit wouldn't do for everyday use, but there were more fashionable alternatives calculated to produce the same effect. Heretofore she had worn chiefly trousers or trouser suits to work, believing them more in keeping with her outlook. No one—until now—had been able to convince her that skirts made her more attractive.

She helped Lois carry the food out to the front room, where Harry and Mark sat talking. Neither man made an offer to help. Neither woman expected them to. When the table was set, they all sat down to eat. Janice felt only a little embarrassed to be naked. When everyone else was the same, it seemed prudish to worry about it. Fried chicken, mashed potatoes with gravy, and corn on the cob seemed quite in keeping with their surroundings. Janice ate with relish. She imagined that she and Lois were going to be the dessert. And despite her earlier sexual excess, she found that thought exciting.

The meal passed in silence for the most part. Janice (and doubtless Lois) didn't want to compare notes or speculate on what would happen next in front of the men. The men, for their part, said little, either because they had decided what to do but didn't want to give the game away, or because they had no plan and didn't want the two women to know that fact. Obviously something sexual was in the air. Otherwise they would not be here. But Janice was beginning to appreciate the value of surprise and the tension it generated.

The suspense was resolved after the two women had cleared away the dishes. Harry and Mark looked at one another, and as if at a prearranged signal they divided their forces. Mark went into the kitchen to (figuratively, since she didn't resist) drag Lois to a fate worse than death. Harry took charge of Janice. She thought at first they might all get together and make a foursome, even though she had never done anything like that and didn't know what the possibilities were. She could only think of two couples screwing in the same room. Novel, for her, but hardly bizarre.

She was surprised when Harry unlocked her leg irons instead and led her through the kitchen and out through the back door into the stable. A literal roll in the hay? she thought. But no. Once inside the stable he led her to an empty stall, where he shackled her by the ankle to one of the posts supporting the roof. Then, to her surprise and chagrin, he turned back into the house. She was left alone to contemplate her surroundings.

There was straw on the floor, but the idea of a solo roll in it was not appealing. The horses they had ridden occupied two other stalls and seemed content enough with their hay and water. The outside door was shut, so she need not fear wolves or coyotes.

Just then the light was switched off. In the resultant darkness she did not feel nearly so confident. The familiar immediately became threatening. She looked uneasily at the doors. Although they would keep out the larger predators, Janice remembered that this was rattlesnake country. The doors were not snakeproof. She listened intently for the characteristic dry rattle that would signal the presence of the reptile. None came, but just as she was about to relax, she thought of rats and mice. Stables were notorious for their rodent population.

Janice immediately clamped her thighs together to deny access to her cunt—though why a mouse should want to take refuge just there she couldn't say. Her reaction was instinctive—part of growing up female in the United States. Her mother (and almost all her female acquaintances) would have reacted in exactly the same way. Janice sat rigid, listening for any rustling noise in the straw.

Immediately she heard hundreds, it seemed—all converging on her. She stood tensely, every sense straining, for what seemed like hours. After awhile, she began to relax, but only after her muscles had begun to ache from the strain of keeping her thighs clamped together. She was nevertheless acutely aware of every sound in the small building, and she had several moments of sweaty panic before she could identify the source of the sounds she heard. Usually it was one of the horses shifting in its stall.

Trying to focus on something else, Janice examined the shackle on her ankle. No, it would not slip off. And yes, it was locked firmly. She should have known that anyway, but she had to be sure. Next she examined the chain. There was quite a bit of it, as she discovered when she pulled in all the slack. She estimated that there was enough to allow her to reach any point in the stable if she had a mind to explore the limits of her prison. Just then she didn't. There was too much dark and too many sounds. The chain itself was fastened to an eye bolt through the post. The nut on the opposite side had been welded and would not turn even if she had happened to have the necessary spanner. All right, no escape that way. No escape, full stop. Wolves, she had heard, would gnaw off a leg to escape a trap. She was not a wolf.

Why had she been left here? And how long would she have to stay? And why was she excluded from the revels she was certain would follow in the cabin? Lois, it seemed, was going to have all the fun. Janice imagined a threesome, Lois being shared between Harry and Mark, one up the front entrance and the other up the back passage. She might have enjoyed that. No, she amended, with a shiver, she would certainly have enjoyed it. It didn't require much imagination to picture Lois with the two men. In fact, wasn't that noise the sound of a woman in climax?

Janice listened intently. Silence. She was letting her imagination run away with her. Unless Lois was an instant starter, she would require more time to reach boiling point. Wouldn't she? Janice moved to the wall nearest the cabin and placed her ear against it. Indistinct sounds came to her through the wooden barrier. A clink, as of glasses. Low conversation, and a single surprised shriek from Lois. What were they doing to her? Were they lashing her? Janice shivered as she imagined the lash on her own body. But no. There were no screams, no sounds of leather on bare flesh.

But as she continued to listen, she heard an unmistakable moan—it was from Lois. And it wasn't one of pain. She heard a surprised "Oh!" from the cabin, and then another, longer one. They were doing Lois! And she was left out here in the (at least figurative) cold. Janice felt a wave of jealousy and anger as she listened to the increasing tempo of the action and imagined Lois impaled on two cocks and writhing in ecstasy. The cries became louder and more continuous. Janice felt her own stomach muscles tighten as she listened to Lois's loud pleasure.

Unconsciously, she reached between her legs and began to massage her labia. And almost at once she felt herself become wet. She realized what she was doing, but she didn't stop. All right, she thought, they tried to keep me on ice for later while they did Lois in my hearing. But. I'll show them. I won't wait. As she parted her labia and touched the hard button of her clitoris with her fingers, she felt a tremor pass through her. Yes, she was excited, but she could deal with it herself, without any help from them. She took her clitoris between thumb and forefinger and began to squeeze it rhythmically, feeling her excitement grow as she manipulated herself. Like most women, she had masturbated whenever she felt the urge, but now she couldn't stop herself as she listened to the sounds from next door.

Lois cried out again, sharply, "Ohhh! Ohgod! That feels so good. Don't stop." She trailed off into a string of incoherent moans. Janice, listening by the wall, plunged her finger into herself, letting a knuckle rub her clitoris while she probed her cunt. At the same time, she used her other hand to squeeze a breast and tease her nipple into taut attention. Her knees felt weak as she teased herself toward orgasm. She put her back to the wall and allowed herself to slide down it until she was squatting on the straw-covered floor with her knees open. Her hands and fingers were busy between her legs and on her breasts. And as she squatted in the dark stable, chained and naked, listening to Lois's cries through the door, she closed her eyes and came herself, shaking and moaning, the spasms spreading through her body from the epicenters in her belly and breasts.

The lights came on suddenly, startling her. The door opened, and Harry, Lois, and Mark came into the stable. They were all looking at her, and none of them looked as if they had been recently engaged in screwing.

"Don't let us interrupt, Janice," Lois said. "We just wanted to watch you do yourself."

Janice came back to earth abruptly, flushing hotly as she realized how easily she had been tricked into revealing her sexual need. "Go away," she said. "Please!" In her embarrassment and chagrin, she didn't want to face anyone. Hastily she removed her finger from her cunt. But she could do nothing to conceal her arousal. The smell alone would give her away.

None of them showed any signs of going away. And none of them seemed to share her embarrassment at being caught masturbating. Harry and Mark had erections, she noticed, and that relieved her own discomfiture somewhat. But Janice was given no time to dwell on her embarrassment.

The two men raised her to her feet, while Lois watched attentively. Janice felt their erections pressing against her front and back as she was placed between them, Harry in front and Mark behind her. Harry lifted her from the floor with his arms around her waist. There was no time for anything but astonishment at the swiftness with which the situation had changed. She could not complain now about being left out of things.

Lois moved closer to guide Harry's cock into Janice's cunt as his arms supported her. As she did so she whispered into Janice's ear, "He's got your weight. Lift your legs and put them around his waist." Her matter-of-fact approach steadied Janice down. Lois guided Janice's legs, crossing her ankles behind Harry's back. "That's it," she encouraged. "Now put your arms around his neck and help support your weight."

In a daze Janice followed Lois's directions, settling herself against his chest. His cock inside her was more satisfying than her finger had been. But as she relaxed and began to enjoy it, she felt another stiff cock prodding her anus.

Lois said, "Just a moment, Mark. She's dry back there."

Janice felt a slippery finger anointing her asshole with cream. Then Mark's cock was sliding into her from behind, and Janice found herself in the threesome she had imagined when she had heard the play-acting from next door. Harry's arms were under her bottom, supporting her, leaving Mark's hands free to work on her breasts and nipples. Which he began immediately to do.

Janice, penetrated front and back, her breasts being held in a pair of firm hands and her nipples being teased relentlessly, was soon fully occupied with her own rising excitement. The standing-up double fuck was a new double first for her. She was making good yet another deficiency in her sexual education, though she did not dwell on it at that moment. She was too busy surrendering to the inevitable.

Harry and Mark slid smoothly into a rhythm. Obviously this was not the first time they had done this. One cock was sliding in as the other was sliding out. Sandwiched between them, Janice sighed with pleasure. She was fully occupied, all her erogenous zones being stimulated at once. The sensations coming from the occupied territories threatened to overwhelm her. The sense of being helpless to resist lent a further dimension to the eroticism of the experience.

Harry bent down to kiss her face—eyelids, cheekbones, mouth. From behind Mark nuzzled her earlobes and the back of her neck. And she came suddenly, bucking between them, her cries muffled by Harry's lips over her mouth, so that she seemed to be screaming into him. Her nostrils flared as she sucked in air. The hard cocks in her cunt and asshole drove her to a shuddering climax. Janice thought she would black out from the intensity of her sensations. But she fought to hold on, not wanting to miss anything.

Both men stopped while Janice came, their cocks fully inside her as she clenched her anal sphincter and vaginal muscles around them. She could feel the twin erections pressing together inside her through the membrane that separated her cunt and asshole—a disturbing but delightful sensation she had never felt before. She clung to Harry while her climax lasted, and when it ended, her two partners resumed their alternate thrusting. Janice caught her breath and rode with them until she felt another climax coming. This one was not so intense as the last, so there was no danger of her fainting. She saw Lois watching them intently. Her mouth was slightly open and her breath was rapid. Just before her next climax, Janice thought Lois was wishing she were the filling in the human sandwich.

Once again, the men stopped thrusting while she came,

but Mark never stopped teasing her breasts and nipples. From his position behind her, he had full access to her front. Janice enjoyed the continuous manipulation of her breasts immensely, but there was another climax on the way, coming hard on the heels of her last one. This one shook her to the core. She cried out as waves of pleasure swept through her. The orgasm was so intense that Janice couldn't be sure whether Harry and Mark had joined her.

Afterwards she knew that Harry had come. He held still while Mark continued to thrust inside her anus. She felt him tense on the verge of his climax, and the feeling of him coming inside her asshole brought on another climax for her. His grunts and Janice's moans blended as they came.

Janice was truly exhausted after that. First there had been the wild ride, then the slower but no less thorough fuck in the pool. And now this. She relaxed her hold on Harry, and he held her up while her legs slowly uncrossed and slid from around his waist. The two men withdrew from her and allowed her feet to touch the floor—a figurative as well as a lit-eral coming back to earth. With his hands beneath her armpits, Harry lowered her until she was sitting on the floor. She was gasping for breath and covered with sweat. Her whole body trembled. And the combined smell of their coupling was strong in her nostrils.

She was not aware of them leaving her. Only when the light went off once again did she realize she was alone again. But this time she did not feel lonely. She was too tired and too satisfied for that. Let them have Lois. Let her have her pleasure. She could afford to be generous now that she was too tired for anything more. Only let them be a bit more quiet, she thought. It wouldn't do to hear them, because it might set her off again. And, as if she had been heard, a long silence descended, and she slept the sleep of the just-fucked woman, lying on a pile of straw on the floor of the stable with two horses for company. She was too tired even to worry about rats, mice, or snakes any more.

It was Lois who woke her the next morning. She looked as satisfied as Janice felt.

"Did you . . . last night?" she asked.

Lois nodded, smiling "They're randy buggers. They had me almost as soon as we got inside. I guess they knew from the smell that I was in heat after watching the three of you."

"Did they both do you at once?'

"One at a time, but that was good enough for me. You might say I died happy. But how about you? Did you sleep well?"

It was Janice's turn to nod happily.

Lois unlocked the shackle on her ankle and led Janice into the kitchen. "Welcome back to the land of the living," she said. "You can help me with breakfast."

They talked as they cooked. Janice learned that Lois and the two men would be going back to the ranch in a short while.

"But what about me?" Janice asked.

"I think they plan to leave you here. Someone will come to collect you before long."

Janice was alarmed at the idea of being left alone in the middle of nowhere. "How long?" she asked.

"I can't say," Lois replied, "but I would guess you won't be here long enough to get lonely." Seeing that Janice was still not reassured, she added, "Relax. They won't let anything happen to you. I'm not supposed to tell you this, but I think it will be Jean-Claude who comes for you."

"With his whip?" Janice was alarmed now at the approach of her own moment of truth.

"Probably," Lois answered. "He usually travels with one, just in case he happens to come across a woman in need of his attentions. You look as if you might fit that description."

Janice's anxiety must have shown on her face.

Lois said, "Don't look so worried! You'll love it. Jean-Claude is a real artist."

"You didn't like it."

"Well, no," Lois said with a sheepish look. "To tell the truth, it hurt like hell. But Hilary enjoys it all the time. So do most of the other women."

"That doesn't mean I'll love it," Janice said.

"Well, you'll have a chance to try it out before you decide. And today's the day. But first, help me get into my pony-girl outfit. That'll take your mind off things for a while."

Janice was still not satisfied, but there was nothing she could do. "Let's get on with it," she said.

Lois led her into the bedroom where her outfit was kept. The shiny leather gear lay on the bed, ready to be put on. Janice touched it and wondered how it would feel to be encased in leather from neck to toe. The main drawback, she thought, was that it made sex impossible for the wearer. It was an elaborate form of the medieval chastity belt.

Lois showed her the two dildoes and the bra part of the outfit. Like the bra Janice had worn the day before, it was lined with tiny prickers. Janice didn't need to imagine what that would do to Lois.

The pony-girl outfit came in two main parts. The lower resembled a pair of tights, but had a wider waistband with a heavy hook-and-eye fastener to hold them up. A zipper ran down the front as well, so the wearer could get into the garment. The top part resembled a pantie corselet with a sturdy zipper up the back. This was designed to lock onto the leather collar so that the wearer could not get out without the key—which, Janice suspected, would not be all that readily available.

Lois inserted the dildoes with a practiced air. Janice helped her get into the lower part of the outfit, smoothing the soft leather up her legs and settling the crotch so that it held the dildoes inside her. Lois inhaled while Janice closed the zipper and did up the hook-and-eye fastener. When Lois exhaled, the leather creaked slightly. The fit was very tight.

"What happens if you gain weight?" Janice asked.

"I have to go on a diet," Lois replied. "Either that or have the outfit altered. That's not cheap or easy. Better not to gain weight."

"We could all say that," Janice remarked drily.

Next came the top part of the outfit. Lois pulled it on and settled the crotch in place. Janice helped her slide her arms into the long sleeves. These, too, had zippers to allow the hands to pass through. Lois drew in her breath sharply as her tits contacted the prickers. Janice could see that she was excited just by getting into her pony-girl outfit. There's no accounting for tastes, she thought, as she moved behind Lois to close the sturdy back zipper.

Lois held out her arms so Janice could close the zippers on the sleeves. She was flushed and breathing rapidly as she handed a leather collar to Janice and gave directions for applying it. Last came a small padlock that joined collar and zipper. As Janice had suspected, there was no key. She locked the zipper, and Lois was imprisoned within the leather outfit with her twin dildoes and the prickers . . . and her evident excitement.

Lois's excitement increased as she picked up a pair of leather mittens from the bed and held them out to Janice. "A surprise gift from Harry," she explained breathlessly. "You'll have to put them on for me."

Janice took the mittens from her and examined them. Unlike conventional mittens, these had no separate place for the thumbs. The entire hand went inside, and a zipper closed the cuffs so that they could not be removed without help. Additionally, a leather thong had been sewn onto the finger part which evidently was meant to be pulled back to a brass ring on the inside of the cuff, doubling the wearer's hand into a thumbless fist when tied correctly. Once the mittens were on and the fingers doubled, Lois would have, in effect, no hands, even if her wrists were not tied together—which Janice suspected they might be anyway. The men who had charge of them would never overlook such a detail.

Lois held out her hands, one at a time, for Janice to put the mittens on her. Janice noticed how Lois's hands trembled with excitement. Janice closed the zippers and laced the leather thongs back through the brass rings on the cuffs of the mittens. Lois allowed her fingersto be immobilized without any resistance. Her breasts rose and fell heavily with her breathing. She was clearly excited now, and Janice imagined her nipples were feeling the effect of the prickers in her bra. She reached up, as Mark had done the day before, to pinch Lois's nipples.

Lois said, "Oh!" loudly as Janice's fingers caused the prickers to bite in. Instinctively, she raised her arms to protect herself. But she immediately lowered them again, as if inviting a further assault on her breasts.

"Does that really feel good?" Janice asked.

"What do you think?" Lois asked tensely. "Do it again. Please."

Janice pinched her again, holding her nipple and watching Lois's face for a reaction.

Lois closed her eyes and moaned with pleasure. She

brought her arms up again and pressed Janice's hands against herself. She uttered sharp exclamations of pleasure as her nipples were pressed against the prickers. Her knees abruptly gave way. She staggered toward the bed and sat down heavily, pulling Janice with her.

Janice could see that Lois was close to orgasm. Amazing, she thought. All from a bit of a massage. But then she remembered her own reaction to the same sort of stimulation. There was no sign of the men, and Janice made a quick decision as she felt her own excitement rising in sympathy. She pressed Lois back onto the bed, urging her to turn over and lie face down.

Lois did so, gasping with pleasure as her breasts were pressed fully against the prickers. Janice made her stretch her arms straight out from her sides so that the full weight of her upper body was on her breasts. Then she got onto the bed and knelt astride Lois' waist, facing the young girl's feet. Janice slid her hand under Lois' crotch and shifted her weight to press it against her own crotch. It was the best she could do to exert pressure on the dildo in Lois's cunt. She was locked into the leather suit and any closer access was impossible.

But Lois got the idea at once, grinding her hips against the mattress and moaning her pleasure as she came closer to orgasm. Lois began raising and lowering her hips as if she were riding a man. She cried out as a small spasm of pleasure shot through her. Janice continued to press on Lois's crotch while her weight pressed Lois's breasts against the prickers. Lois cried out suddenly, "Oh!" Then a full climax swept over her, and she couldn't contain herself. She didn't scream, but she bucked and heaved for a long time while Janice continued to press her sensitive bits as well as she could through the tight leather of the pony-girl outfit. Lois's cries were muted as she kept her face down on the mattress, but Janice could tell that she had come strongly.

Lois lay still for a long time on the bed. Then she said weakly, "Let me up, please."

Janice got off her and helped her sit up. Lois smiled at her. "Thanks. It was a lovely surprise." She was breathing heavily, and her face was flushed with the aftermath of her climax.

"Want to do it again?" Janice asked.

But before Lois could answer, a shout came from outside. "Hey! You two! Aren't you ready yet?"

"I guess not," Lois said ruefully. "But we'll meet later." She put her arms around Janice and kissed her on the mouth.

It was a handless kiss, but a heartfelt one. Janice returned it, surprised by the turbulent sensations from between her legs as she hugged the girl in her tight leather suit. "What now?" she asked.

"We harness me to the cart," Lois said matter-of-factly. "Or rather, one of the men does. You can watch. But first, help me into my boots. I have to cover some rough ground." Lois nodded toward a pair of black lace-up leather boots with high heels that stood by the bed. She sat down once more as Janice eased her feet into them and laced them up. When she was done, Lois stood again and waited for Janice to open the door for her.

They went out into the bright sunlight of the yard, Janice conscious once more of being naked while everyone else was clothed. But she was curious to see Lois perform her own ritual of slavery, so she stood to one side as they brought the cart from beside the stable and set it down near the young woman in the pony-girl outfit. Janice was acutely aware of the sexual tension in the atmosphere. Lois would have to draw the cart back to the ranch with the dildoes and prickers spurring her on. She herself would have to wait here to face Jean-Claude and his ubiquitous whip whenever he chose to come for her. Nevertheless, she felt a new woman. She could not remember this sense of being on a great adventure since her days with William—a lifetime ago, it seemed now. But the fire had not died. It only needed some encouragement to blaze up again.

Lois stood quietly as Harry fit the harness to her head and body. A wide leather waist belt came first. A stout leather strap hung from each side. While Mark held the poles of the cart off the ground, Harry backed Lois between them and fastened the straps to them. Mark let go of the cart now that Lois was supporting the poles. Harry buckled one end of a long rein to the front of Lois's collar and led it back to the cart, between her legs.

Seeing Janice's look of inquiry, Lois explained its use. "That's my reward if I do well. Harry pulls it tight and it saws against my crotch. You can guess what that does." She sounded cheerful.

"Now comes the head harness," she said as Harry lifted it from the cart. Once more she stood quietly as he buckled it onto her head, taking the two side reins back to the driving seat as well. "The scold's bridle," Lois said just before Harry put the leather-covered bit between her teeth and buckled the straps behind her head. He pulled them tight, at the same time pulling the bit deeply between Lois's teeth and distorting her cheeks into a grimace. She was now effectively gagged. The reins were fastened to either side of the bit. She was ready to go. But before setting out, Harry produced another padlock from his pocket. He pulled Lois' arms behind her and locked her mittens together by their brass rings.

"Will you take care of Janice, Mark?" Harry asked.

Mark nodded.

"We'll be off, then. See you back at the ranch." Harry

climbed into the seat and shook out the reins. Lois leaned forward in her harness and drew the cart toward the trail leading back to the resort.

Janice stood watching them until Mark touched her arm.

"Time to sort you out," he said, nodding back toward the cabin.

She followed him inside with butterflies in her stomach. Mark went to the saddlebags they had brought with them the day before. From them, he produced two dildoes with rings in their bases. From their relative sizes (and from the fact that she, like most women, had been constructed with two openings), Janice deduced their purpose at once. But there was more. Mark also had an electric dog collar of the type Hilary had worn. And a coil of thin wire. She saw at once the hand of Jean-Claude in these arrangements. She was going to be wired up, as Hilary had been. And she was going to learn what Hilary had felt during her abduction and subsequent encounters with Jean-Claude. Her stomach muscles tightened in apprehension, flavored with excitement.

Mark locked the dog collar around her neck while Janice practiced not panting with excitement. He connected the two dildoes to a length of wire and inserted them in her cunt and asshole. "Hold them in," he ordered her. Janice obediently clenched her internal muscles and stood with trembling legs for what she knew must come next. Mark led the wire to her collar and connected it, leaving no slack that might catch and pull the wire loose.

Then Mark paused to tie her wrists together in front of her. Janice wondered at that. If she were going to be left alone, she would have to be tied so that she could not get free. She had seen enough movies in which the captives had been able to cut or untie their bonds with their teeth. But she soon saw that

Mark had his own ideas. He led the rope between her legs and threaded it through the rings of her dildoes. She trembled as he touched her, but he was all business this time. He pulled the rope up behind her, drawing her bound wrists down until they rested against her belly. Keeping the rope taut, he tied it around her waist, with the knot behind her back, out of her reach. As a final touch, he hobbled her ankles with another piece of rope.

As he did so, Janice thought, this is how one keeps a horse from straying. He's treating me like an animal. She felt she should be angry at that, but she wasn't. At least he's treating me like an animal he wants to keep, she added silently.

Janice pulled against the rope between her legs to test her bonds. She discovered that the rope rested against her clitoris. She also discovered that she could produce a rather pleasant *frisson* by continued tugging. This, she guessed, was not entirely accidental. Continued tugging caused the *frisson* to become a downright pleasure. Although Mark was clearly going to leave her tied up alone, he had provided a pleasant diversion. A real gentleman, Janice thought.

"Now what?" Janice asked, breaking her self-imposed rule of silence out of great curiosity.

"I need to saddle the horse, but I'll be back to see you before I go. Sit down and wait if you like." He went through the kitchen toward the stable.

Janice stood instead. She guessed that she would not be able to get up again with her hands tied as they were. Instead, she paced slowly through the cabin, idly examining—but unable to touch—the furnishings and curtains. Her inability to use her hands produced a curious excitement in her. Another first: left bound and naked to wander about the house. She thought about how she would feel if she were left like this in her own apartment, among her familiar things but unable to touch them, waiting for her lover-captor to come for her. She couldn't decide whether she would prefer it to be William or Jean-Claude.

In the bedroom she struggled to open the closet. If anyone had asked, she could not have said exactly why she took such trouble to perform such an everyday task. It was just there, and she was curious to see what was inside. It might contain other bondage gear, or clothes—anything really. It turned out to be stocked with several pairs of women's shoes, in various styles and sizes, not new. On the shelf was a leather hood with a rubber penis gag, the type she had worn while being transported to the ranch. She shivered as she remembered how it had felt to wear that hood—speechless and sightless and helpless.

At the sounds of Mark's return, she hurriedly closed the door. Again, she could not have said exactly why she didn't want to be seen prying. Maybe just good manners, though the men didn't seem to worry much about manners.

"I'll be going now," Mark told her.

Janice felt a wave of apprehension at the thought of being left alone. "But what if someone comes and finds me like this?" she asked Mark.

"That's just the idea," he replied. "Someone *will* come and find you. You're meant to enjoy the suspense until he does." He left her standing by the closet and went outside.

Shortly, Janice heard the sound of the horse's hooves receding, and she knew she was alone, naked and bound in a strange place, in the middle of nowhere, and just anyone might happen along and find her. There might be wolves, or snakes. . . . She shook herself mentally. You didn't object. Get hold of yourself. You'll be all right until Jean-Claude comes, she reminded herself firmly. Yes, with the whip, a part of her added, and she shivered again. The sound of the horse faded and died away. Janice was alone.

Last Ordeal

10

Janice walked back to the front room, taking short, careful steps because of her hobbled ankles. There was no reason to go there, or anywhere. She was drifting, waiting for events to occur, passive. As she walked, the rope between her legs bore down on her clitoris and reminded her of the dildoes inside her. She flushed hotly as she thought again of being left alone and helpless, waiting for a man with a whip to come for her. She had spent much of her time this last week in enforced waiting, unable to do anything else. But then, she reminded herself, she had also spent so much of the time having wild sex, wilder than she could remember in a long time. I'm glad I came, she thought, surprising herself by accepting fully her passivity, her captivity, her newly discovered sexuality, for the first time since her abduction. A slave to the cock and the rope and the whip, that's me. I'd never have thought it possible a week ago.

From the front room, Janice could see the diminishing figure of Mark riding away from the cabin. He was mounted on one horse and leading the other. She watched as he turned round a bend and was hidden by a grove of trees. So, she thought, now I am really marooned here, even if I could get my hands free. No idea of where I am and no way to get to anywhere else. She turned from the window. The cabin was empty, the silence and emptiness full of fear and anticipation. She felt a sudden tension in her stomach, recognized the signs of sexual arousal—even in the absence of anyone else.

She moved restlessly to the front door, impelled again by no motive she could identify. She felt she had to break the spell somehow, felt she should go outdoors, drawn perhaps by the very emptiness of the land all around. And then she remembered how it had felt to walk naked and bound in the woods with the sunlight warm on her skin. That was a thrill she had missed without knowing it, until now. Now she would do it again.

Janice struggled to open the door, taking the knob between both her hands and twisting it by slow degrees until she could pull the door open. Stepping carefully back, she opened it wide and looked out at the wild country, the trees and the hills and the sand that surrounded her. There was no one in sight, and she felt the pull of all that emptiness. But first, the more practical side of her said, some shoes. The ground was rocky and would not be kind to bare feet. She went back to the bedroom closet and looked in. She tried several pairs of shoes, dragging them out one at a time with her foot, before she found a pair that fit her. They had moderate heels, the best she could find for what she wanted to do.

Walking shoes would have been better, but Janice knew she would never be able to get into them, let alone lace them up, with her hands tied at her belly. She slid her feet into the shoes one at a time, balancing carefully since she knew she would have a hard time getting to her feet again if she fell. Shod, she made her slow way across the front room and out onto the porch. The land was empty under the warm sun. Go on, she told herself, suddenly reluctant to leave the shelter of the cabin. Down the steps slowly, moving both feet onto each step to keep from tripping herself on the short rope that joined her ankles. Onto the uneven ground with only a slight stagger. Janice moved slowly away from the cabin, looking back from time to time like one who fears losing sight of a sanctuary. Then she felt the fall of sunlight warm on her naked body and was heartened, relaxing as if she had received permission for her foray.

Janice walked down the path that led away from the cabin, not because she particularly wanted to go back to the ranch, but because it represented the easiest route. As she walked farther from the cabin, she felt a tension growing in her. She knew that she was walking farther and farther from sanctuary, and she relished the growing excitement. At some point, she knew, the tension would become so great that she would stop walking, turn around, and start back. In the meantime, she tried not to look back at the cabin lest she lose her nerve. She was enjoying the game she had devised. It was almost as if she were daring herself to go on, to deliberately expose herself to the risk of being discovered naked and bound by some chance passerby.

The risk was not great, she knew, but it did exist, and that made her excited. What if, she asked herself, a man came and found me? What would I do? Nothing much, she knew, feeling the rope tight around her wrists. What would he do? That didn't require much imagination. She imagined being thrown across his saddle (he would be on horseback, of course) and carried away to what used to be called a fate worse than death. And as she imagined herself being abducted yet again, she felt the dildoes inside her, shifting as she walked. Janice pulled on the rope between her legs and was rewarded by a sharp wave of pleasure from her clitoris. She stumbled, nearly falling, her knees suddenly weak.

Janice tried to regain her balance by lifting her arms, but of course she could not. However, the increased pressure on her clitoris brought her to orgasm. She hunched over, her fingers just able to reach her cunt, and she used them to drive herself over the edge. "Oh! Ohhhhh!" Her soft cries were carried away on the light breeze, unheard in the wilderness as Janice closed her eyes and surrendered to her excitement. She fell to her knees in a sandy patch, the rope sawing deeply into her as she bent forward, clenching her vaginal muscles and anal sphincter around the dildoes inside her. She came again, shuddering in the sunlight, powerless to arrest the spasms in her belly and thighs. As if from a distance, she heard soft mewing cries and knew they came from her. But she was past caring.

When the racking spasms at last ended, Janice remained for a long time on her knees, too weak and dizzy to rise. She opened her eyes and looked at the empty land. It looked the same as before. The change was in her. She had surrendered to its call, had walked naked in the sun, driven herself to orgasm in the vast empty space. She felt grateful for the solitude that had allowed her to regain the wonder of her youthful ardor in the deep woods. Oh god, she thought, how did I ever forget how wonderful it was?

The world has been too much with me, she thought, paraphrasing Wordsworth's lines. But no longer. I will change myself utterly, she vowed, grateful to the unknown colleague who had seen her need more clearly that she ever could—and had provided the interlude she had needed. No more mere getting and spending, she thought. There has to be time for all this, too.

At last Janice looked up. The cabin seemed miles away. Had she really walked that far? Seemingly. Else how had she gotten here? She struggled to her feet, swaying slightly. Then she began the slow return. The sun blazed down now, rising to the zenith. The way was slightly uphill, and Janice began to sweat in the heat. Her hair grew damp, and sweat ran into her eyes. She could do nothing to wipe it away. The cabin began to seem more desirable. It offered shade, if nothing else.

Then, as she made her slow way back, Janice felt the dildoes inside her come alive, buzzing and vibrating in her cunt and anus. She stopped abruptly and looked wildly around. Her mood changed in a flash. Where she had been thinking it was exciting to be outdoors while naked and bound, she suddenly felt exposed and very vulnerable. There was no one in sight, but Jean-Claude had to be somewhere in radio range of her dog collar. She cried out, "Jean-Claude, are you there?" As soon as she cried out, she realized how foolish she sounded. Of course he—or someone—was there. But there was no response except the continued vibration of the dildoes. She knew then, with a flash of alarm, that he had come for her.

Feeling thoroughly naked and exposed, Janice looked toward the cabin. Now it seemed to offer refuge. The response was instinctive: get indoors when threatened. The rational part of her said the cabin was no refuge. In fact, Jean-Claude might well have gotten inside while she was walking foolishly about. He might well be waiting for her with his whip. But the rational part of her was not in charge of her instincts. They told her she was a helpless animal seeking refuge. She stood irresolutely, the dildoes buzzing inside her as her confused thoughts seemed to buzz in her head.

Then, like the flick of a whip, Janice felt a sudden jolt in her cunt and anus as the dildoes were switched to shock mode. She staggered and almost fell. Her breath was squeezed from her lungs in a surprised "Oh!" And then, as abruptly as it had come, the current stopped. Shaken, Janice sought to regain her breath and her composure. There was another jolt. This one brought her to her knees. And this time she screamed, her voice lost in the empty landscape. It seemed to last forever. She felt her muscles going into spasm. In a moment, she knew, she would topple completely. And then, as abruptly as before, it stopped.

In the midst of her mental confusion came one clear thought: she was being driven toward the cabin. Like an animal. The dildoes had been vibrating pleasantly so long as she was walking. The shock had come when she stopped. And then, as if to underline the idea, another, briefer shock squeezed a small shriek from her, as much surprise as pain. Janice did not need to be told again. She struggled to her feet and resumed walking toward the cabin. The rational part of her said there was no refuge there, but the threat of another shock was too much for her.

As soon as she began to walk again, the dildoes resumed their gentle vibrations, as if to say, good doggie; come along. And she did, hating her body for being so cowardly. But her body soon began to betray her in another way. As she walked, she became steadily more aware of the dildoes inside her. There were small flashes of pleasure from her clitoris and deeper waves from inside her cunt and anus as the plugs slid and shifted and buzzed. Janice already knew that she was powerless to remove them, and now that thought excited her deeply. She felt a sudden eruption from her cunt and belly that spread through her body as she came, staggering this time with the pleasure of it. Her back arched and her hands jerked involuntarily, tightening the rope between her legs and driving the dildoes deeper inside while the rope sawed against her clitoris. "Hah! Hahhhh! Haaaaahhhh!" Sharp explosions of pleasure were forced from her as she shook in the throes of her climax.

Janice was still reeling from her orgasm when she was stung again by the collar. She jerked erect with a moan and began to move once more toward the cabin. Another short shock and she redoubled her efforts to get there. In her haste, she forgot the hobbles. She almost fell and was rewarded by another shock. Recovering her balance, she plunged on, almost weeping in frustration. The cabin seemed miles away still. She asked herself how she had managed to get so far from it in the first place, forgetting her earlier exaltation at being naked in the sun, forgetting everything else as she was driven toward her rendezvous with the whip.

The dildoes resumed their maddening vibration as she stumbled toward the cabin. And once more, her body responded. Janice felt as if she were two persons, one driven by the pain, the other made frantic by the insistent plugs in her cunt and asshole. She cried out in confusion and arousal as she struggled toward the false sanctuary before her. She knew there was no refuge from the radio signals that drove her onward. And what if Jean-Claude was waiting for her in the cabin with the whip? She stopped again, irresolute. And was felled by another jolt of white fire inside her. This time she fell, rolling on the dusty ground, bucking and heaving as she tried to tear the dildoes from her body, screaming thinly as the breath was squeezed from her lungs.

The throbbing, searing pain stopped abruptly, and she knew what she had to do to avoid any more of it. Moaning, Janice struggled to her knees, the dust clinging to her sweaty body, thick in her mouth and in her hair. Squatting, she managed to get her feet under her. From that position she was able to rise and go on.

Slowly, she drew closer to the cabin. If she had not been hobbled, Janice would have broken into a run over the last short distance in order to end the torment. She cursed the rope that joined her ankles as she struggled onward. Then she was at the steps. She mounted them carefully, the wood creaking in the silence. Slow careful steps across the porch. The door loomed like the entrance to a cavern that she knew she must enter. She gathered her courage and moved forward.

She was felled by yet another explosion inside her that spread pain throughout her body. Helplessly, she jerked and bucked on the wooden floor, gasping for breath and screaming it out whenever she managed to get a lungful. Janice rolled onto her back and drummed her heels on the planking, her whole body vibrating. And still the torment went on. Why is he doing this to me, she thought. Can't he see I'm doing my best?

Janice was on the verge of blacking out when the shocking pain ceased, to be replaced immediately by a renewed buzzing and vibration from the dildoes. To her, it seemed as if they had been turned up a notch, if that were possible. Or her cunt and arsehole had been sensitized by the alternate pulses of pain and pleasure. For whatever reason, she knew her body was about to betray her again to ecstasy. And again, she surrendered to it wholly. You've earned it, she told herself as the first waves of pleasure rippled through her belly, and she tightened herself around her maddening, throbbing plugs.

The answer, she thought in a fleeting moment of coherence, before she was overwhelmed by the sensations from between her legs. That's the answer. That's why he's doing this to me. Oh god, it's so good, ohgod, ohgodohgodohgod. Helpless in her bonds, unable to stop herself, Janice rolled into a fetal ball around her center, drawing her knees up against her belly as she came with a shuddering, rippling explosion. As soon as the first orgasm had spent itself, she felt another coming. And another after that. She lost count as her body, betrayed by ecstasy, transformed her into a wrenching, heaving puppet who couldn't stop coming.

From a distance she heard someone groaning, "Ohgod, I can't come anymore. Please stop. It'll kill me. I can't go on." But it did, and so did she.

An indeterminate time later, Janice regained her senses. What had happened? she asked herself dazedly. Then she remembered. And as she remembered, she became aware that her dildoes were quiet, neither shocking her nor driving her mad with pleasure. That's what woke me up, she thought. She still lay on her side, her knees drawn up, her body aching. The planks of the porch pressed into her as she lay. I'll have to get up, she thought. And then, why? Janice sat up abruptly as she remembered the penalty she had paid for failing to move. But nothing happened. Had Jean-Claude gone away—abandoned her in the empty land as Mark had done?

The thought of being alone again frightened her now. What would she do when darkness came? She had a confused image of herself fleeing from pursuing wolves, hobbled, hands bound at her belly, stumbling blindly in the sandy, rocky semi-desert that offered no refuge. The cabin! She had to get into the cabin! There she would be safe. Sort of. She wormed her way to the edge of the porch, where she was able to dangle her legs over and get to her feet. As soon as her feet touched the ground she realized she had no shoes on. She looked around and saw one of them lying near the door. There was no sign of the other one. Janice shuddered as she realized she must have kicked them off in the throes of her orgasm. She had no clear recollection of anything but the racking pleasure.

Janice moved gingerly to the steps and mounted them again. She crossed the porch and reached the door, but as she was about to open it, she remembered the last time. She hesitated, waiting for something to happen, for some sign from Jean-Claude. Nothing. Gathering her courage, Janice pushed the door open and entered the front room of the cabin. Everything was as she had left it. Nothing moved. No sounds came to her as she stood listening. She set off on another tour of the cabin, checking each room for some sign that she was not alone. She found nothing.

Passing a mirror, she caught a glimpse of herself and was appalled. She was covered in dust, which had run down her body in rivulets of sweat. Her hair was damp and awry. You look a fright, she told her reflection. But she could do nothing about it. She tugged on the rope between her legs, just in case something had come loose during her recent struggles. It hadn't. Then a sudden thought struck her: the kitchen. There must be knives in the kitchen. In all the movies that's how the captive managed to free herself.

Janice made her way there. Where might knives be kept, she wondered. The counters were bare, the cupboards closed. Then she spotted the drawers. She stood as close as she could, straining to reach the handle. Inch by inch, backing away as she pulled, Janice managed to get the top drawer open. There were no knives. She opened each drawer in turn, squatting to reach the lower ones. No knives—nothing she could use to cut the ropes that bound her. They must have foreseen the possibility of someone's escaping that way.

Janice struggled to her feet once more and thought about her circumstances. The search for a knife had been more ritualistic than hopeful: something she had to do rather than something she hoped would succeed. She admitted to herself that she would have been disappointed to have found a knife. Much as she feared the approaching rendezvous with Jean-Claude and the whip, she would not have wished to escape it so easily, by the back door, as it were. Now she had made the search and knew she was truly a prisoner. A feeling of relief flooded her. She need make no more efforts. Whatever happened next, she could not escape. Her fate was entirely in the hands of others.

But there was something else she needed to do. Her stomach reminded her that she had eaten nothing since the meal last evening. Moreover, she was thirsty after her walk and her forced exercises, the pleasant as well as the painful. Opening a can was beyond her capabilities, even if there had been one to hand. But the fridge looked promising. She opened the door, backing away slowly as she pulled, to reveal well-filled shelves. Her stomach rumbled as she contemplated packages of cheese and sliced sandwich meats, orange juice, and of course, the inevitable cans of Coca Cola—most of which were beyond her extremely limited reach. There was also a plastic bowl of potato salad, left over from the meal last evening. That would have to do.

Squatting once again, and straining so that the rope between her legs felt as if it were cutting her in two, Janice managed to grasp the bowl of potato salad between her bound hands. She inched it toward her, tugging it to the edge of the shelf. There she lost control. The plastic bowl slipped from her grasp and fell, spilling its contents on the floor and rolling to one side. She contemplated the mess with a mixture of anger and despair, but she knew what she would have to do. The spilled potato salad was the only accessible food. Anything else she managed to get would have to be eaten from the floor since she could not raise her hands to her mouth or use them to place food on the table.

Janice got down on her knees beside the heap of food. She bent at the waist, the rope cutting into her crotch as she leaned forward to get her mouth near the floor. "God damn it!" she swore when she saw that she still could not reach the food. Even the dubious dignity of eating while on her knees was denied to her. Resignedly, she lay down on the floor and wormed her way to a position where she could take mouthfuls of the potato salad. And she learned that animals are much better at eating without hands than humans are. Having no snout, she was obliged to use her tongue as a shovel, spilling as much food as she managed to eat. When she had eaten all she could manage, her face and hair were smeared with the spillage. And she was thirsty.

The matter of water was more difficult than the food had been. There was plenty of it. All she had to do was turn on the tap and drink her fill. Which of course she couldn't do. Then she remembered the horses. They had to have a means of drinking that didn't require hands. She might be able to use that. Janice wormed her way over to the wall and leaned against it as she struggled to her feet. The door to the stable opened easily enough when she tugged at it. She looked around again at the room where she had been chained all the previous night after the ménage à trois. The shackle hung from a nail in the stall. The two horses were gone, of course. She was truly alone. And there appeared to be no water inside the stable.

Outside, she thought. It has to be outside. She made her way to the outside door. It was more resistant to her efforts, warped in its frame by the sun. Finally she got it open, panting and sweating. She stepped outside once more, then froze. She waited in trepidation for another of those paralyzing shocks. It didn't come. After a few minutes, during which she gathered her courage, she moved away from the door and out into the backyard of the cabin. And there was the horse trough, filled with water and looking like one of the fountains of paradise. She almost tripped over the hobbles in her haste to get to it.

She froze again. A rattlesnake, looking huge to her naive eyes, was drinking at the overflow channel of the trough. Janice was thirsty, but the snake terrified her. She felt herself go cold all over. Horripilations, she remembered, the word coming to her through her terror. Gooseflesh to the untutored. Why am I thinking this? she wondered. Her mind was playing its own games. But she could not move. Knowledge of arcane words was no defense against the instinctive fear of snakes. As she had last evening, she clenched her thighs tightly together and watched the intruder.

Lawrence's lines came to her—he, too, had encountered a snake in similar circumstances, and he, too, had acknowledged the instinctive fear she now felt. And so had Emily Dickinson— a narrow fellow in the grass, she had called the snake.

Janice had to get water. She had no choice. Go away! she thought at the snake. It didn't move. "Go away!" she shouted, with the same lack of results. She stamped her foot. The snake looked at her, and she froze again. Then, lazily, it shook its rattle. The dry whirring sound sent a chill through her. For a seeming eternity the snake and the bound, naked woman regarded one another. Eve meeting the serpent in reality, Janice thought inanely, sweating with fear, unable to move.

The snake uncoiled itself and moved slowly away. Janice almost cried out in relief. She watched the snake as it made its way across the dry ground toward a clump of brush. Would it be sagebrush, she wondered. That's what they had out West, she remembered. Whatever the brush was really called, the snake disappeared under its shadow. Janice unfroze and made a careful circle around the water trough, looking for other thirsty reptiles. There were none, thankfully.

Janice hurried to the trough and knelt beside it. She plunged her head into the water, washing the food from her face and hair. Then she drank her fill. She felt better at once— more confident. She had walked about in the nude. She had managed to feed and water herself, mastering new techniques. She had faced the snake. She had not given way to panic (well, not completely, anyway, she thought, remembering the rattle). She had. . . . Suddenly she had to go to the toilet. What goes in must come out.

But how would she manage, with her two openings plugged so completely? Just do it, she thought, standing up. And wash up afterwards. She allowed her sphincters to relax, and after a few moments she felt the warm water running down her legs. She forced herself to finish, thanking fate she had not needed to shit as well. Then she sat on the edge of the trough, swung her legs over into the water and eased herself in until she was kneeling in the trough. The water came halfway up her thighs. Not enough. She squatted back on her heels and let the water rise still further. She was afraid to lie down because she didn't know if she could get out again, so she had to content herself with what she had.

Janice let the water wash away the dust and grime. And she felt herself relaxing as if in her own bathroom, which had somehow had its roof removed without losing its privacy. She remembered the skinny-dipping she had done with William, the dip in the pool that had preceded her abduction, the fuck in the mountain spring with Mark. I could get to like this, she thought.

It *was* a struggle to get out, but she managed. I'm learning a new skill every minute, she thought, pleased with herself. Janice walked around to the front of the house and sat on the edge of the porch, drying out as she soaked up the sun. She could feel the water cool on her bare skin as it evaporated. Nothing moved in the barren land under the light of late afternoon. If it weren't for the ropes that bound her and the intrusive presence of the dildoes, shifting as she moved, she could almost believe she was alone in the world.

A sudden stirring in her cunt and anus reminded her that she was *not* alone after all. Janice jerked erect and slid off the porch to her feet. She made her best speed to mount the steps, cross the porch, and get inside the cabin. That, of course, did not guarantee her immunity from another shock, which she feared, or from the nearer approach of Jean-Claude and his whip. Another instinctive reaction, she chided herself as she stood inside the door. I'm certainly learning about my instincts. The vibration ceased, and she felt a momentary disappointment, recalling the way she had come earlier.

She stood motionless, waiting for some further signal. None came, and eventually she moved across to the couch and sat down. The outdoors had been spoiled for her. She knew she was being watched. Although she had been startled by the vibrations from her dildoes, Janice had absorbed enough sun to begin to feel drowsy. She sat on for a while, but eventually decided to lie down. Using her teeth, she moved a cushion so that she could use it as a pillow. She then swung her feet up, stretched out, and closed her eyes. If Jean-Claude wanted her, he knew where she was. The effect of the sun and the morning's sexual activity caught up with her, and she slept.

When she woke, it was dark outside. She had slept through the rest of the afternoon. And Jean-Claude was seated in an armchair across the room, watching her. Janice was vaguely alarmed at the idea of him watching her as she slept. It went against the most primitive instincts to be observed while helpless. And she was about as helpless as it was possible to be: naked, bound, hobbled, alone, asleep. She shook herself and attempted to sit up. It was not an easy task. The couch sank under her and she could not manage to sit erect. Jean-Claude watched her struggles with an amused smile. "You could help me," she said acidly.

"Why? he asked. "I enjoy watching your struggles. It's erotic. Don't you think so?"

Janice found that she could share his view now. The erotic aspects of a bound woman struggling to perform even the most basic of tasks was stimulating to her now, where a week ago she would never have believed it. Eventually she got her feet to the floor and sat up. The next move, however, had to be his. She caught sight of his whip, coiled alongside his chair. She felt a thrill of fear—and just the slightest touch of anticipation. Her moment of truth had come, and no one was there to postpone it or interfere in it. Dry-mouthed, she faced him across the uncrowded room.

"What are you going to do?" she asked him. Even as she asked, she knew the question was foolish. But she had to break the silence, somehow reduce the tension that made her voice high and breathless.

"I am going to give you ze most intense sexual experience you 'ave evair 'ad," he said.

His matter-of-fact reply unnerved her. But she forced herself to speak. "And 'ow," she asked, imitating his accent, "do you know so much about the intensity of my sexual experience?" It sounded like a challenge, and Janice was pleased that she had the courage to sound challenging in such unpromising circumstances. Shows I'm not to be taken for granted even yet, she told herself with some satisfaction.

But they both knew it was an empty challenge. Jean-Claude didn't rise to it. He only said, "Wait and see." He crossed the room and lifted Janice to her feet. He regarded her with a faint smile, then unexpectedly bent to kiss her on the mouth.

Janice, who had been expecting the whip at any moment, was taken by surprise. She returned his kiss unthinkingly, knowing her body was going to betray her again. Even as she drew back, she felt a stir of excitement in her belly. She compared him mentally to Harry and Mark and George. And she realized that this older man was the most attractive of the men she had met at the resort, even though (because?) he promised her the greatest pain of them all, in return (he had said) for the greatest sexual pleasure.

Jean-Claude moved behind her and untied the rope around her waist that held her bound hands against her belly. As it fell away, Janice repressed a shudder of fear and anticipation. She stood still while he withdrew the dildoes from her cunt and anus. As the latter came out, Janice felt the by-now familiar urge to shit. She managed to exert control, but she knew she would have to go. She told Jean-Claude, who nodded his permission.

In the bathroom, Janice sat thankfully on the toilet. She remembered George's remark about the pleasure of excretion as she relaxed her iron control and let herself go. Not in the league of real sexual pleasure, she thought, but pleasant enough for all that. Then she found that she couldn't clean herself with her hands bound. She was forced to enlist Jean-Claude's help, standing while he wiped her asshole and dried her cunt. It was at once the most intimate and degrading of experiences, but she somehow managed to find some excitement in it.

Jean-Claude grasped the rope trailing from her bound wrists and led Janice into the front room. This is it, she thought with a tightness in her chest and belly. He strung her up to a hook in the ceiling, pulling her up by the rope until she was stretched tautly. Then he spread her legs and tied her ankles to opposite ends of a sawed-off broomstick. Seeking refuge in the minor details, Janice thought that they should have something more elegant than that. After all, they (or at least Jean-Claude) did this all the time. Surely they would have made something for the purpose. But maybe they like the impromptu approach, she thought—something grabbed in the heat of the moment, a wild, spontaneous response to lust. In any case, rough stick or not, it worked. She couldn't bring her legs together, and with a shudder she imagined her cunt exposed to the whip at the apex of her spread thighs. Indeed, her whole body was open to the whip. But her cunt seemed especially vulnerable as she remembered how Hilary had screamed when the whip found her there. She knew that the whip would find her in the same place, and she knew that she would scream, too.

But she couldn't know if she would feel the ecstasy Hilary had claimed to feel. There was no way to know beforehand. She would just have to go ahead and find out for herself. Janice's stomach muscles knotted in dread and anticipation, and she had trouble breathing because of the tightness in her chest. She knew that if she spoke, her voice would sound high and breathless, and she resisted the impulse to say anything to Jean-Claude. In any case, she knew that nothing she said would affect what was going to happen to her. With her acquiescence, she realized. With her complicity. With her consent. Janice knew her body was flushed, for she felt hot all over. Even her eyes felt hot, and as she looked around the room its outlines seemed blurred. The furniture appeared to advance and recede before her. She waited in a lust that had been newly

aroused during this last week of bondage and domination—
and of intense sex. Would this be even more intense, as Jean-
Claude had promised? How could it be?

Jean-Claude moved out of her range of vision. Janice tried
to turn her head to follow him, thinking wildly that he would
not lash her if only she could make eye contact with him and
let him know how she dreaded this. But she couldn't,
wouldn't, say anything to him. Her pride would not allow her
to beg. She remembered that Hilary had begged, but her plea
had been for more: more pain and more ecstasy. Would she
soon be making the same plea?

The lash caught her across the back, and Janice screamed
in surprise, and a moment later, in pain as she felt a line of fire
drawn across her flesh. He struck her again, higher up this
time, just below the armpits. She screamed again as the tail of
the lash curled under her arm and caught the side of her
breast. She continued to scream as he worked over her back,
over her bottom, and down the backs of her straining thighs,
until she was breathless, her lungs burning, and her chest
heaving as she tried to draw breath to scream again. Ohgod,
where was the pleasure in this? Her resistance in tatters, her
pride gone, she would have begged him to stop if she had only
had the breath.

Then, suddenly, Janice was aware of something between
her legs, something hard and sticklike rubbing against her
labia, parting them, sliding deeper into her cleft and finding
ohgod her clitoris, swollen and hard at the top of her cunt.
Jean-Claude was using the whip handle to arouse her, and she
found, incredibly, that she was responding. Where a moment
before she had been screaming in pain, she now felt the flush
of warmth spread through her belly as the handle caressed her.
Janice's hips moved involuntarily, backward and forward, as

the whip caressed her. In a moment of lucidity she knew she was making love to the whip, and she understood then the phrase she had read somewhere—and marveled at. The very instrument of her torture became the instrument of her pleasure, and she knew that Hilary must have learned this same lesson, learned to love the whip, the pleasure wrapped in pain that it represented, and even the hand that tortured her and gave her such pleasure at the same time.

The whip handle slid between her legs, rasping against her labia, her clitoris, inflaming her beyond anything she could have believed possible even a few minutes ago. Catching her breath, Janice begged him to enter her, fill her, make her come until she burst with pleasure. "Ohgod, Jean-Claude, please. Come inside me. I want to feel your cock inside me." Hilary, she remembered, had made the same plea. And he had not heeded it. Nor did he heed hers. The whip handle was withdrawn, and she felt a burning emptiness in her cunt, a desire to be filled full and driven to the most intense orgasm ever—just as Jean-Claude had promised. But he held back, leaving her hanging on the edge. This was what Hilary had meant—what hurts worst is being left on the edge, burning with lust but unable to come.

Wildly, Janice thrust her hips backward and forward, trying to find the whip handle again, trying to make herself come if he would not help her. She moaned softly, in heat, in need, her voice sounding high and thin and strange in her ears as she begged him once again to come to her.

A sudden line of fire across her belly brought her back to reality. Jean-Claude, she saw as her eyes focused suddenly, had moved around in front of her and was raising the whip to lash her again. The blow landed across her stomach, the tip curling around to lick her bottom as well. Thus he worked up the front of her body, lashing her thighs; letting the tip curl around her legs; up her belly and stomach; and finally to her heaving, bobbing breasts, the nipples taut with her arousal and now being lashed with the whip. Once more Janice screamed in pain as the blows left their red marks on her skin and made her wonder anew how anyone could endure this day after day, as Hilary did.

And this time she did beg him to stop. "Ohgod it hurts, please don't hit me again; please stop. Aieeee!"

The lash curled up between her legs, finding her where it had caressed her a few moments ago. Janice felt an explosion of pain in her abused cunt, and she screamed until she thought her lungs would come out. Red explosions behind her eyes blinded her; she saw everything through a red haze of pain. And in the midst of the pain she felt herself start to come, incredible pain bringing the most intense pleasure, and she tried to scream again in release. She had no breath left, her chest heaved, and her body shuddered as the orgasm swept through her.

Jean-Claude stopped lashing her, allowing Janice to experience the full pleasure of the orgasm he had induced in her. She jerked and moaned, pulling against the ropes that held her stretched tautly, almost lifting herself off the floor in her blind ecstasy. She twisted and turned, working her body as the waves of pleasure shook her.

Jean-Claude waited until she hung limply in her bonds. Then he lifted the whip again. The lash snapped against her belly, leaving another red mark: I'm still here, he was telling her.

Janice's eyes flew open in surprise and pain. "No!" she said, despite herself. "Please, no!"

He paid no attention. The whip swung back, this time

landing on the fronts of her thighs. Methodically then, he resumed lashing her, moving around to reach her back, her sides, her bottom, her breasts, and her legs, returning once again to her cunt. Janice shrieked in agony and struggled to pull free, begging him to stop all the while.

And eventually he did, using the whip handle once more between her thighs, rubbing her labia and her clitoris with the hard leather until her hips began to move involuntarily in rhythm with the strokes, once again making love to the instrument of her torture. Once more she moaned in pleasure, her skin on fire from the lash, her cunt on fire from the delicious friction between her legs. He stepped closer so that his free hand could fondle her abused breasts. The nipples came up hard and taut under his fingers, and Janice moaned anew as she was aroused and driven once more toward orgasm.

Helplessly, she surrendered to his ministrations as her body took fire, flushing as the familiar sensations spread from her clitoris and her nipples. "Ohgod ohgod ohgod ohh ohhhhh." The sensations were more intense than any she could remember: "the most intense sexual experience ever," as Jean-Claude had promised. Now she knew, and she didn't want it to stop. Nor did it. Jean-Claude prolonged the arousal, playing upon her body like a musician—her nipples taut and sensitive, her breasts heavy and full in his hands. The hard leather whip handle between her legs found her swollen clitoris, sliding against the hard button, and she couldn't stop coming, couldn't help herself or control the wild pleasure that ran through her like an electric current that set all parts of her body on fire. Briefly, she remembered the real electric current that had assaulted her earlier. This was nothing like that.

Then he withdrew, and Janice cried out, "Oh no no no no, don't stop!" When he struck her again, across the belly, she couldn't tell whether the sensation was painful or erotic, so confused were her senses. Her body was still in the throes of orgasm, and the lash had the effect of making her come again, the pain making the pleasure sharper. Janice heard someone— herself—moaning, asking Jean-Claude again not to stop, to drive her out of herself and into this new, wild country she had discovered within herself.

She wanted Jean-Claude to take her as he had taken Hilary, penetrating her as she hung from her bound wrists, her body aflame with the stripes of the whip and her own desires. But he didn't. Janice felt a faint surprise as he untied her ankles from the broom stick that held her legs apart. Then he let her down, leading her stumbling into the bedroom by the rope that bound her wrists.

He laid her on the bed on her back. Through the haze of her arousal Janice felt him lifting her arms above her head, tying them to the headboard. He spread her legs and tied her ankles to the posts at the foot of the bed. But he was not yet finished with her. Jean-Claude fitted the leather hood from the closet over her head, put the rubber penis gag into her mouth, and laced the hood tightly onto her. Janice had a moment of fear then: why was it necessary to gag her just now? Was he going to do something even more painful to her? But at the same time, she felt a thrill of anticipation and knew that she would welcome almost anything he did. Unable to speak, she nevertheless formed the words in her mind: take me, fill me, drive me wild again.

But no one came to her. There was no movement as she lay there, waiting for something to happen, unable to influence it in any way. No more independent decision making, no more control. Even her body was no longer her own. She could touch no part of herself, could not move or see or speak. And her body felt as if it were on fire—partly from the lashing, but partly, she knew, from the aftereffects of the violent sexual orgasms she had experienced. It would be hard to imagine herself more helpless than this, more dependent on someone else. And the idea made her ache with desire.

Janice did not sleep this time—could not. Her riotous thoughts alone would have kept her awake, even without the edge of fear and the discomfort of her abused body. She had do idea how long she lay there, tormented by her desire for more of the wild, out-of-control sexual arousal and fulfillment to which Jean-Claude had introduced her. Would he never come back? Had he abandoned her? The thought of never seeing him again was intolerable. She knew now why Hilary longed for him. She, too, felt the need of him and his own particular brand of sex, wanted him with an ache she could not remember feeling before, even for William. She only remembered him. Jean-Claude was here and now.

Only she wished he were here now. She imagined him standing by the bed watching her, studying the lines of her body. So strong was the sense of his presence that she tried once more to call to him: "Unnnnhhh annhhhh!" The wordless plea echoed in her ears while she hoped he would come to her. But no one came. Janice lay back, frustrated and helpless. Sleep would have been welcome, but she was beyond that. Futilely she tugged at the ropes that held her, even though she knew that getting loose would not satisfy her most immediate need: a cock, his cock, inside her; his body on hers; his maddening foreplay driving her mad with desire. And of course, the wild release she had felt under the lash. That, too. That more than anything. She lay there helpless and open and vulnerable, her legs held wide apart and her cunt exposed to anyone who might find her.

A sound, soft and distant—or near and muffled by the leather hood? Another. Definitely a footfall. Janice strained her ears. "Ummmnngghhhh?" A hand on her stomach, tracing its lower outline, going between her legs, lightly touching her pubic hair and toying with her labia. Janice lay still, half in fear and half in hope that Jean-Claude had come back for her. She had a sudden, chilling thought—suppose a stranger had found her naked and helpless? She twisted her head from side to side, pulling at the ropes on her wrists. Her visitor continued to toy with her sex as if she had not moved. "Ummmmmnnnnggghhhhhh!" she said, straining to speak despite her gag.

The hand went away, but Janice lay tense, knowing he was still there. Watching her. Suddenly the mattress sagged as he climbed onto the bed beside her. A hand on her cunt, opening her, and then a cock nosing inside her. No foreplay, just entry. Janice stiffened, undecided whether to fight it or allow his entry. As she dithered, the penetration was complete and the question moot. Not that she could have put up much of a fight. He lay atop her, her breasts flattened against his chest, her sensitive nipples excited by the touch of his wiry hair.

Her visitor began to move, thrusting in and out, sliding almost out of her on the upstroke. Janice said, "Ummmmmmmmmmm," a long moan of satisfaction as she felt herself filled full. The slow thrusting was exciting as she imagined how she would appear to her partner, tied to the bed invitingly. What man could resist such an invitation? Hands on each side of her face, the fingers strong through the leather hood, holding her head in place as he fucked her. Janice wished she could see him, wished he could kiss her, wished ohgod ohgod ohgod. Her climax swept through her with no warning, ambushed her, and swamped her thoughts. She shuddered and moaned, the gag muffling the sounds of her pleasure. She wanted to scream, but couldn't. The gag acted like a cork in a champagne bottle, keeping her excitement inside and making it build instead of being screamed out. When he came at last, the pleasure was almost more than she could bear.

It was time for Janice to leave. The week had passed in a haze of lust and pain and pleasure, going so quickly that she could hardly believe so much had been packed into the time. And she didn't want to leave, even though she knew that staying was impossible. Like almost everyone else, she had to earn a living. But she would no longer see work as she had before. There was something more important now. She had learned several important things during her stay at The Last Resort. There had to be time for more pleasure like that.

She also realized that her temporary exile would make the return that much more pleasurable. As Frost had remarked, it would be good both going and coming. Too much of a good thing could pall, she told herself. But she would be back. It made the thought of leaving more bearable.

Now she waited in Jean-Claude's room, her wrists handcuffed behind her back, wearing leg irons, the leather hood lying on the settee beside her. Dressed once again in her own clothes, the ones she had worn before this fateful week, her bags packed, Janice missed the sense of nakedness she had felt during her stay, even when wearing the maid's uniform. It helped somewhat to recall Jean-Claude's lecture on the naked and the nude. Beneath her clothes, whatever she wore, Janice would know that she was naked, helpless before the strength of her newly awakened desire, needing only a touch to arouse her.

The sound of the door opening broke her reverie. Hilary and Lois had come to say goodbye. Both were still nude— naked, Janice corrected herself. They wore only leg irons.

Janice rose to greet them, shrugging her shoulders to indicate her inability to make any other gesture. Hilary came to her, took her face between both hands, and kissed her on the mouth. Lois hung back, but Hilary motioned her to do the same. Shyly, she did so.

Janice kissed her warmly. "Be sure to call me when you get back home. If you still want to try your wings in the big city, I'll do all I can to help." Lois smiled and said, "Thanks. I'll be in touch."

"You'll be hooded again when you leave," Hilary told her, "so you won't be able to guess where this place is. It's a matter of keeping the resort a secret until you decide to come back. The feeling is that anyone who returns freely is safe. After your second visit, you will be shown where the resort really is—if you want to know. Some of the girls don't want to know. They like being taken to a place they can't identify. It makes the abduction seem more real, more exciting. You can do it that way if you like."

"But how do I make contact when I want to come back? I know secrecy is necessary, but surely not so important that we can't find the place."

Lois held up an envelope for Janice to see. "When you want to come back, call the number on the note inside. Tell whoever answers your name and the date you will be ready to travel. You will be abducted shortly thereafter, so have a case packed, ready to go at any time. They'll come and take you from work or from home, or even off the street. You'll never know when it will be. That's how I do it." She tucked the envelope into Janice's handbag.

"That's a relief. I wouldn't like to be exiled permanently," Janice said.

"But there's more for you," Hilary said. "Sam has given you some clues in case you want to find William, so you'll have something to occupy your time between now and your next visit here. Even if you find him, we all hope you'll come back for another visit. Mind how you go."